The Dragon King

Death Series
Book 3

Penelope Barsetti

Hartwick Publishing

Hartwick Publishing

The Dragon King

Contents

Chapter 1

Calista

All Queen Eldinar had to do was give a subtle nod, and her men scattered like a school of fish. Uncle Ezra did the same, stepping off to the side, his hands behind his back with his eyes still locked on Talon.

Talon moved away as well, heading back to where Khazmuda remained at the campsite.

Since Queen Eldinar stared at me so hard, I knew she wanted me to stay. We stood alone together, in the clearing outside the forest, her eyes locked on mine with the same sheathed hostility she always wore. "There is only way to execute this plan—by having the Death King enter Riviana Star. This greatly displeases me, but I see no other way."

"He said he wishes you no harm—"

"Because of his affection for you—and a man's affection can change in an instant."

My heart gave a painful squeeze. "I don't think he would have fought in your war if his affection were so weak." I'd betrayed him, and he still saved me. "I turned my back on him, but he's never turned his back on me." The guilt was heavy in my throat, like a rock that couldn't be swallowed.

Her eyes narrowed.

"And I don't think my uncle's affection for you could ever change."

"You insult my husband with the comparison. What we have is love, and what you have is a mixture of lust and convenience. I won't deny the Death King is a beautiful man, so I understand why you've been cast under his spell. But make no mistake, the depth of his affection for you is barely skin-deep."

A rush of anger hit me hard like an arrow against armor. "With all due respect, you know nothing about him—and you know even less about us." My fury lit up quicker than a match against flint, the flames higher than the treetops. I might have agreed with her if this had been weeks in the past, but now, everything had changed, our relationship had deepened, and I would fight for it tooth and nail.

She stared at me long and hard, a hint of disapproval in her gaze. "I hope I'm wrong, for your uncle's sake."

It was the first time I realized Queen Eldinar was more than a monarch...but also my aunt. No maternal affection came from her, not a hint of it in her gaze. And I wondered if that was because she knew her love with my uncle would be a mere second in her very long lifetime and a relationship with me was simply not worth the effort.

"I will permit the Death King to enter our forest, but he will be under my supervision at all times. Guards accompany him wherever he goes, without exception. I know that your relationship with your uncle has barely had the chance to bloom, but I see that it's meaningful to you. For that reason, I trust that you will protect this forest, if need be."

"I would protect this forest even if he weren't my uncle," I said. "Riviana Star is a beautiful place, and it's an honor to call it home. But as I said before, the Death King would never hurt your forest or your people. Your concern is needless."

"We're a very capable race. Great allies for the battlefield. I'm sure he's realized that."

I stared, unsure what she meant by that.

She seemed to sense my confusion because she continued. "He conquered your lands because he needed an army for his war. His chances would be even greater if he had the elves to serve him. For that reason, I will always be suspicious of him."

"He wouldn't do that—"

"Why not?" she demanded. "What's the difference between us and the humans?"

I held her gaze without an answer because there really wasn't one.

"I hope that by giving him access to the dragons, whether they agree to his war or not, he'll leave us in peace."

"I don't see how he could force you anyway. You're much stronger than humans."

"He can command the army of the dead, can have us executed by our own kin. He could threaten to destroy or invade Riviana, the gateway to Caelum, in order to ensure our participation. It causes me great pain to permit him into our forest, but I fear it's necessary because the dark elves are a greater threat at the moment."

"I know this doesn't mean much to you, but I really don't think he would do that."

"You're right. It doesn't mean much to me," she said. "Because you have no evidence for your claim. He said himself he's not evil, has only done evil things to survive. I think that enslaving the elves for his war falls into that category."

I still didn't believe it, didn't believe he would ever do such a thing, but I let the argument die.

"Do not let him near the Realm of Caelum—under any circumstances."

"I don't even know where it is."

"It's the Great Tree, the source of power of the forest, next to the cemetery that's been disturbed by his dark magic." Her eyes widened. "Guards will be stationed there at all times while he's in the forest. But if he ventures anywhere close, I will kill him myself. If you wish him to live, I suggest you keep him away."

I gave a nod. "I'm sure it won't be a problem."

She turned her gaze to look behind me, probably to lock her gaze on Talon.

A moment later, he approached, casting a shadow over me when he blocked the sun.

"I will permit you into the forest, under the watchful eye

of my men. You're only allowed in Calista's accommodations and the royal palace. Is that understood?"

He stared down at her as well, his hard gaze locked on her eyes. He clearly wasn't used to being spoken to like an inferior, but he didn't lash out with an insult as he normally would. "Yes." He said it with a bite in his tone.

"We would welcome Khazmuda into our forest, but there's simply no room for him."

"I understand," he said. "He prefers the open sky to the closed canopy anyway."

Her gaze shifted to me, and just as she did with her husband, she held a silent conversation with me. *I'm counting on you.* Then she turned away and began her trek back into the forest.

It was a long journey to the center of the forest, and we spent that time in silence. The guards flanked us, allowing the queen to walk ahead with Ezra at her side.

Talon looked out of place in the midst of grass and flowers, his armor like a shadow of darkness. The birds normally chirped from their branches above, but Talon's presence seemed to drive them away. It was the first time the forest was quiet...utterly silent.

Not a word was spoken. Talon stared straight ahead, and if he felt out of place, he didn't show it.

We didn't take a break like we normally did, because the queen was eager to return to the royal palace as soon as possible. I noticed she didn't speak with my uncle, not once, their eyes focused ahead.

I heard the forest before I saw it, heard the music slowly growing louder, an ethereal sound that was felt through all the leaves in the trees.

Talon had no reaction, like he either didn't hear it or didn't care to hear it.

Then the center of the forest came into view, elves on the paths and in the market, but there was a solemn pain in the air, the aftermath of the war felt in everyone's bones. It wasn't the same magical place as it had been, not when it had been tainted by the rise of the dead.

Some of the elves immediately turned our way, and instead of regarding Queen Eldinar with admiration, their frightened eyes turned to Talon—the Death King. They stared, their fair faces pale like snow, and they all stopped what they were doing to look, horrified that the enemy had entered their forest with open arms.

Talon ignored them, staring straight ahead like public opinion meant nothing to him.

We were escorted away from the royal palace and farther into the forest, where my tree house was located off the main path, high up in one of the enormous trees. There were other tree houses in the vicinity, but they were all facing in different directions so everyone had complete privacy.

We approached the vines that acted as a staircase. "These are tricky—"

Talon stepped onto the vines and carried himself up like he'd done it before. He conducted himself just as Luxe had, with the grace of an elf. He rounded the other side of the trunk and continued up, carrying the weight of his pack. His weapons had been taken from him to be kept in the queen's possession until she deemed it necessary to return them.

The soldiers took their stations around the trunk of the tree, making it impossible for Talon to escape without their knowledge.

I followed him, moving at a much slower pace because I still hadn't mastered the vines, even though I'd gone up and down many times. It was a long walk to the top, so long that it acted as a deterrent to leaving. Sometimes I stayed in my tree house for days because the trek to the bottom and back up again just seemed like too much.

I made it to the top and found him standing there, looking at the armchair he'd occupied in our previous conversations, when he'd sat there in nothing but his sweatpants, when he'd touched me with only his stare.

After a moment, he walked away, carrying his pack to the bedroom where I slept alone. He tossed the bag onto the armchair then stared at the rumpled bed, the sheets kicked back because I'd left my bed in a hurry.

When he turned to look at me again, it was with a hint of anger.

"What is it?"

He severed our connection and walked around me to the kitchen, looking at the dining table where he'd sat across from me—Luxe in between us. He rested his fingers on the surface, and he stared before he pulled out the chair and took a seat, slouching, knees wide apart, looking out the open window to the forest beyond.

I took the seat across from him.

He wouldn't look at me.

We were so close outside the forest, but now we felt like strangers once more.

"Why are you angry?"

After a moment, his stare flicked back to mine.

"Talon."

"Did you fuck him?"

"Who?" I blurted, eyebrows lifted up my face.

His stare hardened.

I quickly realized he was asking about Luxe, the man he'd seen in my tree house, the man he'd despised at first sight. "Talon—"

He yelled without raising his voice. "Answer the fucking question."

"*No.*"

"No, you won't answer the question, or no, you didn't—"

"I didn't sleep with him."

He looked away, still angry.

I never asked what he did when we were apart, but I assumed another woman had taken my place the second I left. I wanted to ask, but I couldn't bring myself to do it, to hear his answer and keep a straight face.

"Did anything else happen—"

"No."

"Did he try to make—"

"I haven't interrogated you about your affairs, so I'm not sure why you're interrogating me about mine."

His eyes hardened on my face. "Ask whatever you wish."

I looked away and stared at the cabinets.

"*Ask*."

"I'd rather not."

"There was no one else, Calista."

I kept my eyes on the hand-carved cabinets, looking at the fine craftsmanship of a carpenter. Flowers and trees were carved into the wood. The tree house and everything inside of it had been constructed of various pieces of timber, everything that had died of natural causes, so nothing matched. But that somehow made it more beautiful.

"I wanted there to be."

I swallowed, picturing the women who serviced him, not just because they were paid to but because they wanted to. Beautiful and enthusiastic, eager to bed the king who'd taken their kingdom in a sweeping victory.

"I was so fucking angry at you, but no amount of anger could make me desire anyone else but you."

I did my best to hide my relief, but I wasn't successful. Our separation had been just as hard on him as it was on me. "Luxe is the commander of the army. Queen Eldinar asked him to keep an eye on me, so that was why he was here."

"A commander doesn't have dinner with his prisoner unless he wants to fuck them."

I turned back to Talon. "Nothing happened, so let it go."

"You know me well enough to understand I don't let anything go." His eyes shifted away, and he breathed a quiet breath.

"I don't want it to be this way," I whispered. "I want it to be how it was before, how it was outside the forest." When we were so close we were practically one person, when the barrier between us was finally gone and our souls touched. He finally let me see who he really was.

His eyes remained averted. "It was all I could think about when I walked in the door, wondering if another man had slept in the bed where I'm supposed to lie with you."

"Well, he didn't," I said. "So come back to me."

His eyes remained directed out the window, looking at the forest in the dying light. Minutes passed, and his anger slowly dimmed like the fading sun. When his anger passed, he looked at me again, the walls down, his eyes dark like midnight but warm like the sands in the desert.

I felt the smile move over my lips. "There you are..."

Chapter 2

Talon

My arms were hooked underneath her thighs, and I pressed a hard kiss to her slick sex, feeling lips fuller than the ones on her mouth. The second she felt the heat of my mouth, she arched her back and released a whimper as her nails clawed into the flesh of my forearms. I kissed her again and again, taking my time because we were on a soft mattress rather than the hard ground, both clean from our showers.

Her taste had been on my lips the moment we parted, a scar that hadn't faded, a memory so vivid it felt like reality. But now, I tasted her again—and my memory hadn't done it justice.

She whimpered and shed her wet tears, thrusting her sex into my mouth. It took just a few minutes for her to release and grind against me, to arch her back hard and flail like she had no control of her body.

Knowing I was her one and only turned me on like crazy, that the pretty elf man had tried to take what was mine and failed. He might be a commander, but I was a king. My lips left hers, and I moved up her body so my dick could relish the fruits of my labor.

But instead of opening her thighs to my hips, she guided me onto my back and moved on top of me. Her wet sex sat on my fire-hot dick, and her lips gave a sexy moan.

I felt the pull on all my tendons, the desperation to be inside that wetness. My hands gripped her hips harder than I should have, and I released a breath louder than I meant to. Every second I wasn't inside her made me more desperate.

Her confidence waned as she grabbed my dick and directed me inside her. I was the one who was always on top, the one who did all the fucking, which I was perfectly fine with. But she wanted to reciprocate, though she still didn't quite know how.

I lifted myself against the headboard to sit up and then guided myself inside her, watching her slide down and sheathe me. My eyes closed because it felt so damn good, like we hadn't been fucking like rabbits for days, and it felt even better because I could see how much she wanted me. How much she needed me. Could feel her forgiveness and her commitment. Her lack of experience made it that much better, because I was the only man she'd ever wanted.

She slid down until there was nowhere else to go, and she released a shaky breath mixed with a wince.

My cock twitched inside her.

Her hands gripped my shoulders, and she brought herself close, arching her back farther than ever. As I'd taught her before, she rose and fell and rocked her hips at the same time, riding me down to the base before she lifted herself once again.

Damn.

She started to move quick and jerkily, her breaths growing heavy, and her nails began to claw me.

I grabbed her hips and slowed her down. "Baby..." I wouldn't last like this, not with the taste of her sweetness on my mouth and her pussy fucking my dick hard because she wanted to come again.

She matched the movements of my hands, resting her forehead against mine, her eyes down on my lips.

Fuck, this was worse.

My hands spanned her waist before I moved one hand into the valley between her tits, feeling her heartbeat right under the skin, feeling the soul attached to it. She was flesh and blood, good and innocent, unbreakable despite all the attempts to shatter her. I was a man who'd pissed away any chance of redemption, and I stood in the shade of her beacon of light because it made me feel whole...even for just a moment.

Her hand moved to mine and squeezed, just under her tit, where her frantic heart continued to race. She was right at the edge of her desire, ready to combust in a fire that would burn this whole forest. A flush entered her cheeks, her eyes glistened like morning dew on a flower, and her body contracted on me before she trembled.

When I felt her come around me, my hand left her chest and moved to her neck instead, clutching her hard enough to feel her frantic pulse under the skin. My dick was hard as steel as her body gripped me like a hand gripped the hilt of a sword. Her hips convulsed, and she turned into a teary-eyed mess on top of me, tits up with hard nipples sharp as daggers.

"Fuck." I squeezed her so hard I nearly choked her. I dumped everything inside that tightness and made her mine for the twelfth time since we'd been reunited. A line of women could have entertained me in her absence, but no woman ever satisfied me the way she did. No woman ever brought me this close to the sun.

I finally released her neck and watched her take a deep breath once her airway was clear. She lay on the rumpled bed beside me, her naked body slightly illuminated by the fireflies that danced outside the window. A sheen of sweat sparkled across her beautiful skin. She lay there and immediately closed her eyes.

I was still against the headboard as I looked down at her, her perfect body on display like she was about to be painted for a portrait to adorn a wall in the castle. Little scars were on her body, but I'd stopped noticing them a long time ago.

I shifted down until I was flat on the bed beside her, listening to the sound of the croaking frogs from the ponds and the chirping crickets hidden in the tall grass. I'd had no expectations when I'd walked into this forest, so I certainly hadn't expected it to remind me of home. But it did.

On summer nights, it used to sound just like this, the critters coming out now that the sun was gone. Enjoying the warm darkness and reduction in predators. The window was closed, so I couldn't feel the breeze, but I could imagine it through my hair and I could hear the waves against the base of the cliff, even though I was nowhere near the sea.

She opened her eyes and looked at me.

And time stopped. Her green eyes could command me the way a king commanded an army. I'd never felt inferior to anyone, felt like a pawn in someone's hand, until I met this woman. I was the darkness, and she was the light. I knew I didn't deserve her, but I also knew I wouldn't let her go, even if she wanted to walk away.

She continued to stare at me. "What's behind those dark eyes?"

Black riptides of death. Bottomless pits of brokenness. Sheer nothingness. "You." She was the only thing left in me.

The corners of her eyes dropped in heaviness, and I saw a mixture of affection and pity in her gaze. Then she smashed against me, the way butter met bread, and she crawled inside me until we were a single person.

My arms hooked around her and held her close, my lips resting against her forehead, smelling her scent because it reminded me of jasmine flowers on a spring afternoon. When her heart was close to mine, I felt better. Everything felt better. A month of loneliness and solitude had shown me that the light in my life didn't come from my fireplace or the fire in my dragon's belly.

It came from her.

"What do you think of the forest?" she whispered.

I stared at the fireflies through the window, their yellowish glow so bright it masked the stars up above. The place was beautiful and full of serenity, but there was a sense of discomfort that pressed against me like the tips of a thousand knives. The air around me was tight, like the forest wanted to eject me from its home with all the force it could muster. I didn't belong there, and for as long as I remained, the trunks of the trees would feel brittle like old bones. "It reminds me of home."

"You lived in a forest?"

"No. Late at night, I could hear the crickets in the grass and the frogs in the pond."

"You still call it home after all this time?"

I'd spent twenty years traveling to different places, taking up different trades, until my destiny could no longer be avoided. "It'll always be my home." I wondered how much it had changed, if the castle was still at the top of the cliff above the city, if the white stone of the buildings remained untouched or if it was scarred by soot and ash. Uncle Barron would have been dead by now if he were a mortal, but after being fused with Constantine, he wouldn't have aged a day. No doubt, he'd destroyed every piece of history that suggested my line had ever lived. The family portraits had probably been burned or thrown in the sea.

"You'll have to show me around...when this is over."

My fingers moved through her soft strands, gliding to the tips before I let it fall back to the pillow. I repeated it, caressing her hair over and over, the way a sailor dragged his oar through the water.

"I wish I could show you the forest, but I know Queen Eldinar would be furious."

I'd been apart from Calista so long that I didn't want to entertain a separation. My nights had been spent in a silent rage, gripping a glass in front of the fire, seeing another man in her private chambers as if he belonged there. "You're all I care about, baby."

I was up before she was.

In just my underwear, I walked into the kitchen where the dining table sat in the center, remembering one of our conversations when she'd had Commander Luxe over for dinner. I found the chopped coffee beans on the counter and boiled a pot of hot water to make myself a hot cup of coffee. I was used to servants doing this for me, but I was resourceful enough to figure it out on my own.

I sat at the dining table and looked out the window, seeing the flowers growing on the vines that hung from the roof. A hummingbird had just slipped its tongue inside a flower, but when it spotted me, it took off so quickly I couldn't see which direction it went.

Distance has never compromised our connection in the past, but the forest has muffled it. I don't feel you as strongly as I normally do.

I watched the steam rise from the cup of coffee. *We're deep in the forest, and the trees are thick.*

Are you well?

Yes.

The trees may be too big for me, but that doesn't mean I can't burn them down to get to you.

That will be unnecessary, Khazmuda.

I appreciate what the elves have done for my kind, but their prejudice against you blinds their sight.

I don't blame them for their hatred. I'm an easy man to hate.

And an easy man to love.

I smirked and drank the coffee.

Minutes later, Calista left the bedroom and came into the morning light that brightened the rest of the house. In just a cotton shirt and her panties, she lifted her arms high over her head as she stretched like a cat. "Morning."

Her shirt lifted to expose her little belly, and my hand immediately went to her hip and guided her onto my lap. "Morning."

Her arms circled my neck, and she kissed me.

My hand went to her ass and squeezed it as I felt her warm lips on mine, as I felt the tremble of my broken heart. She thawed the ice in my blood, reminded me of a joy I'd long forgotten.

She looked at the mug on the table. "You made coffee." She grabbed the mug by the handle and took a drink.

"It's all yours, baby."

"We can share." She took another drink and set it on the counter. "Want some breakfast?"

"Depends."

"On?" She left my lap and stood beside the chair.

My eyes went to her ass that was nearly at eye level. "Not in the mood for seeds and thorns, whatever these people eat."

"Well, I promise there won't be thorns in it." She headed to the kitchen counter and got to work, putting together a vegetable skillet that consisted of hearty potatoes with mushrooms and root vegetables. She cooked it in a sauce made of some kind of plant-based milk. The combination of the ingredients and the spices made a smell waft through the house that wasn't half bad.

Minutes later, she brought two plates to the table along with her own mug of coffee. I sat at the head of the table, and she took the seat beside me, beautiful first thing in the morning when her eyes were rested and her skin rejuvenated.

We ate in silence.

The potatoes were charred on the outside but soft on the inside, and the other vegetables had a good taste mixed with the ingredients she'd thrown together without a recipe book.

"What do you think?"

"It could use some thorns."

She stopped eating and released a quick chuckle. "Did you just make a joke?"

I continued to eat like nothing of the sort had happened.

"I don't think I've ever heard you do that, except when you're being sarcastic."

My eyes remained down on the plate to avoid her stare.

"You should make jokes more often."

I finished my plate then sat back to drink my coffee. In the castle, my breakfast usually consisted of meat and eggs, or I didn't have breakfast at all.

She finished her breakfast a moment later and looked out the window at the sunshine and the flowers. "It's still hard to believe you're here. When you visited me before, it felt like a dream."

A dream with a hefty cost. "Thank you for breakfast."

"Wow, you have manners too."

I smirked. "Don't get used to it."

"I like this new version of you."

It wasn't new. Just buried for a very long time.

She must have watched my eyes fall because hers did too. "You disappear so quickly..."

"There's very little left of that version of me."

She didn't ask why, and I appreciated that.

"If we find the dragons and they agree to fight for our cause and we take back the Southern Isles...then what?"

Taking back the Southern Isles wasn't the ambition. Just usurping the ruler who'd taken it from me. "The dragons will be free. Scorpion Valley will be yours once again. The world will be as it should be."

"You expect me to stay in Scorpion Valley while you're in the Southern Isles?" she asked with pain in her voice.

No, that wasn't what I expected at all. "I don't know what will come, Calista. It's hard to think about the aftermath of a victory that I haven't earned yet. That I may never earn." I might gamble the lives of free dragons and Calista and lose it all. Then my life and soul would be forfeit...all for nothing.

She turned quiet, her pretty eyes contemplative.

A knock sounded on the front door.

I immediately rose to my feet and headed to the front of the house.

"Aren't you going to put something on?" she asked as she stepped out of sight of the door.

"No." I opened the front door and came face-to-face with Commander Luxe, who was completely adorned in his dark green armor and his black cape.

I'd hoped it would be him. "Yes?" I was taller and more muscular, probably because I ate a man's diet instead of foraging for berries and nuts like a fucking rabbit.

His eyes flicked back and forth as he recovered from his surprise, as if he'd expected Calista to open the door in appropriate attire. "Queen Eldinar requests your presence in the royal palace. I'll escort you there."

I shut the door in his face without saying a word.

Calista left the kitchen and came into view. She must have heard what he'd said because she went into the bedroom to get dressed.

"Hold on." I came up behind her and shoved her onto the bed.

She hit the mattress and looked at me in surprise. "What are you doing?"

I moved on top of her and pulled her panties off her ass so I could sink into her tightness. I shoved my boxers down before I adjusted her underneath me.

"They're waiting for us—"

I sank inside her, greeted by her slickness. "And they'll wait."

We walked down the path, Commander Luxe in the lead while flanked by two of his men. The rest of the soldiers walked behind me, keeping a tight formation all around me like I might snap and destroy this forest with my bare hands.

Calista walked beside me in an olive-green dress with flat sandals, her hair combed back to reveal her beautiful face on this sunny day. I felt the attraction the first moment I saw her, but she was in her element here, looking like a princess of the forest. I understood her affection for this place.

After a short walk, we approached the entrance to the royal palace, a building that had ivy and flowers growing up the sides, a statue in the front, either of Queen Eldinar or the Riviana, the God of Caelum. It was hard to know which.

We were escorted inside, Queen Eldinar sitting upon her throne with a spine stiffer than the trees outside the dwelling. In a white dress with the image of flowers interwoven in the fabric and white flowers braided in her hair, she was a woman of unnatural beauty, her appearance blessed by the nearly immortal blood that ran through her veins.

But she was still no match for Calista.

The General of Riviana was at her side, sword on his hip while his palm rested on the pommel. His resemblance to Calista was obvious in that moment. Their eyes were the same. Same color and shape...and same heart. He seemed to have recovered from the battle, with the exception of the scar on the side of his head.

Queen Eldinar stared at me with her nose turned up like I was a cockroach that had crawled into her bed.

As the ruling monarch, she refused to speak first, so I folded just to get the conversation going. "How may I be of service, Your Majesty?"

Her nose upturned slightly less at my gesture of respect. "We hoped to have more time to recover from the battle, not just physically, but emotionally as well. But according to our scout reports, the dark elves approach our border with the unmistakable intention of breaching it. Tension has existed between our two races, but it's been a very long time since they tried to infiltrate our borders. They must know that we're weary from our battle with the Behemoths at the border and have taken this opportunity to strike."

A smart move. "Then I will meet them in battle and protect your border." One look at me and they would scatter like a pack of squirrels. I would raise an army of the dead to act as a barrier between their lands and the elves'—and no one would cross it. I probably wouldn't even have to lift my sword.

"Under no circumstance are you to disturb the dead, Talon."

"King Talon." I wouldn't allow another monarch to belittle my power, not after everything I'd done to earn it. "If you want me to respect your crown, then you will respect mine. If you're unwilling to do that, then I'll leave you to be overrun by these creatures. Khazmuda and I will find the dragons—eventually."

She sat with her arms on the armrests, her blue eyes angry in provocation. But she didn't refute my request. "You can't call upon the dead to fight for you. They've been disturbed once, and I won't allow you to disturb them again."

"Then you shouldn't have asked the Death King for aid."

She continued her angry stare.

I stared back.

"I will not change my mind, King Talon."

"Then you expect me to defeat an army of elves without magic or Khazmuda."

Her intelligent eyes were pointed but veiled, the truth of her thoughts shrouded in mystery.

I felt the smile move across my lips. "Or you expect me not to..."

"If you're nothing without your curse and your ally, then perhaps you're nothing as well."

"Perhaps." I felt the smile slowly fade away. "I will defend your forest—without the dead. And when I'm victorious, you will kneel before me and thank me before your subjects. Are we in agreement?"

She could express so much with just her gaze. For a beautiful woman, she could look so vicious, her eyes like daggers in that pretty face. Her hatred cut through flesh and bone, a storm cloud that billowed around her. "Yes."

"When your men are ready to march, so will I."

General Ezra presented my sword and scabbard in his open arms.

I took it and secured it across my back where my cape was attached to my armor.

Then he presented my dagger and bow.

I took them and returned them to my body.

Then he presented another dagger, the hilt the color of his dark hair and the blade solid black. "The blade is short, but the heft is substantial. Can pierce most armor if it's used in the correct manner."

I eyed it before I took it.

"A gift from my queen."

"An odd gift to bestow upon someone you hope doesn't return."

The general ignored my words and walked off.

Calista came to me next, the storm clouds of worry so heavy in her gaze it looked like it would rain. "I don't like this."

"Nor do I."

"Then maybe we shouldn't do it."

"The dark elves march as we speak. Even if your queen offered me nothing in return, I would still fight—not for her, but for you."

A sad affection moved into her eyes. "I want to come with you."

The statement was so ridiculous I didn't even respond to it.

"Talon—"

"Don't worry about me."

"But what will you do without your army? Without Khazmuda?"

"Khazmuda may not be here, but his blood is still in my veins. Queen Eldinar will be relieved that the dark elves have been defeated, but she'll be disappointed when I return with only a few scratches."

"You don't think she actually wants you dead, right?"

"I do."

"Why would she want that?"

"So she gets what she wants without having to uphold her end of the deal. The Death King will be gone from these lands, and the location of the dragons will remain a secret, while her greatest enemy has been defeated. I may not like your queen, but I respect her strategy."

Despite the fact that the clearing was full of soldiers, including Commander Luxe and General Ezra, Calista came close to me and grabbed my hand because it wasn't sheathed in my glove. She blanketed me in affection without touching me, the depth in her eyes bottomless. "I just got you back..."

I cupped her face, and I brushed my thumb over her cheek.

She closed her eyes and relaxed into my touch, her hand tightening on mine.

When I held her like this, I forgot the circumstances of my life, the events that had brought me here because, for a moment, I only knew peace. I searched for it in violence and in revenge, but I found it in her.

She opened her eyes and looked at me again.

I didn't promise her I would return because I wouldn't make a promise I couldn't keep. But I wouldn't let my story end here, in a battle that didn't further my own interests. It was a stepping-stone to what I needed—and I wouldn't trip going up the steps. "Gather your armor and sword. Be prepared for battle."

"Then you think you'll fail—"

"The winner of the battle is not necessarily the strongest, but the most prepared." I'd learned that the hard way. I cupped her cheeks and pressed a kiss to her mouth, claiming her as mine in front of everyone who stood there. "I'll come back to you."

I marched beside General Ezra as we left the forest to the west, the army of soldiers marching behind us. Instead of marching in lines and ranks like I'd been taught, they were scattered because of the trees, but still a single entity.

Queen Eldinar stayed behind with her guards and let her husband fight in the name of her crown.

A cowardly move.

We marched in silence. I felt my connection to Calista dwindle the farther apart we became. Commander Luxe was down at the end of the line, leading a different section of the men.

"General Ezra."

He looked at me as he continued to march forward.

"Tell me everything about their kind." I remembered the message that King Constantine had delivered to us. It had arrived too late, didn't give us enough warning to act or flee. It said the dark elves had conquered the minds of the dragons and taken control. Were these the same race as my enemy?

He looked forward again and remained quiet for a while. "A long time ago, they lived among our kind. They were no different from us. But Alaric was hungry for power and tried to take the crown from Queen Eldinar. This was long before my time, and all I have is the tale. It was a coup, but my wife was too smart to fall for the scheme. She banished Alaric from our lands, and his followers went with him."

I listened to the story and waited for more.

"They returned years later and attacked Riviana Star, but this time, they didn't come for Queen Eldinar. It was clear their eyes were set on the Great Tree, the Realm of Caelum. It was then that Queen Eldinar realized Alaric had never wanted the crown—just the gateway. Some of them made it through, and the ones who didn't were cursed by Riviana herself. Their skin was marked with the curse by turning gray, the color of death. Their punishment for trying to steal the afterlife was to be permanently banished from it. As you can imagine, that infuriated Alaric and his followers even more."

"Did the curse affect them in other ways?"

General Ezra glanced at me. "I don't understand your question."

"You said they're made to look like death. But did the curse bestow any other effects or abilities?"

He still seemed confused by the question. "Not that I know of. But it's been a thousand years since we've interacted with Alaric and the dark elves. Perhaps they abandoned their crusade until they learned about the Behemoths on the border and assumed we were compromised."

So, if the dark elves had the ability to control minds, General Ezra and Queen Eldinar didn't know about it. *I march with General Ezra and the army to defeat the dark elves that compromise their border.*

And you tell me this now?

Under no circumstance are you to attempt to help me.

I will do as I please.

If these dark elves are the same as those who took my kingdom, then we can't risk their invasion into your mind.

I defied their attacks, Talon.

But I would rather die than risk it.

Khazmuda was quiet.

It's not worth it.

"I don't like you."

I turned back to the general when I heard what he said.

"I don't like you for my niece...is what I mean."

I marched by his side and continued to hold his gaze.

"I appreciate what you've done for her. I appreciate the way you've protected her. But we both know you're the wrong man for her. She's suffered enough, and I don't want her to suffer anymore."

The flush of anger was enough to make my blood boil underneath the surface. "When you discovered that Scorpion Valley had been conquered and your brother slain, what did you do?"

He held my gaze.

"Answer me."

He looked ahead and remained silent.

"Nothing—that's what you did. There wasn't enough love or loyalty to your brother to get you to leave this forest and search for the only family you had left. An orphaned little girl was forced to survive on her own—and you couldn't get off your ass."

His eyes remained locked ahead.

"I didn't kill her father. He handed her over to his commander and offed himself. A fucking coward."

General Ezra stopped.

And instantly, so did the entire army.

He looked at me, the rage in his eyes.

"Her father abandoned her. You abandoned her. But I never have. When an army marched upon your forest with her inside it, I flew across the land to raise my sword in her defense. She told me she never wanted to see me again, but I still came. You may not like me, General Ezra. But every man in her life has failed her—except for me."

General Ezra raised his hand when we approached a large clearing.

The entire army stopped.

We didn't march with heavy footfalls like most men. The elves were quiet, slithering through the grass and around the roots of trees like snakes. It was dark, and I spotted the torches in the distance on the way here.

Now, I saw them up close, a line of torches across the wide gap between the trees. It wasn't large enough for a battle to take place, but it was a clear divide between the two borders. The trees were different here, shorter in height with less vegetation.

We stood there for minutes. The soldiers waited for orders.

I waited to spot the enemy, refusing to engage in battle without understanding their numbers or formation.

General Ezra continued to stare ahead.

Then someone appeared through the trees, starting as a shadow before the light of the torches struck his face. The only evidence that he was an elf was his pointed ears, but the rest of him looked human. He was thick and muscular, much bigger than any of the elves who stood behind me. He was dressed in black armor that blended in with the darkness around him. He had long black hair that was combed from his face—and a long scar down the center of his eye.

He stopped at the line of torches and looked straight at us, like he could see in the dark.

General Ezra took a step forward.

My hand went to his shoulder, and I steadied him. "Allow me."

He threw my hand down. "I'm the general of Riviana Star, and you follow my orders."

I lowered my voice. "I remember your wife asking me to handle this—not you."

He said nothing, but his eyes did all the talking.

I walked forward and broke the line of trees.

The dark elf immediately shifted his gaze to me when I emerged, and that arrogant smile slowly faded as I drew near. The disgusting glee left his face, and he turned serious once he realized he faced more than the elves.

I stood several feet away, my face visible in the torchlight.

He stared at me with wide eyes, his skin the color of stone in the mountains, his eyes dark and lifeless. But he was tall and burly, a creature that existed off meat instead of seeds and berries like his relations. "You're cursed." His voice was deeper than I expected, like the hum from deep in a mountain. "Cursed just like us."

"Yes."

He glanced at the army behind me before he looked at me once again. Then he changed his tongue, speaking in the language of death. "*Scion hueim ahieu schiem buros.*" The Death King has conquered Riviana Star.

I spoke back in the same language. *Yurot ahugn viuah Riviana Star. Buffios niuiss vitti zurois cuaoloum.* I have not conquered Riviana Star. I'm an ally of the forest.

"Impossible. Queen Eldinar would never accept aid from a necromancer."

"She fears you—so she must."

A smile moved across his face. Not a normal smile like a child could wear, but a demented one, a mad one. "As she should."

"What do you want in the Realm of Caelum, Alaric?"

His eyes bored into mine as if he was hypnotized by my stare. "To be the God of Caelum. To make Riviana serve me on her knees. To banish Queen Eldinar and every elf who has ever supported her to an eternity in the underworld. That is what I wish, Death King."

"That's quite ambitious."

He smiled again. "Not as ambitious as you."

"And how do you intend to subjugate a god?"

He stared at me with that same smile. "Riviana may be invulnerable among us, but in Caelum, she is touchable. She is vulnerable. I will chain her wrists and her ankles. I will fuck the pussy of a god and take her crown."

I didn't fear this creature. Not his size or his ambition. But his words were vile...and made me sick. I remembered my wife's tears when she told me what happened to her. And I would never forgive myself for what happened to Calista because I felt responsible for her tragedy.

His fingers moved to his temple. "When she cursed us, she bestowed upon us a gift, a gift to attack with the mind." He tapped twice before he lowered his hand. His smile was wider than ever. "She may be physically superior, but her mind will break under my hold."

A rush of fear moved up my spine. We were thousands of leagues across the sea from my homeland, but some of these dark elves must have left the forest and moved elsewhere throughout the last thousand years. It was too much of a coincidence. "Why haven't you used this ability against Queen Eldinar?"

"Because it doesn't work on mortals."

That meant it would work on me. Or Khazmuda.

A hint of a smile was still on his lips. "What did Queen Eldinar offer you in return for your service? There is no other reason the Death King would choose an ally that's beneath him."

I was certain that General Ezra and the others could hear us speak, but they didn't understand the content since the language was unknown to them. Very few knew it because it had to be bestowed upon you as a gift or a curse. "My kingdom across the sea was taken from me.

My family was executed. I need to find the remaining free dragons to fight alongside me as I take my revenge. Queen Eldinar knows their location and will share it with me in exchange for your defeat."

His smile was back. "And you believe her?"

"She made the vow in the presence of her people. If she doesn't fulfill it, she'll be a liar."

"Being a liar is one of her better traits."

I didn't care for her either, but I wouldn't insult her in the presence of her enemies.

"She's not the only one who knows the location of the dragons."

I'd marched through the forest to fight with my sword and my speed, not with my mind. Now, I was locked in a dangerous chess game where every single move counted. "If that's true, why haven't you gone to them?"

"To do what?" he said. "If the dragons burn down the forest, they burn the gateway to the Realm of Caelum. The forest is too dense for their kind to fight alongside us, so they're worthless in this regard."

"How do you know where they are?"

"Because I was there when we freed the dragons from the humans and granted them asylum. I was one of the

Guardians of Thalian until my service was completed, and I was allowed to return to Riviana Star. There is no other safe place for the dragons, so I know they haven't changed the location."

It might be foolish to believe him, but I did.

"Join us. Raise your army of the dead. Help me take the Realm of Caelum, and I'll give you what you seek."

Uncle Barron wouldn't have succeeded in his plan without the aid of the dark elves. If Riviana had never cursed them, this gift of mental subjugation never would have been bestowed and none of this would have happened at all. I wasn't sure who deserved the blame—Alaric or Riviana.

In either case, I was the one who'd paid the price.

He pressed me when he grew anxious. "What say you, Death King?"

"I can't betray my alliance. I'm a man of my word and have to preserve my integrity."

He blinked several times as he stared, trying to hide his disappointment. "I understand. Then excuse yourself from the battle, and I'll still give you what you seek."

They didn't seem to fear the elves. Only me.

"Don't trust her, Death King. She may shake your hand in public, but she'll stab you in the back when no one is looking. The safety of those dragons is her responsibility, so there's no scenario in which she trusts it to an enemy of Riviana."

"I'm not an enemy to Riviana."

"You're sired by Bahamut, God of the Underworld. You're forever under his command, so yes, you're an enemy to Riviana." Alaric continued to stare at me. "I will give you their location this very moment if you agree to stand aside. That is a small sacrifice to have what you want above all else. I offer my hand, and it would be unwise to push it away."

I continued to stare, my heart racing with my predicament. Those dragons were all I needed and I could continue my war, but what price was I willing to pay for them?

Alaric's stare was locked on my face, his eyes shifting back and forth as he waited for my answer with palpable desperation.

At that moment, General Ezra joined us. "I grow tired of these secrets." His hard gaze pierced the side of my face. "What says he?"

Alaric acted as if he weren't there.

I said nothing.

"Speak," General Ezra commanded.

Alaric smirked.

"You've been at war with Queen Eldinar for a millennium," I said, still speaking to Alaric. "If you go to war with Riviana Star, those of you who perish will never reach the afterlife. The battle is not worth the risk to your vulnerable mortality. The Realm of Caelum is heavily guarded, and you have no chance of breaking through that defense. I give you one week to vacate this forest and reside at least a hundred leagues elsewhere. It's time to move on, Alaric."

"Perhaps you're right." Alaric continued to wear his disturbing smile. He gave a slight bow before he turned away and walked back into the trees from which he came. "Thank you for your mercy, Death King."

Chapter 3

Calista

The tension in my heart made it shrivel. It hardened my blood to stone. My lungs ached to breathe but couldn't capture the air. More than a day had passed since Talon left, and we'd received no news.

I did as he asked and wore my armor and carried my sword. It didn't feel heavy at first, but with every passing hour, it made me sink into the soil from the weight. It became harder to breathe. I barely slept and hardly ate, poor preparations for battle, but I couldn't do much else until I knew he was okay.

I couldn't ask Khazmuda if Talon was alright because we were too far apart to speak with our minds.

Then we finally got word from a scout that the army had returned.

I waited at the royal palace with Queen Eldinar, hoping that both my uncle and Talon would return in the same condition as when they left. In their absence, I hadn't spoken with the queen because she would offer no solace. She acted like I didn't exist, offering no maternal support because she was clearly disinterested in a familial relationship. She would always blame me for the Behemoths who marched on their lands.

I wouldn't waste my time trying to change it.

The soldiers began to file in, and the first person I saw was my uncle. But before I could run to him, Queen Eldinar left her throne and got to him first. I hadn't seen her show him affection in public, but she immediately cupped his face and brought their heads together.

I looked past him and saw Talon, his black armor making him stick out like a spot of blood on a white sheet. His intense gaze was locked on mine, and I grabbed on to his even though he was still twenty feet away.

I didn't care who saw or what they thought, I ran straight to him.

A small smile came over his lips, and he looked so handsome.

I moved into his chest and rose on my tiptoes to kiss him.

Both of his arms circled me, and he brought me close as he kissed me, not squeezing me like he usually did because the plates of his armor were as solid as stone. He pulled away and pressed a kiss to my forehead before he released me.

"I can see there was no battle," Queen Eldinar said. "The armor is untarnished. There were no injuries. So, what happened?" She turned her gaze on Talon as if he was somehow at fault.

He stared her down, me standing at his side.

General Ezra turned around and gave him the angriest look I'd ever seen. "I don't know what happened, Your Majesty. Because the Death King communicated with Alaric in a language I've never heard."

"You heard what I said to him," Talon said. "I gave him a week to leave your forest and settle somewhere at least a hundred leagues away. Their kind will no longer be a threat to you, and no lives will be lost in the process."

Queen Eldinar slowly walked up to him, dressed in her pristine white armor and ready for battle. "And he agreed?"

I stepped away because it seemed as if they were about to swipe at each other.

Talon held her gaze. "It appears so."

"I asked you to *defeat* them. Not ask them to leave."

"If they're a hundred leagues away, then they're as good as defeated."

"And why would they listen to you?" Her eyes narrowed. "We've been at war with them for a thousand years, and all it takes is the Death King to ask nicely?"

"They fear me."

Anger flashed across her eyes. "If they fear you, you should have killed them—"

"Without my army and my dragon, I am far more vulnerable. Why would I risk injury and death if there was another option? Perhaps if you hadn't handicapped me, you would have gotten what you wanted."

She shook her head slightly from side to side, her jawline tight as she clenched her mouth to suppress her ire. "You're worthless—"

"You thought you could outsmart me, when I will always outsmart you, *Your Majesty*. I'm a man of my word, and now it's time for you to be one of yours. Take us to the location of the dragons."

She turned around, walked back to Uncle Ezra, and stared him down. "How long did this secret conversation go on?"

"Minutes." Uncle Ezra turned his accusatory look on Talon.

"And then they switched to the common tongue when you approached?" she asked.

"Yes."

Queen Eldinar turned back to Talon. "Why do two strangers have so much to talk about?"

Talon said nothing.

She walked back toward him. "What was said?"

"Nothing that concerns you."

Even I didn't like that answer, and I felt uneasy.

"You're my ally, and they're my enemy," Queen Eldinar said. "You should want to tell me."

"Show me the location of the dragons, and I will."

"How dare you hold this against me—"

"Like how you're holding this against me?" His eyes narrowed. "I'll tell you one thing, Your Majesty. He told me not to trust you—and now I wonder if I should heed that warning."

I stood there and felt the tremor in my heart, felt so much unease I wanted to explode. I was so relieved when he'd come back unscathed, but this showdown was just as strenuous.

She stepped back. "When you're ready to share the details of that conversation, let me know. In the meantime, you can make yourself comfortable in one of our cells." She gestured to General Ezra. "Take him away."

No.

General Ezra moved for him.

Talon was faster than all of them, drawing his blade and throwing an elbow into the face of one guard before punching another in the face. It all happened in the blink of an eye, and then he managed to grab my uncle and spin him around, holding the blade to his neck. "I saved your forest from guaranteed annihilation. Behemoths would have claimed this forest for their own, and the dark elves would have infiltrated the Realm of Caelum by now—and you would all be dead. I understand my reputation precedes me, but I have never given you a reason to distrust me. Khazmuda is fused with me by choice. Inferno was always given a choice. And then you send me to battle with my arms tied behind my back, and I make your enemies run like minnows in a pond—and this is how you treat me?" He continued to hold the blade to my uncle's neck.

Queen Eldinar remained remarkably calm despite the blade to her husband's throat. "If you want me to trust you, then tell me what was said."

"He told me not to trust you. I already told you that."

"Talon..." My voice broke on its way out because I was scared, scared of what could happen to the two men I cared most about.

Talon didn't look at me, but his hardness faded.

"Talon, please let him go."

He clenched his jaw like he was furious then released my uncle. Threw his blade on the ground and stepped back.

My body finally relaxed.

"Tell me what was said, King Talon," Queen Eldinar demanded. "Why do you resist—"

"Because our conversation doesn't concern you," he snapped. "I didn't betray you. Here I stand, still your ally, when I probably shouldn't be. You played games with me, and you still continue to do so."

Queen Eldinar stood with a stiff spine and didn't check on her husband's neck, which didn't suffer a bleed. Her eyes were reserved for Talon. "You're right. I don't trust you." She gestured to the men. "Take him away."

"No." I moved to the queen. "Your Majesty—"

"This doesn't concern you." She didn't even look at me.

The guards surrounded Talon and grabbed him by the arms.

Talon quickly twisted out of their hold. "Trust me, if I wanted to get out of this, I could."

They led him away to the building beside the royal palace.

I went to General Ezra next. "Please stop this."

"Calista—"

"He did as you asked."

"You didn't hear them." He grabbed Talon's sword from the ground then turned to me.

"And neither did you."

"I couldn't understand the words, but I understood their behavior. Alaric had a vile grin on his face almost the entire time. They spoke to each other as equals, almost as friends or comrades. Talon issued no threat."

"You don't know that."

"I think Alaric propositioned him for a plot to overthrow us, and Talon agreed."

"He would never do that."

"Calista, I understand love makes you blind. I love a woman I'll love my whole life, and she'll love me for a second. It's complicated and messy, and I get that. But you don't see who this man really is."

I felt the tears behind my eyes. "I see him for all that he is."

"I didn't need to understand them to know what transpired. Talon asked them to leave, but I think it's a red herring."

"A red herring for what?"

"For the fact that they'll return and try to take Riviana. And when they arrive, Talon will help them."

"Why? Why would he do that? What does he get out of that?"

He hesitated.

"There is no motive, Uncle Ezra. You're making baseless assumptions out of fear."

"Alaric knows where the dragons are. I'm sure he figured out why the Death King marched with us and offered him the location if he turned on us—and he did."

"He did not."

He gave me a look layered in disappointment. "Because you can't see, Calista."

"He would never betray you or me."

"Do you understand that he's sired by Bahamut?"

Talon had told me the origins of his power, but he didn't tell me the tale. He said it was too beautiful of a night to discuss something so heavy.

"Bahamut and Riviana are enemies. Have you noticed that the music in the forest has changed? Because every moment that one of Bahamut's servants dwells in this forest is agony for her. As a puppet of the God of the Underworld, Talon wants to destroy the afterlife as much as the dark elves. It was a mistake granting him access to our forest. Alaric and the dark elves are coming, and we must be prepared. If our scouts report that the dark elves have left the forest by the deadline, then we'll release Talon."

"If they've decided to stay, that still isn't enough to incriminate Talon."

"I disagree."

When I looked at Talon, I didn't see a master of shadow or the embodiment of evil. I didn't see a puppet of an evil god. I saw a broken man with a broken heart...but a heart, nonetheless. "I understand your concern, but you're wrong about him. I would put my life on it."

He continued to look at me with pity. "Then it's a good thing you don't have to."

The prison had no other prisoners besides Talon, so Queen Eldinar stationed guards outside the building.

I entered the building and found him behind iron bars, leaning against the wall with his arms and ankles crossed, still wearing his heavy armor like it weighed nothing. There was a small window at the top of a stone wall that allowed some light to come through. He was staring at it when I walked inside.

I stood at the bars and looked at him.

He continued to gaze out the window instead of at me.

"They said if the dark elves leave within the week, they'll release you."

He seemed uninterested in that.

"And if they don't, I'll get them to release you."

"I can leave this cell whenever I wish." He slowly turned to look at me. "But that would require me to do things that would piss off your queen." His dark eyes looked at me with heavy disappointment.

He would raise the dead to set himself free. Or he would have Khazmuda burn the forest.

"It's interesting. They say they don't trust me, but we all know I'm only in here because I'm a willing participant. Because I have too much integrity to disturb the dead now that I understand how much grief it caused their people."

"Why won't you tell them what Alaric said to you?"

"Because." He looked at the window again.

"Because why?"

He didn't answer.

"Will you tell me?"

After he stared at the window for a while, he turned back to me. "Someday."

"I—I don't understand."

"I told you how my family was killed. I told you the dragons were subjugated by a foul creature with magical abilities. Well, those beings were called dark elves, and they're the same as the ones in this forest."

My eyes immediately dropped.

"Not the exact same ones, but...they're the same kind."

"Why wouldn't you want the queen to know this?"

"The reason they have these abilities is because they're cursed, and Riviana is the one who cursed them. So, did I lose everyone I love because of the dark elves, or because of the god that lives in this forest?"

My blood ran cold at his words.

"I haven't decided." He looked out the window again.

Now I understood why he didn't want the queen to know, because his allegiance was unclear. Would he want revenge against the monsters in the forest...or against the god they worshipped? "There's only one person to blame, and that's the person who conspired against your family. Once we have the dragons, we'll kill him."

He continued to stare out the window.

"Talon."

He slowly turned to look at me.

"Did Alaric offer to tell you where the dragons are?"

He didn't hesitate before he answered. "Yes."

"And did you take it?"

Now, there was a hesitation, a long pause. "I told him to leave."

"That didn't answer my question."

"I told him to leave, and I returned in the hope that your queen would honor her obligation. But she didn't. I'm treated as the villain in this story when your queen is a manipulative liar. I didn't take his offer, but now I wish I had."

"Why don't you tell her this so you can walk out of here?"

He tilted his head slightly, almost as if he didn't understand the question. "Because she wouldn't believe me and would try to kill me—so I'd have to kill her."

Chapter 4

Calista

"Release him." I stood before Queen Eldinar in the royal chambers where she sat upon her throne, wearing her armor and short swords at her hips instead of her elegant dress. It was clear she expected Alaric to march on her forest rather than leave like Talon had asked. "You must realize that he could escape that prison whenever he wishes. He could call upon the dead to rip off the door or have Khazmuda come to his rescue. But he refrains from doing both out of respect for you and your kingdom."

She listened to all of this with a bored look on her face.

"Queen Eldinar—"

"Yes, I heard you." She sat with her legs crossed, her fingers drumming on the armrests. Uncle Ezra wasn't present at her side, so he must be preparing for the battle that might arrive at their doorstep. "If he wants out, all he has to do is tell me what was said. His unwillingness to share information makes me question his intentions."

"I think your questions are questionable, Your Majesty."

Her eyes narrowed so fast.

"We both know you sent him out there in the hope he would die."

Her fingers continue to drum on the armrests. "I still believe the world would be better off without an angry necromancer."

"Then your forest would be ruled by Behemoths as we speak."

"Your father would be alive and you would rule Scorpion Valley if he hadn't taken power, so your argument is untrue."

"He still saved your forest—"

"Because you nearly destroyed it." She raised her voice, her words echoing off the stone walls covered with ivy. "I don't trust him. I can't escort him to the dragon haven when such a doubt festers in my heart. I fully understand that our cell won't hold a man such as the Death King, but I must restrain him until the battle is finished."

"What battle?"

"Did you really think Alaric and the dark elves would leave this forest?" she asked incredulously. "I suspect they forged an agreement that will compromise the gateway to the Realm of Caelum. We'll be subjugated and killed. And if the Death King is free of his prison, he will raise his sword and his army against us."

"How many times do I have to say it?" I snapped. "He would *never* do that."

"You're young and deep in the forest of lust. Even the weeds look like roses in a garden."

My physical attachment to him went deeper than the flesh. I felt cleansed by his touch, made whole by the healing powers of his eyes. "It's more than lust."

She stared at me for a long time, her thoughts locked behind the gates of her intelligent eyes. "Then he must have told you the details of that conversation."

My heart squeezed when it missed a beat, and a cloud of suffocation moved over me and blocked out the sun. Talon hadn't asked me to keep his secret, but I knew he'd shared it with me because our trust was ironclad. "No."

She cocked her head slightly, her eyes homing in on my face. "And you didn't ask?"

"I knew he wouldn't tell me."

Her fingers had been still on the armrest for the last few minutes, but they started to tap once again. "I don't believe you. If your relationship is so deep, then it's based on trust, loyalty, and love. That means he wouldn't hesitate to tell you—and he wouldn't hesitate to believe that you would guard his secret."

I held her gaze and did my best not to harden my expression.

"Keeping this information to yourself when I granted you asylum in my kingdom undermines your character."

Talon's voice came into my head. *Your queen is a manipulative liar.* "You granted me asylum because you didn't trust me. Don't pretend you did it out of the goodness of your heart. I love your forest and I admire your commitment to protecting a race that's not your kin, so I would never do anything to compromise your kingdom or your people."

I returned after sunset, bringing him dinner I'd made in my kitchen. I slid the bowl through the bars on the floor then dropped the fork inside it. I also brought a canteen of water, along with some wine.

There was an armchair in the corner, and he sat there, covered in shadows. Fireflies were visible through the window. Some of them came into his cell and hovered there, acting as a beacon in the dark building.

One came close, and then his face was illuminated. The light highlighted his sharp jawline, his bottomless eyes. He stared at me, his ankle resting on the opposite knee, looking like he sat upon a throne rather than an old chair.

"I talked to Queen Eldinar today. Tried to negotiate your release."

"Don't waste your time, baby."

I sat on the floor on the other side of the bars, wishing we weren't separated by the metal. "How does Khazmuda feel about this?"

He released a slight chuckle. "If he knew, you would know exactly how he felt about it." He left his chair then joined me on the floor. "He would burn down this forest and everyone inside it." He sat with a straight spine and took a bite from the bowl. It was a medley of vegetables and I'd tried to make something as hearty as possible, but I knew it wouldn't satisfy him the way meat would. But he didn't complain. "Thank you for dinner."

"I wasn't sure if they were feeding you."

"They gave me a bag of seeds like I'm a fucking bird."

An uncontrollable chuckle escaped. "Another joke?"

"It's only a joke if I'm kidding." He took a couple bites then opened the wine I'd provided.

"I'll get her to release you."

"She knows she can't keep me long. I already see her plan." He spoke in between bites.

"What's her plan?"

"If Alaric and the dark elves vacate the lands, she'll release me. If they don't, they'll march on this forest. She'll keep me confined through the battle to ensure I don't assist Alaric. She wins in any scenario, because if I release myself from this prison, I would have to violate her one rule, and she'll use that to justify her hatred."

"Do you think Alaric will come?"

He stared down at his bowl as he finished off the last few bites. "I don't know. But I can't leave until I have the location of those dragons, so I'll wait until I have that answer. Whether there is a great battle...or there is no battle at all."

"I'll keep trying to get her to release you."

"Don't waste your time, baby." He grabbed the wine and took a heavy drink.

"I just got you back." I looked at the bars that separated us, the solid metal that neither one of us could pierce. My bed was supposed to be warm with him beside me. I was supposed to feel smothered by his kisses to my mouth and neck. I was supposed to feel safe when his mountain loomed over my valleys. Once I had him in my grasp again, I never wanted to be apart, and then he was ripped right out of my hands. "It's hard for me." He might be the cause of all my misery, but he was also my savior, the only man who proved his loyalty, the only man who could protect me from my nightmares.

He set the wine aside as he looked at me. "I'm right here, baby."

"It's not the same." I grabbed on to the bar, cool to the touch.

His hand moved to mine, where it rested against the metal. "Baby, look at me."

I continued to focus on our joined hands.

He didn't command me to meet his stare the way he did before. Now, he was gentle, giving me the time to find my courage on my own. His fingers were warm against mine, still strong with undying confidence.

I finally looked at him again.

He rested his forehead against the bar. "I'm right here."

I did the same, feeling parts of his skin against mine.

"I'm always here."

I woke up beside him on the hard floor of his cell.

It was morning, the song of the birds more distracting than the sunshine. Our hands were still together through the doors where we'd left them the night before. I stared at him beside me, even more handsome when his guard was down.

I lay there and studied his face, seeing the shadow on his jawline, the little scar on his neck that must be from the tip of a knife. If we were in my tree house, we would be naked under the sheets, and the second he opened his eyes, he would be on me again, smothering me with the same kisses he'd given me the night before.

I hadn't thought I'd enjoy sex after what happened with General Titan, but I craved it whenever I was with Talon. It was an experience so surreal it felt like a dream. The connection was greater than our bodies, involving our souls. Sex had broken me, but with Talon, it healed me.

I gently pulled my hand from his and left the prison to return to my tree house. I wanted to shower and make him breakfast. After the long journey up the vines of the tree house, I showered then worked in the kitchen, trying to make him something he might like, but all I had was oatmeal with berries. He probably preferred something hearty for breakfast, like eggs and bacon, but that simply wasn't possible.

I donned my armor once again and headed back down the vines, but when I reached the bottom, I knew something was amiss—because there were at least twelve guards there.

I stepped off the last vine with the bowl of oatmeal in my hand. "Did you need something?"

"Queen Eldinar requests your presence," one of the guards said.

"And she needed twelve of you to deliver that message?" I asked sarcastically.

The one in the lead gestured to the path. "Leave that here, and let's go."

I left the bowl at the bottom of the stairs to be retrieved later and let them escort me to the queen, treating me like a prisoner when I'd done nothing wrong. When I entered the royal chambers, I could feel the tension like humidity on a summer day.

The queen wasn't seated in her chair. She stood before me, in her armor and weapons like she was ready to march to battle. The look she gave me was as icy as a winter morning full of fog. "The enemy marches for Riviana Star."

Disappointment was heavy as a stone dropped in my stomach.

"The Death King's request seems to have fallen upon deaf ears." The look in her eyes was borderline maniacal, her stare so full of accusation like all of this was entirely my fault. "The dark elves do not march alone. They've struck an alliance with the Behemoths who fled the last battle. Our armies are evenly matched, and the outcome of this battle balances on the edge of a knife."

The sweat on my palms was instant. The fear in my heart was palpable. "Shit."

"You claim the forest is your home, so you will fight with us." It wasn't a request, but a command. "Every able-bodied elf is called to battle. Our army is simply not enough to challenge the foes who seek to destroy not only our kingdom, but the afterlife as well. Many of us will die, but if the Realm of Caelum is protected, we will live on. Can we count on your sword?"

Talon had trained me in the blade and I was a decent swordsman, but I was no soldier. I was also no coward, and leaving Riviana to its fate wasn't an option. "Of course you can, Queen Eldinar. And I know you can count on the Death King's as well."

Her eyes narrowed. "The Death King's allegiance is uncertain. He'll remain locked in his prison during the battle. Since the prison is located so far to the east, he'll remain unaware of the battle until its victory has already been determined."

My heart had already dropped once, but it managed to drop again. "If you already doubt your ability to triumph, then it makes even less sense to ignore his aid. Let him fight for you."

"No," she said. "And to make sure you don't defy my wishes, you'll stay at my side."

"This is a mistake—"

"Letting him into my forest was the mistake." She turned to General Ezra. "Equip her with her sword and daggers."

General Ezra retrieved my weapons and presented them to me.

I looked at the sword that Talon had given me and hesitated before I took it. It was heavier than I remembered, probably because I would need it in battle rather than training, probably because I would need it to protect my own life. I secured it at my hip and slipped my daggers into my greaves.

My uncle stood before me. "I asked her to pardon your participation, but since all elves have been called to fight, it would be a blatant form of nepotism on my part...and she's right."

"I understand, Uncle Ezra. I want to fight. I would just prefer to do it with Talon at my side." It was selfish, my desire for self-preservation, but I knew Talon was the only one who could watch my back and his front at the same time.

All he did was give a nod and step away.

I felt an icy chill move up my body despite the beautiful morning. The tranquility had been destroyed by the impending doom headed this way. When Talon woke up and realized I wasn't there, he would be suspicious. And when I didn't come back before this evening, he would grow more suspicious.

He would probably figure it out entirely on his own.

He would call upon the army of the dead, break his vow to the queen, and save us all.

They arrived at nightfall.

I couldn't see their flesh, but I could see their fire. Torches glowed in the distance, so many of them that they looked like stars in the dark sky. They appeared between the trees then disappeared again, only to pop up a second later.

I wanted to pretend I wasn't scared, but I was.

Queen Eldinar and General Ezra marched to the Great Tree with her personal guard of twenty-four soldiers. They were bigger than the other elves, more muscular with heavier armor and sour faces.

I was among them, unable to leave because their eyes were always on me.

When I looked upon the Great Tree for the first time, I could see the magic with the naked eye. There was no fire on her trunk or limbs, but she was illuminated by an internal glow that seemed to come from deep within. The Great Tree stood alone in a large clearing of grass, distinctly separate from the neighboring trees that were at least a hundred feet away. It possessed a thicker trunk, with branches as wide as the nearby trees and a height that reached way into the sky.

And the music...it was louder here. But it was also warped and pained, like Riviana could feel the intruders step into her lands.

In the center of the tree was a door made of withered branches, stretching across the front to make a solid barrier. The branches looked sturdy and gnarled, so it would take a long time to clear it, even with a sharp axe.

Queen Eldinar stopped in front of the Great Tree and gazed upon it with a mother's love. "I will protect you with my life, Riviana." She moved to the tree and placed her palm on the center of the door. Then she whispered under her breath words in her native tongue.

The song changed, turning soft like a lullaby.

My uncle watched her from where he stood, one hand resting on the hilt of his sword, looking at her with the same love she gave the tree.

When Queen Eldinar turned away from the tree, she went straight to my uncle.

"*Fleur Nia,*" he said quietly. "You don't have to do this."

"I will not let this tree fall." She looked at him with calm determination, a hint of resignation. "I suspect it'll claim my life, but as Queen of Riviana Star, it is my duty. I can't let this tree fall."

Uncle Ezra struggled to find words, visibly overcome with emotion he couldn't express in the presence of his men. His eyes dropped down to the ground between them, and he inhaled a heavy breath. "I will do my best to hold the perimeter." He raised his chin and looked at her again, his pain suppressed as much as possible.

She cupped his cheek. "I know you will."

He grabbed her by the wrist, and he turned into her palm, placing a kiss against the inside of her hand. He rested there, just holding her wrist as he stared at her, the undying love like a beacon of light in his eyes. Then he moved into her and cupped her cheeks before he kissed her, his fingers slipping into her hair, kissing her like they were alone rather than on display in front of an audience.

My stare felt intrusive, so I looked away.

Uncle Ezra eventually walked away and left the tree, knowing he might never see his wife or me again.

I looked at Queen Eldinar.

She stared at him until he disappeared from the clearing. Then she was back to her callous expression, her eyes full of blood lust and her mouth set in hard determination. Her armor was formfitting, showing her petite size with the muscles in her arms and legs. For a monarch who seemed to sit on the throne all day, she appeared strong.

After a few minutes passed, I addressed her. "I know he would protect the tree, Queen Eldinar."

She stared into the clearing, her eyes trained on something that wasn't there.

"Please..."

"He couldn't care less about this tree, Calista," she said. "He couldn't care less about how it affects us all since he's barred entry."

"What do you mean, he's barred entry?"

She continued to stare ahead.

"Queen Eldinar—"

"I will not change my mind, Calista. He would be the first to set this tree ablaze."

"He's not the villain you think he is—"

She turned to me, her expression furious. "Calista, I just said goodbye to my husband for probably the last time. Do you think I give a damn about your underworld lover right now? My only concern is protecting the afterlife for all those whom I love. Because once Alaric gets inside, we'll all be damned."

"He would protect this tree, Queen Eldinar."

"You know nothing, child."

"The tree may mean nothing to him, but if it means something to me, then he'll do whatever it takes to protect it," I said. "You're making the wrong decision."

She looked ahead again. "This conversation has concluded. Do not speak to me again."

I wanted to fire up and unleash a line of insults, but I knew nothing I said would change her mind. Instead, I stared into the clearing lit by fireflies and hoped Uncle Ezra and his soldiers were enough to stop the enemy from entering the forest.

"They're here." Queen Eldinar hadn't moved from her position, standing with a straight spine and staring hard into the night.

I noticed the music had stopped, and I feared what that meant.

"Riviana is afraid." She seemed to say it to herself rather than the men who flanked the tree. And she seemed to have forgotten I was there because she didn't look at me once.

Then I heard it...the sound of battle.

The sound of steel on steel. The screams of victory and the screams of anguish that indicated defeat. Blood spilled into the dirt and poisoned the roots of the trees.

The fires from the torches had taken hold of trees in the distance, and I watched them light up into the sky.

The battle had only begun—and it was too much.

I'd experienced battle two times in my life, but both events had been brief. I'd either run for my life, or someone had come to my rescue. But in this instance, I was cornered, unable to run to Talon because one of the twenty-four guards would apprehend me.

I was unable to run to the one person I needed.

The cries of battle grew louder, and I was scared that my uncle's voice was among them.

The fires continued, torching the trees, and those flames inched closer and closer.

Queen Eldinar remained unintimidated.

I wasn't afraid to admit it—I was fucking terrified.

The music had died, but now the tree began to scream. A wail of anguish, a petrified chorus that repeated endlessly.

"They're in the forest," Queen Eldinar said. "Prepare yourself."

"Fuck."

My uncle's commands echoed into the forest and the clearing. "Move to the north. The others block the enemies coming from the south."

That did not sound good.

Eleven soldiers appeared in the clearing, making a new line to protect the tree from the enemies who were able to flood into the clearing.

My knife remained in my scabbard because I was afraid to draw it. As soon as I did...this would be real.

Once Uncle Ezra had the elves in their lines, he ran straight for us and stopped in front of the queen. "Alaric has other allies. We're outnumbered. They'll break the perimeter in the next minute." He spoke without being out of breath, either because of his fitness or because of the adrenaline.

Queen Eldinar remained calm, and she seemed to be the only one. "Who are the allies?"

He didn't answer straightaway.

"I asked you a question, General."

He grimaced before he said it. "Goblins."

I'd never heard of a goblin. Didn't even know what they looked like. But fuck, that sounded bad.

"I'm not surprised Alaric would befriend such creatures." She pulled her short blades from their scabbards. "We need more elves to protect the tree."

"The enemy has the forest surrounded on most sides. If our men don't reduce the flow, we'll be overrun."

Queen Eldinar issued no other order, like she had none. "Then we'll do what we can."

We were fucked.

When screams pierced the night, Queen Eldinar looked at the clearing again. A dark pool of enemies carrying torches broke past the perimeter and the tree line and started to flood the grassy area. Even from this distance, I could distinguish the differences in the dark elves, the way their skin looked sickly and gray. I recognized the Behemoths from the edge of the forest, the creatures that were seven feet tall. But the goblins...they were a terrifying sight to behold. Their skin was black and shiny, two fangs protruding from their mouths, slightly hunched with lanky arms and legs. They didn't release deep cries like the Behemoths, but high-pitched screams I couldn't even describe.

We were all about to die.

Queen Eldinar turned to her men. "Hold your ground. If we lose the tree, we lose it all."

While her back was turned, I looked at my uncle. "Uncle Ezra—"

"Run, Calista," he whispered. "I will tell no one."

"I'm not going to run." I was scared enough to flee, but my obligation to the elves was stronger. "But if you want me to live, then release Talon."

Queen Eldinar remained distracted by her men, getting them into formation to protect the door to the Realm of Caelum.

Uncle Ezra stared at me, the enemy growing bigger in the distance behind him.

"He's the only one who can save us, and you know it."

He continued to stare, the decision weighing on his mind.

"I promise you." I moved my hand over my heart. "He will fight for us." There was no doubt in my heart or my mind. No matter how much Talon wanted those dragons, he wouldn't let the elves perish. He wouldn't let the afterlife be taken by those who would corrupt it. He wouldn't betray the people I cared deeply for.

Without saying a word, Uncle Ezra turned toward the east—and ran.

More enemies poured into the clearing, coming from different sides where the ranks had broken. The line of elves before the trees was quickly decimated by the feral creatures that cut down the elves like they were on a chopping block.

The Behemoths formed a line then charged, breaking down the elves and making a path straight for the trees.

Queen Eldinar was ready. "Stay behind me, Calista. I will do what I can to protect you."

I gripped my sword with both hands, wishing I had the surge of strength Inferno had given me when we were fused. I had been infinitely stronger, infinitely faster. Now, I faced an army with death in their eyes, and I felt powerless to stop it.

If Talon didn't arrive in the next minute, all hope would be lost. Queen Eldinar would be skewered, the door would be compromised, and I'd probably be dead.

The Behemoths were upon us, and the guards in service of the queen immediately rushed to her protection. The orcs barreled down on them while I stood back to get out of their way. The queen was clearly the superior fighter because she took out an orc entirely by herself, while one of the guards was cut down dead within a single swipe.

She might be shorter and smaller than the others, but what she lacked in strength, she made up for in speed. She moved so quickly and faked her dodges that she tripped another Behemoth before she sliced him across the neck. Her prowess was impeccable, but the victory was short-lived because a pool of enemies poured into us now that the path to the tree was clear.

It was chaos—dark elves, goblins, and Behemoths all coming at once.

All I could do was try to stay alive, swing my sword at anything that came too close. A goblin screamed before he rushed me with a bloody dagger in his hand, but Talon's training took over as muscle memory and I struck him down.

Another goblin jumped on me and stabbed his blade into my chest, but my armor was strong enough to stop the blade before it penetrated my skin. I shoved my black sword straight through his chest, and he screamed before he rolled off and died.

I pushed myself to my feet and already saw a pile of dead bodies before the tree.

Queen Eldinar was facing off with five enemies entirely on her own, and she already had a dagger sticking out of her arm where she'd been stabbed. She cut down the sword of a Behemoth, but a goblin got her from the side and stabbed her armor with a sword that then broke off into two pieces.

I looked at the tree when I saw a dark elf approach, carrying an axe with a smirk on his face.

Queen Eldinar screamed when a blade swiped across her side and sliced her flesh.

Most of the guards had fallen, their dead bodies on top of the monsters they'd already slain.

I had to make a choice, and I had to make it fast. I pushed myself to my feet and sprinted at the dark elf who had reached the tree. I grabbed my dagger and stabbed it right into his neck, making him release a blood-curdling scream. He twisted sideways with his axe to strike me, but I ducked just in time to avoid the hit. I slammed his arm down on my knee and made him drop the axe before I grabbed the dagger and stabbed him once again.

This time, he fell to the ground.

Queen Eldinar was the last one standing, and somehow, she was still alive—but barely.

She continued to hold her sword, but she swayed. A dark elf slammed her shoulder with his sword, but she was too slow to dodge it. The dark elf kicked her next, sending her to the grass, her white armor smeared with her own red blood. He grinned as he stood above her, savoring his victory with a cruel smile.

She was too weak to fight, her body finally giving out.

"Your Majesty." He raised his sword to stab her right through the chest.

"No!" More enemies swarmed into the clearing, trying to get to the tree, and I was blocked from the queen. All I could do was raise my sword and try to stay alive, but I knew I would be next.

But then I saw him appear out of nowhere. With his black sword and matching cape billowing behind him, he sliced his blade clean through the dark elf's neck and severed his head from his shoulders. "*Calista*!" He couldn't turn to look for me, his blade cutting down all the foul creatures that came for him, handling more than Queen Eldinar had but without taking a hit. I knew Khazmuda's strength had fired off in his veins, and he was an opponent who couldn't be matched.

Uncle Ezra reached the queen before I could. He ripped a chunk of his cape and secured it around where she bled.

A goblin tried to descend upon them from the rear, but I sliced him through the back and made him drop. "Talon, I'm here!"

He defeated another group of enemies with a sword that moved quicker than lightning, cutting off heads and arms, having the strength of more than twenty soldiers combined. When he killed the last one closest to him, he turned to look at me.

Time seemed to stop as he stared at me, his stare so pissed off it was violent, but also so relieved at the sight of me. "General Ezra, protect the door. Calista, attend to the queen and be the eyes in the back of my head."

General Ezra released his wife even though it probably broke him to do so. He unsheathed his blade and struck down the goblins and elves who stabbed and clawed at the door made of branches.

I rushed to the queen and supported her head. Where the cape was tied around her waist, I applied pressure to stop the bleeding. She breathed hard, and her eyes started to mist over. "Stay with me, Your Majesty." I looked up to watch Talon.

He single-handedly kept the entire army back, moving from side to side to cut down the foes who tried to break the ranks and get to the tree. The few who made it through were cut down by Uncle Ezra.

I watched Talon work, watched sweat pour from his forehead and his cape whip around as he moved with strength and grace. The gift of his dragon gave him a power that couldn't be matched by enemies a foot taller than him.

But I knew there were too many.

He knew it, too, because he turned to the queen. "If I don't call upon the dead, we're all finished. Do I have your permission?"

She continued to breathe hard, her face going pale.

Talon turned away and executed a flurry of blows too fast to watch. He stabbed a Behemoth in the chest, straight through his armor because his blade was made of dragon scales, and then beheaded another goblin, exerting such strength that every strike was a one-hit kill. "I will not die for nothing. Do you want me to save your fucking tree or not?" He looked down at the queen without an ounce of pity for her slow demise, the rage like bonfires in his gaze.

She breathed hard before she opened her lips to speak, but nothing came out. All she could do was nod before her eyes closed and her body weakened in my hold.

Talon turned away and lifted his palm as I'd seen him do in the past. His fingers closed into a hard fist before he slammed it hard against his chest.

I heard the collective scream through the forest, the God of Caelum screaming in protest at the defilement.

Talon turned back to the battle and slashed his blade across his foes, keeping them away from the tree. It only took a few minutes for the tide of the battle to change, where Talon was met with fewer foes as he protected the tree.

The dark elves and their allies were forced to turn their attention to the army of the dead who popped out of the ground to fight under Talon's command. It divided the monsters into sections, all fighting on different sides.

Uncle Ezra kept his position at the Realm of Caelum, his back to the door. "*Fleur Nia*?"

I checked her pulse. "She's still alive." Her eyes had closed, and her breathing had decreased.

"Hold on, *Fleur Nia*," he said. "For me."

Her eyes opened briefly, but then they closed again.

I continued to apply pressure while stopping the bleeding in other places.

Talon cut down more of the enemies, stopping anyone from approaching the queen or the tree. But then the enemies disbanded, leaving a large opening as a dark elf approached, his armor black like oil, his eyes sinister as they locked on Talon.

Talon spun his blade around his wrist as he stared at the challenger.

The dark elf kept his distance. "Queen Eldinar hovers between life and death. You may be able to raise an army of the dead to fight for you, but they cannot speak. She won't give you what you seek once she's beyond the veil, not that she ever intended to give it to you anyway. Step aside—and I'll give you what you want most."

Talon remained still, his cape blowing in a gust of wind. His face was hidden from me, so I didn't know his reaction to those words...if he was tempted or disgusted.

The elf continued to stare him down. "Give me the Realm of Caelum, and not only will I give you the location of the dragons, but I will also *give* you the dragons." He raised his fingers and tapped them against his temple. "If they refuse to serve you, I will make them serve you. You will reclaim your lands in full glory. You will control the minds of your enemies. You will be the greatest king who ever lived."

Queen Eldinar started to breathe harder in my arms. "No..." Her voice escaped as a painful whisper. She tried to leave my arms, but her body was too weak to cooperate. "Calista...stop him."

"I don't need to stop him..." I believed—and I believed with all my heart.

The dark elf continued. "The Realm of Caelum is forbidden to us. We can change that. We can defeat the God of Caelum and make it exactly what we want. You can have it all, Talon. Your revenge—and your salvation."

I didn't fully understand the elf's words. They spoke a language I could understand, but the message was still foreign to me.

"All you have to do is step aside." He raised his arm and gestured to his right, like he wanted Talon to step off the stage and let the curtain close behind him. "And you'll have everything you've ever wanted."

I waited for Talon to raise his sword, but it didn't happen.

Talon continued to stand there, his cape whipping around him, the battle going on right before his eyes, elves still being cut down as they sacrificed themselves to protect the forest and the tree.

My heart started to wane. My grip on faith began to slip. I was just about to say his name when he spoke first.

"I decline your offer, Alaric." He spun the blade around his wrist then moved forward.

Alaric hesitated for a split second, seemingly surprised by Talon's decision. But he unsheathed his sword and blocked Talon's blade before it slammed down on him.

He turned with his own blow, and the two of them became locked in a battle with blades that danced quicker than could be watched.

Unlike the other monsters that challenged Talon, Alaric was actually skilled with the blade and quick on his feet. Talon's blows never met their mark because his speed was equally matched. The men circled each other as they tried to find an opening in the other's armor. Both of their capes whipped around them in an elegant dance, their swords clashing and grinding when they slid past each other.

Uncle Ezra stepped forward and defeated the enemies that tried to make it to the tree, protecting us and the doorway on his own. My uncle was a general and a great swordsman, but the difference between his abilities and Talon's became obvious when it took him three or four blows to strike down his enemy rather than one.

I did my best to keep the queen alive, but there was only so much I could do. Enemies surrounded us as they tried to make it to the tree, and Talon was locked in a battle with his equal. The forest continued to be ravaged by monsters and fire. Smoke wafted into the sky and blocked out the stars. Screams continued to pierce the night.

Alaric evaded Talon's attack and stepped back. "Why do you defend this bitch?" he snarled. "She will never give you that location. If you kill me, it'll be gone forever. Do you understand what you're doing—"

Talon took the opening and sliced his blade clean through his neck.

Alaric's head dropped to the ground, and his body crumpled underneath it.

He turned back to face me, his cape spinning behind him, and marched to me with the same rage on his face. "Ezra, get the queen to a healer. Take Calista with you. I will defend the tree until the enemy is defeated." He turned back around to face the dark elves, Behemoths, and goblins that still wanted to claw at the tree. He spun his blade around his wrist once more then attacked, striking down his enemies with ease.

General Ezra didn't question Talon and scooped his wife into his arms. "Come on, Calista." He began to turn away.

But I stayed and looked at Talon, not wanting to abandon him.

"Calista." My uncle's voice captured my attention. "He'll be alright."

Talon slew another enemy before he turned to me, and our eyes locked. "*Go*."

Uncle Ezra ran through the forest to take her to the east, where the most vulnerable members of the elven society were to remain until the battle was over. The healers were there already, treating some of those who had been removed from the front line.

But once the queen was brought in, they turned all their focus on her.

They immediately removed the pieces of armor that were still intact, and with no regard to her dignity, they cut her clothing free. Her pale skin was visible from her neck down to her hips. Her breasts were on full display, but no one seemed to care because of the circumstances, not even my uncle.

I looked away out of respect for her.

"Save the queen," Uncle Ezra ordered. "Save my wife."

I stepped outside because I didn't want to watch my uncle suffer. I wasn't a healer, but I had watched Queen Eldinar inch closer to the end as I held her in my arms, watched the light grow fainter with every passing minute. Her injuries seemed too dire, her loss of blood too great. When I looked down at myself, all the blood on my armor was hers.

I gazed into the distance and saw the fires burning the forest. Listened to the cries of battle raging on. I knew it would all end soon, because the Death King would save us all. I continued to look into the distance and then noticed a great rush of wind blow through the entire forest—and then the fires were extinguished.

I knew who had conjured the wind from nothing. "Riviana..."

Chapter 5

Talon

I stabbed the goblin through the heart then kicked his body to the ground so he would slide off my blade. Black blood covered the blade to the hilt, and I watched it drip before I looked at the army of the dead that stood there, idle in their places, staring at me with only their eye sockets.

I knew the battle had ceased because it was quiet. Whatever enemy remained had begun to flee back to the hiding places from which they'd come. Their leader lay dead in the grass where I'd executed him. "Your service is fulfilled. Go be in peace." I was used to the dead, used to their exposed bones and dry joints, bodies without heads, some with flesh still on the bone. All my loved ones were dead on the other side of the world, so it didn't disturb me. But if my loved ones had been here...it would disturb me greatly.

They slowly walked away, heading back to the cemetery where they'd been ripped from their graves by my command.

I felt a presence behind me, an enemy that tried to sneak up on me when my guard was down. I spun and whipped my blade around, blocking an attack that I assumed was aimed at my neck.

But the enemy was neither a Behemoth nor a goblin. It wasn't a dark elf either.

It was a woman with red hair that glowed with her own light.

I felt invisible knives stab me everywhere, pricking my flesh without drawing blood, inflicting physical pain that I could feel but not see. Her eyes were green like the forest, but they were different from any other color I'd ever seen. Her beauty was unmatched, and her presence was as powerful as a hurricane. She continued to stare at me with a guarded expression, the light so brilliant around her that her expression was unclear.

I knew who she was without an introduction—Riviana, the God of Caelum.

When she spoke, her voice came from everywhere but her lips, all around her as if the trees spoke on her behalf.

"Bahamut is your master, yet you risked what life you have left to serve me."

With the black blood still on my blade, I sheathed it across my back.

When I didn't say anything, she stepped forward and raised her palms. The wind had been nonexistent a moment ago, but it picked up instantly, and a swirl of air passed through the treetops and snuffed out the fires instantly.

I hadn't seen Bahamut since I'd entered these lands, and I knew it was because he was forbidden from this forest. It was the only time I'd been free of him since I'd sailed to his island deep in the Southern Sea.

Riviana turned back to me, her red hair flowing in the wind. "You didn't just protect the living. You also protected those who have already lived. Peace continues to reign in the Realm of Caelum—because of you." She continued to stare at me with eyes that possessed more intelligence than any mortal I'd ever met. "Your love for Vivian continues to burn, even though your heart now beats for another."

Her name was like a dagger to my heart. A pain so potent it would ache permanently. "It'll always burn..."

Her hair continued to whip around her without wind, flowing beautifully. "But you've chosen a different path. One that will separate you from her for eternity."

"I don't regret my decision."

"Talon Rothschild, you're worthy of both love and forgiveness. A lesson you learned too late."

"It's a lesson I'll never learn."

Her eyes softened slightly, like she pitied me. "I hope you find peace, Talon. Someway. Somehow."

The only peace I felt was in the quiet moments with Calista, when she looked at me and I looked at her. When I didn't have to hide who I was. When she believed I was the hero and everyone else thought I was the villain. "If you hadn't cursed the elves, I wouldn't have lost my family."

She stared at me.

"My uncle wouldn't have used the power of the dark elves to subjugate the dragons. Everything I've lost...is because of you."

Her stare lingered for seconds. "But you still raised your sword and fought in my name. Revenge has sustained your ambitions all these years, but there is also love. Even with a broken heart, you still love a woman with all of yourself."

"I will always love my wife—"

"That is not who I speak of."

A new pain washed over me, a high tide over a dark shore.

"Do not feel guilty, Talon."

I looked away, her words hitting my most sensitive tissue.

"If you achieve all of your desires, your time together will be very brief. Make sure she knows your love before you can no longer share it."

"That's cruel."

She stared at me once again. "She does not know..."

"No."

"And Khazmuda?"

I didn't know how she knew that either. "No."

She turned quiet, her eyes judgmental and piercing. "That is cruel."

I looked away, ashamed to meet the gaze of an all-knowing god. She was very different from Bahamut in her temperament, but also similar in her presence and stature. If I closed my eyes, their auras would feel the same. "I wish to speak no more of this."

"Bahamut gave you a curse. Let me bestow upon you a gift."

I looked at her again.

"I want you to feel my gratitude."

"What is a gift from a god?"

"What your heart desires most," she said. "And I can feel your heart much easier than most because of how true and kind it is."

I waited for her to present it.

"It breaks my heart to know that a soul so good will never enter my kingdom."

"I said I don't regret my decision."

"Even when you leave behind the woman you love and your best friend?"

I said nothing, not wanting to think about it.

"I suspect you'll regret it then."

My voice came out weak. "I can't change it now."

"No."

Silence trickled by. My thoughts heavy.

She continued to stare at me.

"What is the gift?"

"You never knew whether you had a son or a daughter. I can answer that for you."

I hadn't expected her to say such a thing, and the mention of my unborn baby immediately brought tears I fought back. I felt my lips tremble. Felt my throat grow thick and wet. How did I love someone so much that I'd never seen? All I'd felt was a little kick in the womb...and I fell so deeply in love.

"Would you like to know?"

I couldn't speak, so all I could do was nod.

"A daughter—just as you thought."

I inhaled a deep breath as the tears welled in my eyes. "Is—is she there?" My voice cracked at the question.

"She is."

The tears became too much and streaked down my cheeks.

"All she knows is peace."

Chapter 6

Calista

The battle ended.

There were too many injured and too few healers. A lot of people lay on the ground outside, bloody and broken, with no one to attend to them. Dead bodies littered the forest floor, both friend and foe. Those who were able-bodied began the painful duty of moving their dead to the graveyard and placing them in shallow graves. There were no headstones, and their bodies weren't covered with earth so their loved ones could identify them.

The slain enemy were carted outside Riviana Star to be buried in a mass grave. Fire had wounded the forest enough so there would be no pyre to extinguish their bodies.

Hours had passed, and I still didn't see Talon.

I knew he was alive because his body wasn't at the base of the Great Tree. Perhaps he searched for me. Or perhaps he needed space. I didn't know why he would need it, but something told me he did.

I returned to the healers to check on the queen. They'd worked on her through the night, and now that it was dawn, I hoped for an update. I hoped she would pull through, not just for the elves she ruled, but for my uncle.

The room was full of other injured elves, so the queen wasn't alone. She didn't have a private chamber to recover, choosing to be among her own in this time of tragedy. I spotted her across the room in a bed in the corner, Uncle Ezra at her side, her hand in his. He was still in his armor, like he'd been there all night.

I approached and waited for Uncle Ezra to look at me.

When he did, he gently pulled his hand away and let it rest on the mattress. She appeared to be asleep, so she didn't notice when he stepped away to speak to me in private. We walked outside under the morning sky.

"How is she?"

"Gravely injured," he said. "But they think she'll live."

"I'm happy to hear that."

"The magic in her blood allows her to heal quickly."

"Magic?"

"The Realm of Caelum is in Riviana Star because the elves are descendants of Riviana, the God of Caelum. Queen Eldinar's bloodline makes her a direct descendant."

"You're telling me elves have the blood of a god?"

"Partially," he said. "That's the reason they're nearly immortal."

"I had no idea." But now, it made complete sense.

"It's a secret among their kind."

It was a lot to soak in, but I slowly absorbed it. "I was afraid that was the end for her."

"As was I." He looked at the trees that surrounded us before he looked at me once more. "You were right about him. If we had listened, the people would have been spared."

I would never gloat about something like that, so I said nothing.

"Where is he?"

"I—I don't know."

His eyes narrowed at my answer.

"My heart tells me he needs space. He'll come to me when he's ready."

Uncle Ezra looked down the path again. "I think he's ready now."

I followed his gaze and spotted Talon a distance away, still in his armor and uniform like he hadn't returned to the tree house to shower or change. He'd spent his time somewhere else, deep in the forest where he could truly be alone.

A rush of feelings bubbled inside me like a warm bath. All the adrenaline from the battle had disappeared, and now my heart was soft as a cloud. I didn't say goodbye to my uncle before I ran to Talon, wanting our bodies to finally come together.

His intense eyes grabbed on to mine, and he squatted down slightly to catch me when I ran into him. He scooped his hands under my ass and lifted me up, my legs circling his waist as we came together. I hugged his neck, and I brought our faces close, so thankful to be reunited.

"Are you okay?" I whispered as I looked into his dark eyes.

"Just a few scratches."

"That's not what I mean." I continued to look into his eyes and saw the way they winced slightly. "You were gone all night." I saw the line in the ground he drew with the tip of his sword. Understood the boundary he didn't want me to cross. Our time together had become intimate and uninhibited, so I understood him better than I had before, understood things he never explained.

"I'm okay," he said. "What about you?"

"Just a few scratches."

"Good. What about Queen Eldinar?"

"The healers think she'll survive."

"Glad to hear that." He lowered me back to the ground, and our eyes were no longer level. He had to dip his chin to look down at me. "Are we needed here?"

"I don't think so."

"Good. Because I'm hungry, dirty, tired—and I want to be with you."

The sunlight came through all the windows and brightened the tree house, but we were both so tired that sunshine wouldn't stop us from sleeping.

Talon showered then walked around the tree house in just his boxers, and that was when the bruises were visible. Down both arms and across his chest and stomach. He didn't seem to know they were there. Otherwise, he wouldn't parade them around. He looked through the kitchen for something to eat.

"I'm making a meal."

"I hope it's steak." He closed the cupboard and dropped into one of the chairs, his hair still slightly damp and messy. Despite the fatigue and the bruises, he looked so handsome sitting in the sunlight, his dark eyes a little lighter than usual.

"I'm sorry."

"Then I'll need to leave soon. Can't eat this shit much longer."

"My uncle and the others manage—"

"Did you see the dark elves?" he snapped. "They're much bigger than your uncle because they have a human diet. Even without the Behemoths and the goblins, I doubt your people would have survived." His foul mood was the cumulation of hunger and lack of sleep, so I didn't snap back. "I'll need to leave the forest soon to have a real meal. I can't exist on rabbit food much longer."

I remembered how angry my father would get when I was a child. Then my mother would put food in front of him, and within a couple minutes, he was back to his old self. She told me the best way to keep my husband happy was to never let him go hungry.

"We should be leaving soon—if your queen keeps her word. But I'm not entirely sure she will."

"She will."

He slouched in the chair, arms across his chest, the foul mood still circling in his eyes.

I finished his lunch and placed it in front of him, trying to make something as hearty as possible with potatoes and root vegetables in a tomato sauce seasoned with rock salt and spices.

With his whole body leaning forward over the table, he ate without complaint. Devoured an entire loaf of bread by himself. Drank a gallon of water like it was a single cup. And when he was done, his stomach was still hard and flat. He was polite enough to remain at the table as I ate my meal, his tired eyes watching a hummingbird that floated out the window.

"You can go to bed, Talon."

He continued to watch the bird move from flower to flower, drinking the nectar inside the petals.

I couldn't eat as quickly as he could, nor could I eat as much. "Did you see her?"

His eyes moved back to mine.

"The God of Caelum."

His stare remained hard as a wall.

"Her wind snuffed out all the fires. I thought you may have seen her."

He let the silence pass with heft, a moment that felt as solid as a mountain. "I did."

My memory of her was still sharp, as if it had just happened. "She's beautiful."

"Yes." His eyes remained on me with calm stillness. "But not as beautiful as you."

A slight smile tugged at my lips. "That's nice of you to say."

"You think I'm disingenuous."

"I think you're smooth."

"I can have you whenever I want you without being smooth," he said. "I meant what I said. She was a sight to behold, a world of color and vibrancy instead of a land of gray scale, but her beauty burns like a candle to your inferno."

My eyes dropped because those words got to me. "Did you speak to her?"

He turned quiet again, the silence suddenly heavy.

I looked at him when he didn't speak.

His eyes had a blank stare, hard as stone. "No."

We both fell asleep the moment we were in bed, and feeling his thick arm hook around my body was the intimacy I'd craved. When the bars had been between us, all I could feel was his hand. When I was forced to leave his prison and stay at the queen's side, I had been desperate for his protection. He was the one person I could count on, and he was taken from me. I'd never allowed myself to need anyone because no one could be trusted, but I knew I could trust Talon with my life.

We slept like that for hours, my leg hitched over his hip, his muscular arm hard around my body. Both so exhausted we didn't move throughout the day, our bodies occasionally twitching because the fatigue had infected our nerves.

When I heard the sounds of crickets and frogs, I knew it was nighttime. My eyes opened to see Talon dead asleep beside me, his face so handsome when it was calm, his jawline less sharp as he relaxed.

After sleeping all day, I was ready to get up, but I hadn't exerted myself and fought the way Talon had. I hadn't saved Riviana Star with my sword and my powers. So I lay there and didn't move, wanting him to sleep as long as he needed.

I just stared at him, and that was enough.

I fell asleep again at some point, and when I woke up again, it was early morning. Talon was still asleep, still hadn't moved, his body recuperating. I watched him take a breath to reassure myself that he was still with me.

I wanted to lie with him forever, but if I didn't pee soon, my bladder would burst. I slowly left the branches of his arms and made it to the edge of the bed without waking him. Then I did my business down the hall and looked out the window, listening to the birds singing their song to the morning light. The forest had changed after the battle, but the wildlife continued to make it a peaceful place.

"Baby." His voice was deeper than usual, his throat still asleep.

I returned down the hallway and found him on his back,

the sheets to his waist, the outline of his hard dick visible under the material. "I didn't mean to wake you."

He pulled back the sheets and patted the spot beside him.

I came back to the bed and snuggled into his side.

But he wanted to do more than snuggle. He immediately moved over me, grabbed on to my panties, and yanked them off. My shirt was spared, and he moved to his boxers next and pulled them free before he made himself at home between my legs, folding me underneath him and pinning me into the mattress before he invaded my lands.

He sank inside as he took in a slow breath, filling me with his size. He went as deep as my body would allow before his hand slid into my hair the way a man gripped the reins of his favorite horse. Every touch was possessive, every stare captured my mind, body, and soul. He made me his in every way possible, made it clear in no uncertain terms that I was his woman, his only woman, and he belonged to me as much as I belonged to him.

I started to cry, not because he hurt me or because he made me come, but because it'd all been too much. "I was so scared..."

He hadn't thrust into me yet, just taking the moment to savor my body. His dark eyes deepened in their intensity, his hand loosening in my hair to cup my cheek instead.

"They took you away from me."

He stilled at my words, his intensity pausing just for a moment, sorrow replacing that stare.

"I was so scared." Life had been hard and unkind. I'd stopped crying a long time ago, choosing to accept my fate. But then life started to get better when I met him, and all those fears came to the surface. While he might be the one responsible for the hardship, he was also the one who had spared me from it. I could never go back to that life.

His thumb caught one of my tears. "I'm here, baby. Right here."

Up in that tree house, it was easy to forget the battle and the aftermath. Once we'd caught up on sleep, we spent the rest of our time in bed, locked in the throes of passion and an intimacy that we'd never really had before.

Talon was always on top, always deep between my legs, eyes locked on mine like he couldn't look away or he would die.

Even when I grew sore, I didn't complain because I wanted him despite the pain, wanted him even if my body couldn't tolerate it anymore. Because this connection was bliss. It was stronger than it'd ever been, more passionate, deeper.

It was so deep, it hurt my heart.

When I lay beside him, my fingers traced his jawline, touched his hard chest, rested over his heart to feel it beat. I memorized every piece of him, from the cuts in the muscles of his arms to the cords of veins that popped in his neck. I even counted them.

He did the same with me, kissed my old scars to make them disappear, worshipped my body like it was a statue dedicated to the Riviana, the God of Caelum.

It was easy to forget the world outside that tree house—even Khazmuda.

I lay beside him, both of us sunbathing in the light that spilled through the window. My thigh was hiked over his hip, and we were face-to-face. "I'm so proud of you."

His eyes narrowed slightly, like he didn't know what that meant.

"Alaric offered you everything you wanted, but you still said no. Lesser men would have taken the deal, but I knew you wouldn't. I realize now how much I misjudged your character when we first met."

"You didn't misjudge me." His dark eyes were packed with sorrow and self-loathing.

My hand moved back to his heart, the beat strong. "I disagree."

"I won't pretend it wasn't a hard decision—because it was."

"If you were tempted, then that makes your decision even more impressive."

"A greater man wouldn't have been tempted in the first place. But Alaric's kind are the reason I lost my family. If they have the ability to subjugate the minds of immortals, then that means they have the power to control the remaining free dragons—including Khazmuda. Perhaps, at some point, they would have taken the free dragons for themselves and history would repeat itself—but someone else would be the victim instead of me. I had to destroy them. I had to protect Khazmuda and his kind."

"So you did it to protect him."

"I did it for a lot of reasons."

I waited for him to tell me what those reasons were, but

he never did. I didn't press him for more because his mood had suddenly turned solemn.

There was a knock on the door.

Talon left my side and pulled on his boxers before he stepped into the hallway.

"You're going to answer the door like that?"

His footsteps receded as he headed to the front door.

I hoped it wasn't my uncle.

The door opened, and then there was silence.

I continued to strain my ears as I waited for something.

"Her Majesty requests your presence." It was Commander Luxe.

Talon held his silence.

I could picture that pissed-off look on his face. Could visualize the vein popping in his forehead and the promise of death in his dark eyes. I was instantly mortified.

Talon shut the door in his face then came back to the bedroom. His expression was exactly what I pictured, tinted red in anger.

"Nothing happened," I said. "You're acting like a lunatic."

He ignored me and retrieved his uniform from where it lay on the ground.

"Talon, this needs to stop."

He turned back to me. "You'd be a bigger lunatic if some woman were trying to fuck me."

"I've seen your concubines fight for your attention—"

"Our relationship is different now, and you know it," he snapped. "If a woman tried to take a piece of me, you'd lose it—and I'd want you to. Because you're fucking mine, and I'm fucking yours." He gave me a violent stare like he dared me to refute his words, and when I didn't, he turned back to his clothes and continued to get dressed.

I didn't pursue the argument, stopped in my tracks because, despite his anger, he'd said the most romantic thing I'd ever heard. Now, I didn't care if he couldn't contain his hatred of Commander Luxe. "Come here."

He turned back to me, eyes still angry, standing in just his pants.

"I said, come here." I pushed off the sheets so he could see my naked body. He'd already had me so many times over the last few days, but I knew he'd want me again if I wanted him.

He stared at me for a few seconds before he dropped his pants and boxers in one go, his dick hard as I'd expected it to be. His knees hit the bed, and he was on top of me, moving between my soft thighs to give me his big dick again. "You're mine. Say it."

I grabbed his ass and tugged him hard inside me. I gasped because it hurt, but it hurt so good. "I'm yours."

Instead of wearing my armor and sword, I wore one of the dresses they'd given me, sage green, with a pair of sandals.

Talon only had his uniform and armor, so he left the tree house with me, looking like he was about to step into battle again. He even had his sword across his back, and when I asked him to leave it, he refused.

After he'd proven his loyalty to Riviana Star, I let him do whatever he wanted.

We walked down the path together and listened to the birds sing their song. There was a foot's gap between us, so to any onlooker, we looked like allies and nothing more, not even friends. There was no indication of the inferno of passion we'd shared the last two days.

As we approached the royal palace, I noticed how much had changed in the forest. I saw fire damage in many places, and the reduction in the population was painfully felt. Far fewer elves were out and about than there had been before. Despite the birds chirping in the sunshine, the music from the Great Tree was full of melancholy.

It was easy to forget the destruction and devastation when I was in my lover's arms, but now, I could feel the sadness in my bones.

We arrived at the royal palace and were escorted inside.

Queen Eldinar was upon her throne, but she wasn't quite the same. Her skin was paler than before, and the usual silent hostility in her eyes was nonexistent. Despite the fact that she held her head high, she wore a look of defeat. She wore a look of permanent weariness.

Uncle Ezra sat at her side in an ordinary chair, her hand enclosed in his, his eyes on the side of her face.

Talon stopped beside me and gazed upon her with a hard face. He didn't speak.

I felt invisible, so I tried to stay invisible.

Uncle Ezra continued to gaze at his wife.

Queen Eldinar stared at Talon before her, her eyes shifting back and forth slightly as she took in his appearance for what seemed like the first time. She usually regarded him with palpable rage, but the daggers were gone from her eyes. "I'm glad to see that you're well, Your Majesty." There wasn't a tongue of sarcasm in her words. Only a quiet genuineness.

Talon absorbed those words for a long time before he responded. "You as well, Your Majesty."

I stared back and forth between them, knowing they'd never been so kind to each other.

"Many blades pierced your armor," he said. "I feared that would be the end of your reign, Queen Eldinar."

"I feared the same, Death King. If you'd arrived just a moment later, I would have fought among the dead you called to battle. My husband would have been a widower far too young and died of a broken heart. But you did more than save me. You saved my people—and you saved what we hold most dear." Her eyes were locked on his as she spoke, regarding him with a look of admiration and respect. She was beautiful under any circumstances, but when her mouth wasn't hard in a scowl and her eyes were kind, she was even more exceptional. She started to push against the armrests to lift herself up, but she struggled in her weakness.

Uncle Ezra immediately rose to assist her. "*Fleur Nia—*"

"I can manage." She brushed away his hold and stood upright, straightening her spine and standing still in case she swayed. Then she stepped forward, wearing a white gown and barefoot as she approached the stairs.

Uncle Ezra came to her side and extended his arm to her.

She refused to take it, descending the stairs on her own, but taking it one step at a time. "I wish to address the Death King as my equal." She stopped when she reached the bottom, pausing for a moment before she finished the last steps and met Talon face-to-face. "Because he has proven himself an ally to Riviana Star—and a friend."

Any remnant of hostility had faded from his gaze.

Queen Eldinar stared at him for a long moment before she slowly bowed to him.

A subtle look of surprise moved into his face—and a drop of emotion.

She righted herself once more and regarded him, almost at equal heights because she was an exceptionally tall woman. "We've lost many of our kin. Trees that have stood here for thousands of years have perished. Our forest will be forever scarred by the blood that has spilled into the soil—from both friend and foe. But the Great Tree still stands tall because you risked your life to defend it. You betrayed your god to serve another. With full humility, I will admit how deeply I misjudged your character, Death King. And for that, you have my deepest apologies. I hope you accept my gratitude as well as my remorse."

He continued to regard her with a hard stare, as if he was doing his best to fight the tendrils of emotion that slowly tightened around him. There were lapses in his determination, shifts in his eyes, moments of uncertainty in his gaze. "All is forgiven if you give me what I seek, Your Majesty."

A small smile moved over her lips. "No amount of bloodshed or fatigue will deter your mission."

His stare hardened. "No."

"If you succeed, will it bring you peace?"

His stare endured for several long seconds, his thoughts hidden behind the vault. "No."

"The King of the Southern Isles is more powerful than any monarch in this land. He will betray the laws of nature to subjugate creatures that are meant to brighten our skies with the reflection of their mighty scales. He is empty of empathy and kindness, but full of cruelty and callousness. You're a man who fights with honor, but he fights with none. I fear that this is a battle you cannot win, even with the aid of the dragons—and it will claim your life." Her eyes shifted back and forth between his as she regarded him. "You have the devotion of a woman who saw your true character before anyone else. You have the love of a mighty dragon who has chosen to share his gift of immortality. If victory will not bring you peace, then perhaps this is a battle that shouldn't be fought."

"After everything I've done for Riviana Star, you still deny me what was promised?" He didn't raise his voice, didn't seem angry, only broken.

"You misunderstand my words, Death King," she said gently. "Not only will I share the location of the dragons, but I will personally escort you there—without a blindfold. You've proven you're an ally to these magnificent creatures and you take up your sword in their defense as you did with my kin. There is only one reason I try to deter you, and that's because I care for you."

His lone reaction was a slight increase in his breathing. His eyes lost their hardness as they shifted back and forth between hers. "My family is dead because of my foolishness. I knew something was amiss, and I should have tried harder to convince my father of the treason that lurked right below his nose. But I didn't try hard enough...and I don't deserve peace. I do it for them, not for myself. I do it for Khazmuda—because those he loves still live. You're right to assume that battle will claim my life, because it will. But that does not deter me in the slightest because I should have died alongside them a long time ago."

Pain gripped my heart the way a soldier gripped the pommel of his sword. The self-loathing in his words was physical. For decades, he'd carried his pain, and it'd only grown worse over time.

The queen continued to watch him with a heavy look of sorrow. "If you should have died with them, why do you live now?"

"I wasn't given a choice in the matter."

She didn't press for an answer but nudged him with her stare.

"Khazmuda saved me, not realizing I didn't want to be saved."

"I see," she said quietly. "I think I speak for everyone here when I say we're happy that Khazmuda made that decision."

His gaze shifted away, the first time he'd broken eye contact.

"Because you were worth saving, Talon Rothschild."

His eyes never found hers again.

A heavy silence passed.

I watched Talon struggle with his emotions, struggle to destroy them and any trace that they'd ever existed.

He eventually looked at the queen once more. "When do we depart?"

She was quiet as she held his stare. "I need a few more days to recuperate. Then we shall ride together."

I knew Talon was impatient, that he would have preferred the details of the location so he could go now, but he didn't want to insult the queen. "I'll wait for you outside the forest, Your Majesty."

My eyebrows rose.

"You're welcome in our forest forever and always, Death King."

"With all due respect, I need greater sustenance than potatoes and berries, especially after such an arduous battle."

She gave a slow nod. "I completely understand. But that's a rule I can't bend to accommodate you. This forest is a sanctuary to all those who live here."

"I understand your beliefs," he said. "Would never expect you to change them for me. But even if you did, I still need to be with Khazmuda. We've been apart for some time, and I know he desires my company."

"That doesn't surprise me," she said, "with a bond as strong as the one you share. We'll meet you at the border when we're ready."

"Thank you." He gave her a slight bow.

For the first time ever, the queen smiled. "Thank you, Death King."

He turned away and left the royal chambers.

I watched him go before I addressed the queen. "It pleases me to see the two of you get along."

"It pleases me as well," she said. "He's a greater man than I previously assumed." She stared out the door where he'd disappeared before she looked at me again. "I know your heart beats for this man. I noticed it before you noticed it yourself. Nothing I say will change what's to come, but I'm compelled to warn you anyway."

"Warn me of what?"

"That this love will be brief." She faced me head on, my uncle still at her side. "Prepare yourself."

"Why do you assume he'll perish?"

She stared for a long time, her eyes dropping before they met mine again. "Because he wants to perish."

Chapter 7

Talon

I stood in the clearing outside the royal palace and looked at the visible tree line. The tops were burned, exposing the dead branches where the leaves had withered to ash. The elves were still burying the fallen. The sensation of knives against my skin was still present, but not as sharp.

Calista left the palace and came to my side. "Let me get my things, and we'll walk to the border."

I stared at the trees for another moment before I looked at her.

She must have felt the unease in my stare because she addressed it. "What?"

"I wish to go alone."

"Oh." The hurt washed over her face like an incoming tide.

"Not because I don't want you there."

"Then...why?"

"Khazmuda is upset with me. Ever since you and I have been reunited, he feels abandoned."

She crossed her arms over her chest, and her eyes looked slightly less pained.

She'd just told me how much our separation had hurt her, how much she needed me always, so I felt like an asshole saying all this. I saw past her tears to the trauma carved into her heart. She accepted me into her heart fully, without an ounce of doubt, and she allowed herself to need me. "I don't want to be apart from you."

"I know." She composed herself, hid the hurt my words provoked.

"It's been just Khazmuda and me for so long."

"I didn't mean to steal you," she said. "I don't want him to be angry at me."

"I wanted you to steal me, baby." Truth be told, I wanted to stay. I wanted to return to that tree house and spend the remainder of our time together in bed making love, feeling each other's heartbeat. Soon, we would leave the forest, and it would be all business from that moment forward. These quiet moments would be gone. And then I would die trying to avenge my family...or I would die after I avenged them.

Her eyes softened.

"And he's not angry at you. His ire is reserved for me."

"You don't deserve it either."

I moved into her and cupped her face, my fingers reaching into her hair. "I'll see you in a few days."

Her fingers gripped my wrist. "Okay."

I hugged her tightly and kissed her hard.

She melted at my touch, like she always did. I could feel the way she'd given herself to me, fully open and vulnerable, forgiving me for every horrible thing I'd done. The slate had been wiped clean, and I was fully redeemed in her eyes.

I pulled away and let her go.

She couldn't hide the sadness in her eyes, couldn't pretend she was okay, not even to make me feel better.

I turned around and walked away, knowing I couldn't take it.

It was nightfall when I reached the border. None of the elves stationed there intervened with my progress or tried to detain me. As far as I could tell, I was free to come and go as I pleased.

Khazmuda wasn't there. *I'm here.*

Nothing.

I could feel his mind, so I knew he was nearby, just choosing to ignore me.

I built a fire out of fallen branches and set it ablaze with matches. The heat immediately drove off the chill. I pulled out my tent and constructed it while I waited for Khazmuda to stop the cold shoulder.

He didn't.

Khazmuda, come on.

Silence.

I'm here to see you.

His voice erupted in my mind, full of his callused anger. ***Only because I asked—not because your heart desired it.***

There'd only been two serious women in my life, and neither one of them ever acted like this. *My heart always desires you, Khazmuda.*

Silence.

I got distracted with Calista, and I'm sorry for that. Due to the intimate relationship I have with her, it's hard for all three of us to be together. I think we would all be uncomfortable.

No man has that kind of stamina, Talon.

It took me an entire day to get here, Khazmuda. Going back and forth is not convenient. But we're about to leave the forest, so this problem will soon be solved.

A moment later, I heard his wings in the dark sky. Then I saw the glow of his scales in the fire as he descended and landed across the campfire. He folded his wings and lowered his head so his face was visible in the campfire. ***What do you speak of?***

Queen Eldinar has agreed to escort us to the dragons.

When?

Whenever she's recuperated. She suffered grave injuries in the battle.

She lives because of you.

I stared at the campfire.

Looks like she was wrong about Talon Rothschild. They all were.

Not Calista. She's always believed in me.

Because she knows your heart—as do I.

I continued to stare at the fire.

You're on the verge of claiming everything you've worked for. It's in your grasp like the pommel of your sword. Yet I can feel your sadness...

My eyes watched the flames dance.

But I can't determine the source.

It was cruel to tell him. It was cruel not to tell him. But what would be crueler?

Talon?

My eyes raised to his. "Queen Eldinar may take us to the dragons, but that's not a guarantee they'll fight for us."

We've searched these lands for the dragons for decades, and we've finally found them. Regardless of what they say, that's still progress. Because dragons are brave and

mighty, I'm sure they'll pledge their scales to our fight.

"I think you're being optimistic."

And I think you're being pessimistic. You've turned the elves to friend from foe. No reason we can't do the same with these dragons.

"Perhaps..."

He stared at me for a while, the flames reflecting off the scales around his snout. ***I've missed you, Talon Rothschild.***

"You don't have to say my whole name, but I missed you too."

It killed me to stand by and do nothing while you fought alone.

"You would have destroyed the whole forest."

The forest can burn to the ground. You're all I care about. And Pretty.

I was hungry, but it was too dark to hunt now. I'd have to wait until morning.

You're different since we've come here.

"Different, how?"

Before we left the castle, you detested Calista so deeply you wanted to abandon her. But the moment you set your eyes upon her again, you've become a different man. You water her like she's a flower. You carry her like she has no legs. You show her a tenderness that a gardener shows his roses. It's a version of you I've never known before. And even when she's not with you, I can still see it.

I leaned against the log, one knee propped while I crossed my arms over my chest.

I feel replaced.

"Khazmuda, you're irreplaceable."

His eyes shifted to the flames. ***I understand how things are. Dragons are no different from humans. We find a mate, and that mate becomes our nest mate, our best friend. When we first met, you were so broken you didn't want to live, but all these years later, you've found someone to live for. Instead of being selfish, I should be happy for you...and I'm sorry I wasn't.***

It'd been easy to carry this lie for so long because success always seemed out of reach. Decades had been spent going in circles, but now we were closer than we'd ever been. The lie felt heavier. "Don't apologize, Khazmuda. Having a woman in my life is no excuse to ignore you."

Perhaps I'll find a mate when we free my kin.

The thought gave me a pain of sadness, because I wouldn't be around to see that happen. "I'm sure you will."

I've always wanted to have hatchlings. Teach them to fly and breathe fire.

My hands squeezed my arms as I waited for the pain to leave my heart. As I fought back the tears I didn't expect to shed.

His eyes locked on mine, probably because he felt my surge of unexpected anguish. ***Why does that hurt you?***

I tried to find the words but failed. It took Vivian and me a couple months to get pregnant, and the discovery was one of our greatest joys. I pictured my life with a son or a daughter, all the things I would show them and teach them. Knowing I had a little girl in the Realm of Caelum, a daughter I would never know, would always kill me. "I hope you experience the joys of fatherhood, Khazmuda." And I wished I could see it. Little dragons with his black scales. Dragons that grew up strong and fast, hatchlings that became fierce predators.

I didn't mean to be insensitive.

"You weren't." My hands relaxed on my arms.

Your dream can still come true, Talon. Calista will be a great mother to your hatchlings.

I couldn't take any more of this conversation. I hadn't had these dreams when I'd sold my soul to Bahamut. I hadn't thought I would ever feel anything for another woman as long as I lived. But then I saw Calista on a starry night...and I was lost. It was a slow burn, from a lit match to a fire in the hearth to an inferno that engulfed the land. And now it burned me alive, burned me from the inside out.

You're still in pain.

"I care for Calista deeply, but she's not my mate."

Then what is she?

"I—I don't know."

He stared at me with his dark eyes, blinking every few seconds. ***It's okay to have another mate if your previous one passes away***—

"Let's not do this."

Did you tell her about Vivian?

"What did I just say?"

Why don't you want her to know?

"It's not that I don't want her to know. I just don't want to talk about it."

Then, would you like me to tell her?

"No."

I think she should—

"Drop it."

Talon, I know you love her—

"If you don't want me to return to the forest, you'll drop this. I mean it." I'd come out here to be with my companion, my closest friend, but now I wished I'd never left the forest. I could be in Calista's bed right now, not saying a word.

Khazmuda would normally press his argument, but he didn't dare risk losing me. He'd been out here alone for a long time, feeling my mind close off from him whenever I was intimate with Calista...which was most of the time.

The fire crackled between us. The crickets chirped loudly. A breeze rushed through our campfire and rustled my hair. Ashes scattered, and the smoke blew in my direction before it went elsewhere again.

Khazmuda's mood was solemn, his eyes on the fire instead of me. ***What's the plan?***

Good, back to business. "When the queen has recuperated, we'll travel to the dragons and make our plea."

And how should we do that?

"I think you should do the talking. They aren't going to care about my motives."

But they're going to need to know why a human is risking their life for this cause.

"Then we'll tell them," I said. "But I think you're more likely to convince them than me."

You've always been better with words.

"But no amount of words will make them forget I'm not one of them."

You're one of us, as far as I'm concerned. And I will make sure they see that. Even if your family was somehow returned to you this very moment, I know you would still fight with me.

I didn't want to picture the hypothetical, speaking to my father again and rectifying the animosity from our final conversation, smirking at my brother and him smirking back at me. I would never have the audacity to look Vivian in the eye after I'd failed her. Anytime I thought of her, I was filled with a shame that was suffocating. "Yes, I would."

I wonder how many dragons there are.

"I'll ask Queen Eldinar."

If there are only a handful, it won't be enough. Not even with the forces you've acquired in Shadow Stone.

"We'll cross that bridge when we come to it."

And we'll need a plan.

"We can't have a plan without knowing the enemy. It's been a long time since we've been there. I'm sure much has changed."

It has been many years. But they may expect us. They searched for us in the wild a long time. They know we got away. Your uncle may have received news that the Death King conquered Calista's lands. He may suspect it's you.

"Maybe."

We have to assume he's prepared—and be prepared in kind.

I returned to Riviana Star, walking through the patches of shade made by the tall trees, feeling the warmth through my armor and clothing when the sun hit me. The music was distant up ahead, but the birds sang their own song in the branches above me.

It was a long walk, but it was a peaceful one.

The elves who patrolled the border didn't halt my passage. Didn't ask me to abandon my sword and daggers. They just let me pass—like I was one of them.

Hours later, I arrived in Riviana Star, and the second I stepped in its vicinity, I could feel the sorrow. This place didn't feel the same as when I'd arrived. It was no longer full of silent tranquility—but death.

I continued down the path and found Calista's tree house. The springy vines were an odd staircase to have, and I worried she would fall over if she carried goods from the market to the top. But soon, we would be leaving, and I wouldn't have to worry about it anymore.

I let myself inside without knocking because this place felt like mine as much as it was hers. My eyes immediately went to the dining table where she sat, having dinner alone, probably a bowl of rabbit food with a green tea.

Her eyes widened at the sight of me, and a burst of affection exploded in her gaze.

I wished I could feel her emotions the way I felt Khazmuda's, but I would have to settle for the sight of her heart on her sleeve. It was hard not to smirk at her joy, how visibly happy she was that I'd returned, how much she wanted me and was unafraid to show it.

She left the table and moved straight into me, her soft body hitting my armor, rising on her tiptoes as she hooked her arms around my neck to kiss me.

I gave her a boost, scooping my arm under her ass to bring her to eye level with me so I wouldn't have to angle my neck down to kiss her. She felt light in my arms, feeling smaller than the two-handed sword I wielded in battle.

Her fingers dug into my hair as she kissed me, showing me how much she'd missed me in the brief time we'd been apart. It had been less than two days, but it felt a lot longer than that. Her hand cupped my face, and she looked at me as her thumb brushed over my cheek, regarding me with a love so powerful it was like looking straight into the sun. "I missed you." Her words were barely above a whisper.

"And I you."

"Did you eat?"

"Yes." Khazmuda had hunted for us both, and we'd shared a meal like old times.

"Do you feel better?"

"I do, but I think it's because of you." A pain had weighed on my heart ever since I'd spoken with Khazmuda. The pain was always there, a permanent part of me like my beating heart, but whenever I was with her, it dimmed considerably. In our most peaceful moments, I didn't notice it at all.

Her thumb rested in the corner of my mouth, and she paused to stare at me, her eyes descending into the depths of emotion. "Take me to bed."

"What about your dinner?"

Her lips came back to mine. "You're my dinner."

A flush of heat ripped through me when I heard the desire in her voice. Women had always wanted me, but the longing felt different when it came from Calista. It hit me deeper, burned me hotter.

I carried her to the rumpled bed she hadn't made and dropped all the pieces of my armor and my uniform, stripping down to my bare skin and hard dick.

She was naked on the bed underneath me, hard nipples aimed at the ceiling, her hair in a beautiful disarray behind her. Her sex was already glistening, like she was desperate for me the second I walked through the door.

I took her invitation and slid between her soft thighs, feeling the warmth of her flesh, and sank inside her as our eyes locked. It had taken a lifetime of patience to have this moment with her, to fix everything that asshole had broken, and now the connection between us was pure fire. It was both physical and emotional, no barriers between us at all, no walls around her heart.

I felt my breath escape when I felt how fucking slick she was, how her body responded to me with a flood of enthusiasm. My dick twitched inside the place I called home as I folded her legs underneath me. Her eyes were already dazed with pleasure, and her lips were already pursed for the moans she knew she would release.

I started to rock into her slowly, not for her benefit, but mine. Because...damn.

Her hands were all over me, sometimes on my chest, sometimes in my hair. She would cup the back of my neck and bring my lips to hers, kissing me as I continued to rock into her, showing me a confidence that was so fucking sexy.

I wouldn't last, not when she was the sexiest damn thing in the world.

"Come inside me," she whispered against my lips, her fingers still in my hair. "It feels so good."

My entire body halted as I closed my eyes. It had taken a lifetime to earn her trust, and now she was a better lover than all my favorite courtesans. But it was also better because it was more than physical. It had the kind of depth I hadn't known in a long time. It was beyond the flesh, deeper than a heated moment between two strangers in a pub. It was so real it fucking hurt. I filled her with a moan I couldn't suppress, feeling the glow of the afterlife my cursed shadow couldn't defeat. Everything turned golden, like sunshine on a summer morning, chasing away the winter weeds.

Her lips parted in the sexiest way, her nipples hardened, and her nails dragged down my chest. "Talon..."

My dick was rock hard like it hadn't just fired, and I rocked into her once again, this time harder, making sure to push against her little clit and steal her breath away. I slid through my own come as I took her, lost in the heaven between her legs. "Baby..."

We slept on and off through the night. A single touch would light a spark between us, and then the flames caught on the sheets. She was beautiful in the moonlight, the beams striking her fair skin. She was more addictive than my scotch and cigars, both of which I hadn't had in a long time and hadn't even noticed until now.

She moved on to her hands and knees beside me then looked at me over her shoulder.

I lay against the headboard and stared.

"Finally had enough?"

No. I grabbed her hip and tried to roll her to her back.

She fought my touch. "Why do you always do that?"

I pulled my hand away and continued my stare.

"Why don't you want me that way?" She pivoted her body to face me, taking away her beautiful ass that reminded me of the nectarines that ripened in the summer. "You can teach me."

"That's how you fuck a whore—and you aren't a whore."

She continued to stare at me. "What if I want you to fuck me like a whore?"

I was lucky my cock was hidden under the sheets because it swelled like a river in spring. "I don't fuck you, baby. I make love to you, face-to-face, eye-to-eye." I took my courtesans with their faces down and their asses up, fucking them mercilessly because they didn't mean a damn thing to me. But Calista meant so much.

She looked at me in the dark, reading my gaze with her deep stare. "Why can't we have both?"

"Because I don't want to have both."

She crawled toward me, coming close with her perky tits on display, so sexy without even trying. "I think you do." She grabbed the top of the sheet and pulled it down, revealing the hard dick I couldn't hide underneath the material. Her fingers went to my balls and gently caressed them like I'd taught her. "Come on..."

A beautiful woman was begging me to fuck her, but I continued to say no. "It's a compliment, Calista. You actually mean something to me." My breaths increased as her gentle fingers moved to my dick and stroked it with her soft skin.

"You don't understand me." She leaned toward me, her lips coming close to mine. "I want to be fucked like a whore—*by you*."

Calista and I entered the royal chambers and saw Queen Eldinar upon her throne, looking far less weary than in the days that had passed. She had a strength to her spine and a sharpness to her gaze that hadn't been there before. She'd always been pale, but now there was a hint of rosiness to her cheeks.

Calista gave a slight bow. "How are you, Your Majesty?"

"My health has been greatly restored. I feel like myself again—can think like myself again." She turned her attention to me. "How's Khazmuda?"

I approached and gave her a slight bow. "Lonely."

"You've been together for so long that doesn't surprise me."

"Will you be ready to make the journey soon?"

"That's the very reason I called upon you," she said. "We'll leave tomorrow morning. It's several days' ride to the north."

My greatest desire was finally in reach—and I'd never wanted it less. It was the very reason I'd remained alive all these decades, but now, that motivation had been snuffed out like a dying fire. The guilt slowly mounted in my chest, rising like a lake after the snow had melted from the top of the mountains. It made my heart beat harder.

"Is that agreeable to you, Death King?"

"Yes," I said. "And Talon is fine."

"You were so insistent on maintaining your dominance when you first arrived here, but now it seems to mean nothing to you." She spoke her observation aloud like she didn't expect an answer.

"A title means nothing among friends."

Her shrewd eyes slowly softened at my words. "May we speak in private—*friend*?"

I looked at Calista.

She gave a nod and didn't seem wounded by the exclusion. She wordlessly left the chambers and went back into the forest.

When she was gone, I looked at the queen again.

"Come." She rose from her throne then moved farther into the chambers, showing a grand table with high-backed chairs that could accommodate twelve guests with plenty of spacing. A slender trench-style vase constructed of wood ran down the table in the center, at least twelve feet across, and white flowers grew from the soil compacted within the container. She took a seat at the head of the table, wearing a white dress with a flower crown upon her head. "Sit."

I pulled out the chair to her left and pivoted it to face her directly.

"This is where General Ezra and I have our meetings—as equals."

Because we were also equals. "You honor me, Queen Eldinar."

"I respect you, Death King." She sat back in the chair, her legs crossed, her hands together on the table. "Calista and I have never connected because of the circumstances of our meeting. I wasn't given the luxury of embracing her as an aunt because of my duty as queen. To make the attempt now would be forced and disingenuous."

"Calista isn't the type to hold grudges. She has a heart that forgives easily."

She smiled. "Because she's young. Despite her hardships, she has a zest for life that only exists in youth."

"Perhaps."

Her fingers stitched together. "Just because that relationship between us doesn't exist doesn't mean my affection also doesn't exist."

General Ezra had made his disdain for me clear. I'd hoped that had changed after the battle, but perhaps it hadn't.

"As I said before, she's young. And you're a man who may seem the same age in appearance but is many decades older in spirit."

"With all due respect, I find this hypocritical, considering the age gap between you and General Ezra is a century rather than a couple decades."

She didn't flinch at my comment, a soft smile on her lips. "And I think General Ezra would have benefited from a conversation similar to this. I did my best to deter his affection, but he was adamant the moment he saw me. It's a selfish love, to use all of his youth, while I barely spill a drop of mine."

I was surprised by her honesty but gave no indication of it.

"But there's a major difference between us. I was able to return General Ezra's affections and agree to a life together. The last conversation you and I had still troubles me because I sense you're unable to give Calista the same—for reasons I'll never know. We are new friends, and I won't interrogate you about matters that don't concern me. I only ask that you consider the devastation you'll leave behind."

I'd underestimated the queen's intelligence and shrewdness and wouldn't make that mistake again. "It weighs on me every day."

Her eyes absorbed my stare along with that answer. "I warned Calista that this love would be brief. It's hard to know if she took that warning seriously, based on the way she continues to look at you—the way my husband looks at me."

A sword pierced me through the chest, the guilt carving into my heart like a sharp knife.

"Each of you is experiencing a different version of this relationship. While you dread its impending doom, she lives for the sunrise. Manage her expectations to protect her gentle heart. For you, this is another moment in your long life, but for her, this is her life—because you're her life."

Chapter 8

Calista

We were given horses to ride to the edge of the forest, stepping out on the eastern side and to the flatlands beyond.

Khazmuda flew from the south to meet us there, and once he soared overhead, Queen Eldinar and the elves in charge of her protection all looked up to admire the black dragon that blocked out the sun.

He glided down, and his heavy body hit the earth with a distinct thud that sent tremors through the ground. He folded his wings and looked down at us all.

I climbed off the horse I shared with Talon then jogged to him. "I'm so happy to see you." I ran into one of his powerful legs with enormous talons at the end and hugged him as best I could, my hands unable to meet on the other side of his girth.

He dropped his head and rubbed the soft side of his snout against my hair, a puff of hot air releasing from his nostrils and making my strands dance for an instant. ***I missed you too, Pretty.***

"I'm sorry for hogging Talon. I know how much he means to you."

He continued to rub me like I was a hatchling. ***Dragons are possessive of those they love as if they were treasure. Talon is also yours, and I need to share. If I found my mate, I know Talon would understand.*** He pulled away so he could look at me with one of his dark eyes.

"You're so sweet, Khazmuda." I pressed a kiss to one of his hard scales. "I know you must be excited to meet the dragons. Perhaps you'll meet a female dragon with scales as beautiful as yours."

Perhaps.

Queen Eldinar dismounted her horse and approached Khazmuda. "It's lovely to see you again, my friend." She gave a slight bow to him, wearing a new set of armor that was as pristine as the original.

I translated for Khazmuda so everyone could hear his words. ***You as well, Queen Eldinar.***

"It's several days' ride to the north. You can meet us at the coastline if you wish."

I wish to stay with Talon and Pretty. We've been separated for so long.

"Of course," she said. "I thought you might say that." She turned to her men, including General Ezra. "Then let's ride."

When I returned to my horse, Talon had already hopped down to the ground to help me back into the saddle.

"I can do it."

He smirked. "You can do it better if I give you a push. Come on."

I grabbed on to the pommel and slipped my foot into the stirrup. When I pulled myself up, he placed his hand on my ass, giving me a push that made it a lot easier to reach the top of the steed.

He moved into the saddle behind me and grabbed the reins, preferring to have me against his chest so I wouldn't fall off. I'd ridden horses as a kid but hadn't been on one since Scorpion Valley was taken...by the very man who held me.

Talon clicked his heels into the steed and took off with Queen Eldinar, handling the animal like he'd ridden horses and dragons all his life. When we'd traveled through the forest, we walked most of the way because of the dense trees, so this was the first time we took off at a full run.

Now, I was happy to be in the front.

When he felt my unease, he hooked his arm across my waist and held the reins with one hand.

I grabbed on to his arm because it felt more secure than the pommel at the front of the saddle. Being wedged between his chest and his arm made me feel so snug, there was no way I could bounce off.

"First time on a horse?" he asked.

"No. It's just been a long time." And my father would never allow me to run, only walk through the trails and enjoy the scenery. Riding atop a powerful steed that ran at full speed was far more terrifying than flying on the back of Inferno.

"Don't worry. I've got you."

My heart gave a flutter. "I know you do."

We rode until sunset then made camp out in the open. Unlike the kingdom on the other side of the mountain, this place was mostly uninhabited. Lots of lush valleys and forests full of mighty pines. No sight of a human or elf anywhere.

The soldiers put together Queen Eldinar's tent and took their station in a circle around it, guarding her from all sides. But it was probably unnecessary when we seemed to be alone in this land—and her husband was the general of the army.

Talon built the little tent we would share, along with a fire. His horse was on a loose rope so he could graze on the grass.

The sky was becoming fainter with every passing second, the colors changing as the sunset deepened to blood-orange. Khazmuda lay on the ground behind us, like a dog that was tired after a long day.

I walked over to Queen Eldinar, whose hair flapped in the breeze as she watched the sunset with visible appreciation. "Your Majesty, do others live in these lands?"

"Yes."

"It seems so open...and empty."

"We're the only civilization that resides in these lands. But others do live here, like the Behemoths and goblins, both of which you've met. There are other beings as well. We refer to them as monsters."

"Why live in a land with such foul creatures?"

She turned to look at me, the breeze continuing to gently pull the strands from her face. "Because no one else wants to live in haunted lands, so we remain at peace. If the humans from your kingdom knew how to pass the mountains and found beautiful soil and unclaimed land, they would invade our forest and cut it down to build homes and castles. The monsters are like spiders—they keep worse creatures at bay."

"The monsters have never challenged you?"

She shook her head. "We never had a quarrel until General Titan decided to use them for his own benefit. They may know we reside in the forest, but after witnessing the defeat of the Behemoths, I'm sure they'll stay away."

"Are they anywhere near us now?"

"No. They live to the west, closer to the mountains. Everything that you see is claimed by nature alone—as it should be."

I looked at the sunset again, which was nearly over, the rim of the sun sinking beneath the horizon. The air felt warm on the summer evening, a nice respite now that the sun was almost gone. After serving a decade in the Arid

Sands, any heat I encountered would feel mild in comparison.

"Get some sleep," Queen Eldinar said. "We leave before sunrise." She turned away, her blond hair dancing in the breeze, dressed in pristine white like a lily.

I returned to the campsite I would share with Talon, and he already had a roast over the fire.

I glanced at the elves and saw some of them stare in disapproval.

Talon sat upon the log in front of the fire and watched the flames dance. "We're outside the forest."

I said nothing before I took a seat beside him.

Khazmuda joined us, resting his chin on the ground as he enjoyed the light from the campfire. ***Did you ask Queen Eldinar how many dragons reside in Thalian?***

"No," I said. "But we'll find out soon enough."

I wonder if they'll be different from me. Will their scales be shinier? Their claws sharper?

"Impossible," I said with a smile.

What if they're bigger than me?

"Then the war will be easily won," Talon said. "Because you're enormous."

You're right. I am enormous.

Talon rotated the meat for even cooking then opened his canteen and took a drink. He handed it to me to share. "It's not water."

"Then what is it?"

"The good shit."

I hesitated before I tilted the canteen back slightly and took a small drink. It was like fire down my throat, and I nearly spat it out.

Talon smirked.

With a look of disgust on my face, I handed it back. "That is *not* wine."

"It's better than wine."

I reached for my canteen and washed away the foul taste with the water.

Do you think they'll like me?

I turned back to Khazmuda. "Of course they will. You're beautiful—on the inside as well as the outside."

Beautiful?

"She means you're terrifying and have scales the color of midnight," Talon said. "They'll fear you and respect you—and that's the foundation of any good relationship."

"I meant what I said," I said. "You don't have anything to worry about. They may not like me and Talon."

No one likes Talon. But everyone loves you, Pretty.

I smiled.

"Thanks," Talon said coldly. He approached the fire and removed the spit to slice up the meat. I wasn't sure when he'd hunted, but he'd caught something in my brief absence. He divided it between us and handed me a plate.

"No, thank you."

He hesitated before he tipped his plate and let my portion roll onto his. "You need to eat."

"I packed food."

"We aren't in the forest anymore, and you aren't one of them."

"I know, but it still makes me uncomfortable."

He let the conversation fade and ate in silence.

I've gotten fat since you've been in the forest. All I do is eat and sleep.

"I didn't notice," I said.

It's hard to notice on a dragon.

"I noticed," Talon said with a smirk.

Khazmuda released a quiet growl.

"You know I'm kidding." Talon finished his dinner then wiped his hands. "If you give me your rations, I can cook something for you."

I grabbed my pack and pulled out the medley of black potatoes and vegetables seasoned with rock salt. There were also some nuts to add a crunch to the dish.

Talon pulled out a pan from his pack and sautéed everything over the fire. It was done quickly, a lot quicker than his meat, and he dumped it onto his plate before he handed it to me.

"Thank you."

It was dark now, the stars bright overhead, brilliant as sunshine because there were so many of them. A streak flashed across the sky, like a star had fallen from its place in the heavens.

Talon stared at it for a while before he looked at the fire once more.

I finished my dinner and returned the plate to his pack.

Khazmuda had closed his eyes like he was ready to sleep.

Someone approached our campfire, becoming visible in the smoke. In his armor and uniform stood Commander Luxe, his long blond hair hanging around his face.

Talon rose to his feet as if he'd been provoked.

Commander Luxe looked at him instead of me.

Talon stared right back, flames in his eyes.

"Death King," Commander Luxe said. "May I have a word?"

My eyes swung back and forth between the two men.

Talon's cape caught slightly on the wind. He stared at Commander Luxe like he was an enemy in battle when they were allies on the same side. "Speak."

"I meant in private."

Talon didn't raise his voice, but his tone darkened. "You may speak in present company."

I stared at Commander Luxe.

Khazmuda didn't lift his head from the ground, but his tired eyes opened and watched the scene before him.

Commander Luxe made the mistake of glancing at me.

"I said, speak."

Now, Commander Luxe stared at Talon and nothing else.

"You've already disturbed my evening. Don't let that be in vain."

After seconds of silence, Commander Luxe made his plea. "I would like to rectify the tension between us because you saved my queen and protected the forest I call home. You're a friend to our queen, and I would like to be friends as well."

"You're no friend of mine."

"Talon." I wanted to cover my face because of the humiliation. It was unnecessary hostility directed toward a man who had only been kind to me.

"Queen Eldinar has earned my friendship. Your forest has earned my respect. But you've earned nothing. Now leave my sight and never return."

Commander Luxe seemed to realize this was a lost cause because he left the campsite without saying a word. He walked off and disappeared into the night.

Once he was gone, Talon returned to the log and stared at the flames as if nothing had happened.

I knew he could feel my hot stare on the side of his face, but he ignored it. I spoke to Khazmuda. Has he always been this way?

He feels emotions deeper than others of his kind. Ever since I met him, I've noticed his emotions are always right beneath the surface. He's always angry. He's always bitter. He's always depressed. And at any moment, those emotions can escape. But with you, those emotions have changed. Now, he's always possessive. He's always protective. He's always emotional. But there are moments of peace in between. Unfortunately, this is not one of those moments.

I was so pissed off at Talon, but Khazmuda somehow made me less angry.

Dragons are the same way. When we find our mate, we'll burn the world for them. We'll burn the world for our hatchlings. We are normally pragmatic and calm creatures, but once we feel threatened, we become the monsters we're feared to be. Talon has the

blood of dragons in his veins, so he feels deeper than most.

I also have the blood of dragons.

And it's easy to see how you feel for him. He raised his chin from the ground and looked at me. ***I've never seen him with another woman besides you, so this side of him is even more intense than usual. Forgive him, Pretty.***

I lay in the bedroll alone, on the hard ground that made my back stiff. But I knew I wouldn't notice such discomfort if I had Talon beside me. I was dead tired after the day of travel and the drama outside the tent, but my mind wouldn't rest until Talon was beside me.

But it seemed like he had no intention of coming to bed.

I crawled to the flap and looked at him in front of the fire, his back to me and his muscular shoulders a silhouette against the flames. "Talon."

He ignored me, not the least bit startled by my voice.

"Come to bed." I sat there and stared at him, longing for him to leave the fire and bring his flames to me.

He didn't react at all.

I continued to wait for something to happen, but it never did. "I'm tired."

"Then go to sleep."

I released a sigh of frustration, annoyed that he was treating me like I was the one who'd done something wrong. But the last thing I wanted to do was fight. "I want you." I couldn't express my longing any better than that. It was a desperation that couldn't be quelled by anything else but him.

But he continued to sit there.

I released the flap and sighed as I crawled back into bed, cold on the hard ground, lonely without the man who gave me peace and butterflies that felt like fire-breathing dragons at the same time. I closed my eyes and tried to relax.

He opened the flap and entered the tent.

Relief washed over me at the sight of him, like he'd just rescued me from an untimely death.

He removed his armor and cape, placed his sword on the ground next to the bedroll, and in only his trousers, he got into the bedroll with me.

The second he was close, I moved into his chest and held him. My legs tucked between his, and I felt the warmth from his body immediately thaw my body and the bedroll that surrounded us.

I felt more tired than I ever had.

His lips rested against my hairline, and he lay still, his heartbeat gradually starting to slow down.

I listened to it like a lullaby and fell asleep.

When I woke up again, it was still dark outside. The campfire burned.

I wasn't sure if I'd been asleep for just a few minutes... or if it was a new day. When I reached for Talon beside me, he was gone, so I assumed sunrise was close. I sat up and groaned, dead tired and wanting to go back to sleep. I noticed the sounds from the campsite as everyone else packed, and I assumed that was what had woken me up.

The flap opened, and Talon appeared on one knee, wearing his armor and his cape. "Time to move."

"It's not even light out."

"The sooner we get there, the sooner this is over."

"That doesn't help me at all right now."

He smirked then grabbed my clothes before he handed them to me. "You can sleep on the way."

"On a horse?" I asked incredulously.

"Come on, baby," he said. "You know I'd never let you fall."

We traveled that way for three days. Our nights were spent camping out in the open, and our mornings were spent in the dark. The horses rode the entire way, covering dozens of leagues every single day, but the trek was so long it took an eternity to get there. When we were close to the coast, I could feel the change in the air, the scent of salt and water, feel the drop in temperature as the world became cooler.

There were no dragons to spot, so I knew this wasn't the end of our journey.

It was nearly sunset when we arrived, the waves along the shore a crystal blue in the light. The wind was a lot stronger this close to the sea, and I could feel it flap through my hair. We seemed to have reached the end of the world without recourse.

Talon said nothing, just waited for Queen Eldinar to explain the next part of the plan.

The elves disbanded and moved to the shoreline, and from locations hidden in the grasslands and near rocks, they pulled out rowboats that could fit twelve men. They placed them on the sand with the oars.

I looked at the tiny little boats then out to the vast horizon over the sea. "I don't like this..."

Talon continued to hold his silence as he stared at the queen's back, waiting for her to finish conferring with her men. His cape danced in the wind, but he remained still as a statue. Khazmuda kept his distance so he wouldn't trample on anyone accidentally.

The queen turned away from my uncle and approached us. "Now, we sail."

Talon glanced at the boats before he looked at her again. "Calista and I will ride Khazmuda above."

"Khazmuda will have to wait here." She looked past Talon to the dragon that sat on the grass. "As much as we'd like to welcome you, there's simply no room where we're going. Our journey is brief, just around the corner to the cliff at the edge." She turned to face the mountainous cliffside to our left, the terrain steep. "Our harbor is concealed from land within the rock. Our galleons and supplies are stored there. The only way to reach it is by rowboat. Once we set sail, you can notify Khazmuda so he can fly as we sail."

Now that Talon knew the plan, he was more agreeable. "Then let's go."

The horses were left with a few guards who would await our return, and the rest piled into the boats before we pushed off into the water. Everyone grabbed an oar and paddled against the waves, water splashing all over us, until we reached the calm sea.

Talon seemed to know exactly what to do, knew how to handle the oar and when to change sides like the others.

We turned left and approached the cliff at the corner of the land, and as we neared, we saw the entry into the chasm. It looked like a shadow from a distance, but as we came closer, the texture changed and the depth was discernible.

We rowed inside, the ceiling rising hundreds of feet up above, revealing an enormous cove holding several galleons with their sails raised. Elves were visible on the ramparts and the docks, watching the queen slowly sail to where they stood.

No one would ever know about this place unless someone told them it was there.

The boats were secured to the edge, and we stepped onto the wooden dock. The galleon closest to us was constructed of warm wood that resembled the color of honey. At the bow, Queen Eldinar was carved into the wood, wearing a flower crown in her long hair. Mesmerized by the sight, I studied the ship and watched it slowly bob in the water.

When I realized Talon wasn't beside me, I turned to find him.

He'd walked farther down the dock, examining the ship with an eye of admiration, like he appreciated the craftsmanship of the galleon. He stepped back and examined the sails, looked at the crow's nest up above, stared at it with wide eyes like he'd seen one of these before...or had never seen one in his life.

"We'll rest here tonight," Queen Eldinar said. "We'll set sail in the morning."

"How long is the journey?"

"It depends on the speed and the direction of the wind," she said. "But it could be a couple days or a week." She turned away and went to General Ezra's side to speak to him quietly.

He nodded at whatever she said, but his eyes glazed over like he wasn't really listening, too infatuated with her appearance to focus. Then they walked away together, General Ezra always slightly behind her.

I turned back to Talon.

He continued to examine the ship.

I came to his side. "It's pretty."

"It is," he said in agreement. "It's very well made."

"How can you tell?"

His arms crossed over his chest, and he continued to stare at the woodwork, his eyes lost in a daze. "Because I used to be a sailor."

We were given accommodations in a private room with a bed and a real mattress. My back was stiff from sleeping on the ground for three nights, and I was relieved I would be spared that discomfort.

Talon helped himself to a shower then stepped into the room in just his boxers. His arms were cut with the lines of muscle, and his abs looked the same, so distinct and sharp. His hair was still damp, but he didn't seem to care enough to dry it.

I sat up in bed, already clean from my shower, watching him carry himself with a straight spine and rounded shoulders. A fire burned in the hearth because he'd started the flames. It brought warmth to a room that seemed to have been vacant for a long time. "How long were you a sailor?"

He stilled at the question before he slowly turned to me.

He never answered my questions about his past. He told me as little as possible, as if sharing parts of his past was akin to giving away bits of his soul. "Almost twenty years."

My eyebrows slowly rose up my face in surprise. "Wow. Where did you sail to?"

"Everywhere."

"And what were you sailing for?"

He hesitated at the question, and that seemed like the end of our conversation. But to my surprise, he answered. "Sailor is too generous a word. I was a pirate, the kind that plunders and steals."

I felt no judgment. Would never think less of him, no matter what he told me. "Did you enjoy it?"

He took a seat at the edge of the bed, directly in front of the fireplace, his eyes on the wall beside me. "I joined the crew as a prisoner, and I didn't have an opinion about anything at the time."

"Why were you taken as a prisoner?"

"I was living in a quiet village when Captain Blackstorm and his crew took over. They'd lost some of their crew on their last mission and needed hands on deck. They wanted to take a boy who had barely become a man, so I took his place."

My eyes softened. "That was kind of you."

"He had a family, and I didn't care whether I lived or died."

The softness faded as a wave of sorrow struck me. I could hear the pain in his voice, see the bottomless pit in his gaze.

"I'd been a fisherman for the previous year, so I was a good addition to their crew. I did what I was told and didn't say more than a couple words for years. But then things started to change. Captain Blackstorm took a liking to me and made me his commander. We sailed the seas far and wide...and I think the ocean healed me in some ways."

"Do you miss it?"

He considered my question for a long time. "I don't miss who I was. I was more dead than alive. Just going through the motions day after day in the hope I would either die or the pain would stop. Captain Blackstorm told me I was the bravest man he ever knew, but I just had a death wish." He kept his eyes on the wall. "But I do miss the simplicity. All we would do was sail and plunder. Over and over. Through the winds, the tides, and the storms. Celebrate our conquests with a big pint at the pub and laugh about all the times we almost died. Khazmuda says it was all a waste of time, just a distraction from what we needed to do, but I was still broken and in shock...and I needed that time to come alive again."

I hoped he would share more about his life, but I wouldn't pressure him into it when it might just push him away. "Thank you for sharing. I'm sure you were a very sexy pirate." Whenever he came to port, the women would have been eager to get a piece of him. He probably had a gorgeous tan and muscles just as ripped as they were now.

He didn't smile, like his mind was still in the dark.

"I'm surprised that you knew how to sail since you were meant to be a king."

"My father said every man should know how to hunt and survive, regardless of his station in life. So, he taught me and Silas how to sail and wish and survive in the wild."

"Silas?"

He hesitated, even his breath stopped. "My younger brother."

I could feel his pain in those simple words, feel how hard it was for him to say it out loud. "I'm sorry..."

"It never gets easier," he whispered. "You just get used to them being gone."

"Yeah."

"If my father hadn't taught me those things, I'm not sure where I would be."

"I'm glad that he did, because it brought you to me."

He let those words hang in the air for a moment before he turned to look at me, his eyes hollow and lifeless...with a light far in the distance. When his sight locked on mine, it stayed there, looking at me with a new depth.

I felt the bumps on my arms, the heft in my heart, the desire between my legs. I never thought I would look upon a man with this much feeling in my soul. To feel a connection that transcended words. To have someone I would die for without having to think twice. My body had been battered and bruised and my heart had been beaten to death, but he healed me.

He leaned back onto the bed before he climbed up my body, moving over me until his face was just above mine where it rested against the headboard. With his signature intensity, he looked at me like I was his sun, his moon, and his stars. He dipped his head and brushed his nose against mine, giving me affection that was somehow as good as a kiss.

I felt the breath leave my lungs, felt my body burn and go numb at the same time. I felt my heart leave my chest and jump into his, where it wanted to stay forever.

He dipped his head and kissed me, a slow touch of our lips, a kiss that was so gentle it was like a leaf that fell onto the calm water of a lake. His eyes were open and still on me as he kissed me, watching my reaction to his touch and letting me see his in return.

He turned his head the other way and kissed me harder, giving me a kiss that nearly bruised my lips. Then there was his tongue, his breath, all of him. All while he held himself over me, his body tight and strong, veins popping out of the strong muscles.

His arm circled under my back, and he lifted me slightly, dragging me down until I was flat on the bed, my head on the pillow.

He moved over me and kissed me harder, his hand fisting my hair while he made me his with just his perfect mouth. He grabbed one of my legs and hiked it over his hip as he fit his body between my thighs, bringing our bodies close together despite the clothes that separated us.

My hands explored the body I already knew by heart, feeling the heat that burned from his skin, the hardness of the muscle that bulged underneath. My lips got lost with his in the passion, and I felt my body melt like snow from the top of the mountains, rushing downstream like a river.

When he reached for my panties, I automatically lifted my hips so he could pull them free because I was eager to feel him inside me, eager for him to feel just how ready I was to take him. I'd had him many times, but I somehow desired him more with every passing day. I pulled down his boxers so his big dick could come free.

His hips slid between my thighs, and I tilted my pelvis so he could fold me, so his dick could find my wet slit and slide inside. The second he reached my entrance, he moaned like he felt it, felt how gushing wet I was for him. "Baby..." He pushed inside and sank nice and slow, his eyes on me all the way down.

My fingers dug into his hair as I moaned for him, feeling him invade me like no other man who had passed through my gates. He erased the mark of a lesser man, made my invisible scars disappear from memory. My ankles hooked together at the top of his ass, and we moved slowly, locked together like we never wanted to break apart.

Chapter 9

Talon

I lay in bed with Calista in my arms, the fire in the hearth barely alive. Shadows were across the walls, but they were dying as the flames slowly started to fade. My eyes were closed, and I was tired from the constant travel over the last few days. I was used to riding Khazmuda wherever I needed to go, but I felt obligated to ride alongside the queen and her soldiers to feel united.

The warmth was suddenly gone, and I felt a jerk that yanked me sideways. The softness of the bed was gone, the quiet room with the low-burning fire disappeared, and it was dark.

My eyes opened, and I heard a hum, the hum of a thousand tongues, a solid baritone that never faded. I sat upon a high-backed chair made of black wood, and my naked body was now covered in the uniform and armor

I'd left on the bedroom floor. I looked at the table in front of me, also black with faded skulls carved by a sharp knife. Tall black candles formed a line along the center, wax bubbling down the sides.

A shadow passed—and then I saw him.

Seated at the head of the table in the midnight-blue uniform he always wore when he appeared before me sat Bahamut, God of the Underworld. His arms were flat on the armrests, and he stared at me with eyes that were gray instead of blue.

It was then I realized there was no color at all. Everything was in shades of black and gray. My eyes flicked left and right quickly, taking in the stone archway that rose high above, the black sconces on the wall that held flames in the color gray. The last thing I remembered was falling asleep in a warm bed, so was this a dream.

"I own you, Talon Rothschild. I can take you whenever I wish."

My eyes found his once more, still unsure if this was real or a horrible dream.

"You were spared my wrath in Riviana Star because I'm barred from those lands, but the second you left that forest, you were vulnerable. If you thought the presence of your companion and the horde of elves that travel with you would prevent my visit, you were dearly wrong. Your soul is indebted to me, and I can take you whenever I wish."

So, this isn't a dream.

His jaw tightened noticeably as he suppressed his rage. There was a sharpness to his eyes I'd never seen, even in the absence of color. "You're *my* servant, but you aided my enemy. A betrayal that runs deeper than a blade through the heart. How dare you defy me?" He cocked his head slightly, his anger rising like steam from lava.

"I didn't defy you—"

"You took up your blade and defended the God of Caelum. We don't interfere with the living, but you decided their fate with your sword." He struck with the speed of a vampire and slammed his fist hard onto the table. "And you thought I wouldn't know..."

I heard a yelp from the other room, a screech from a frightened human. I wanted to glance to see, but my eyes remained on Bahamut. "You weren't my concern, Bahamut. If the Great Tree had fallen and the Realm of Caelum was overrun by dark elves who sought to claim the afterlife for their own, then the souls of my family would have been at risk. The souls of the people I care for on this side of the veil would have also been at risk. Just because my soul is forfeit doesn't mean I want the same for others. It was my choice—and they deserve to have the same choice."

His eyes were still packed with rage.

"I don't regret what I did." And I would do it again. "You said you don't interfere with the living, but if I fought with the dark elves, I would have also interfered. No matter what I did, it would have been an interference—"

"You could have stepped aside and let the mortals settle their quarrel."

"Stepping aside is still a choice—a choice that affects the living. I know I made the right choice, and you will receive no repentance from me."

He continued to stare at me with a quiet rage he struggled to sheathe.

Footsteps sounded, slow and with an uneven gait, flesh against stone. Then someone, or something, appeared. Hunched forward with a spine so bent it nearly doubled back on itself came a creature that seemed human...at one point in time. Dressed in brown rags with flesh that looked burned by fire, it continued to make the painful walk toward the table where Bahamut sat, carrying a bowl in its shaky hands. Its breaths were deep and labored, like the unnatural bend of its spine made it hard to draw breath.

I shouldn't stare, but I couldn't not stare.

The creature reached the table and placed the bowl in front of Bahamut. It appeared to be a soul, judging by the steam that wafted from the surface toward the high-vaulted ceiling. The figure hissed in its breathing before it turned around and began the painful shuffle back to where it came from.

Bahamut hadn't taken his eyes off me once.

It was the first time that unease prickled my skin, that I felt cold from the lack of light, that I saw a glimpse of the underworld. Every conversation I had with Bahamut had happened in the lands of the living, under the clouds and the sun. But now, I didn't know where we were.

He grabbed his spoon then slid it into the bowl. When he lifted it, a ball of black slime stretched from the spoon, looking like burned cheese or black spinach. He stared at it and slowly watched the material stretch until it plopped back into the bowl with a small splash.

Then I noticed the smell...of burning flesh.

"Would you like some?"

I knew it was a question I shouldn't answer.

"How does a god remain immortal?" He scooped the spoon into the bowl and repeated his actions, revealing the black sludge that slowly slipped off his spoon and splashed back into the broth again. "Souls."

Fear didn't latch on to me easily. I could normally deflect it with calm and determination. But it burned right through me and left a hole in my stomach. It made every muscle in my body feel tight, made me taste rotten fruit on my tongue, made me feel like a thousand spiders crawled across my body that very moment. Sensations I didn't feel in the land of the living. "I haven't fought my war. I haven't met my uncle on the battlefield. Nothing has come to pass. I would like to revoke our deal. You can take back your command of the dead, and I will fight without it." I'd come to rely on the ability so deeply, because I could unleash an army to fight my enemies within a second's notice. It would be invaluable in the war to come, to occupy Barron's soldiers on the ground as I focused on the sky, but I would do without. "I would like to dissolve our agreement."

Bahamut rested the spoon at the edge of the bowl, and then a smile slowly crept into his face. He showed all of his perfectly straight teeth, the joyless mirth in his gaze. "I've noticed the woman in your bed."

A shadowy creature had gazed upon me without my knowledge, haunted us like a ghost in the wind. Discomfort moved through my whole body. I felt violated without being touched. I'd signed my name on the dotted line without understanding the terms.

"But you should have thought of that before you came to me."

"I was a different man when I sailed to your lands."

The smile remained, like he enjoyed my resistance more than my cooperation. "Nonetheless, you conquered Scorpion Valley and Shadow Stone with the powers I gifted you—"

"And the dragons whose allegiance I earned on my own."

"You protected Riviana Star, not once, but twice. It wouldn't have been possible without your command of the dead. You sail to the hidden location of the dragons, information you earned from Queen Eldinar because of the battle you won. All these events wouldn't have come to pass without my aid. What's done cannot be reversed, Talon Rothschild. Just because you've come to love a woman doesn't change the terms of our deal. I warned you the day we met. I told you that this is binding and cannot be undone, and you looked me in the eye and pledged your soul to me for eternity." His voice slowly started to rise as the angry passion flooded through him. "What is done cannot be undone. If the battle is won, you will have a brief moment to savor your victory before you're brought here for eternity, to harvest the souls from those who are unfortunate enough to meet me. You will prepare them for me night and day so I can maintain a power so great it can be challenged by none other than a god. And if you lose the battle and this is all for naught..." He continued to smile like he enjoyed every moment of my suffering. "Then your fate will remain the same."

Forfeiting my soul felt inconsequential when I had nothing to live for, but now it felt like the gravest mistake of my life. Khazmuda's dark eyes were visible in my mind, the insurmountable sorrow he would feel when he saw my body on the ground, dead without injury. The tears he would shed would look like diamonds in the sun.

And then Calista... I couldn't bear the thought.

"Enjoy the time you have left, Talon Rothschild." He scooped his spoon into his bowl, and instead of letting the contents drop back into the liquid, he took a bite. Eating the soul clean off the spoon. The room darkened... and objects started to blur...and then, for just an instant, I saw rows of razor-sharp teeth from a dark mouth, a face large and jagged like pinnacles of rock, eyes red like a blood moon, and a snarl that could crunch bone. "Every soul tastes different—and I look forward to tasting yours."

And then the world changed, and I stared at the fireplace once more. The flames had died long ago because the hearth was cold. The scent of smoke was absent from the room. My breaths were quick and labored, like I'd run straight from the underworld back to this room. I turned to the bed, where I expected to see Calista sleeping.

The bed was empty.

I looked at the bathroom and saw the door was wide open, and no one was inside.

I was rooted to the spot, unable to move, unable to get the image of the monster out of my mind.

Where did you go?

The sound of Khazmuda's voice made my eyes clench shut, desperate to rid my thoughts of the unspeakable things I'd seen.

You're afraid. What's happened?

Just had a bad dream.

Talon...you've been gone for a day.

Dread dropped into my stomach, and the unease followed.

Our minds always touch, no matter the distance. But I couldn't feel yours.

I opened my eyes and lifted my chin. Against the wall, he stood, dressed in his midnight-blue armor, eyes blue like the ocean. That same satisfied smile was upon his handsome face, basking in my misery.

Talon?

I continued to meet his gaze, haunted by a god who would feast upon my soul.

The door flew open, and Calista stumbled into the room. "Talon."

Bahamut disappeared like a wind blew away the smoke.

She rushed to me and gripped me tight, her face moving to my chest. "You have any idea how scared I was?" She stepped back, her eyes both vicious and emotional. "Where did you go? Khazmuda said he couldn't feel you, and I was afraid you drowned or…" She couldn't think of another explanation because there was none. There wasn't a single story to explain how I'd left the hidden port without taking a boat, how I'd broken the connection with Khazmuda without breaking the fuse, how I'd been gone for an entire day as people searched for me. Her eyes shifted back and forth between mine, angry and desperate for an answer.

I was in shock from what I saw and unable to speak.

I've never felt such fear in your heart. What has happened?

"Talon," Calista pressed. "I felt you leave the bed, and you were just gone..."

Tell me.

I'm fine. Now, give me a moment. "I just needed to be alone."

"To be alone." She said the words slowly like she didn't understand. "Why? Why would you need to be alone?"

"I just did."

"And how could you be so alone that Khazmuda couldn't feel you—"

"Because I closed my mind to him."

"Why would you disappear for a day when we're supposed to set sail for the dragons? Queen Eldinar had men searching for you in the water—"

"I'm sorry I alarmed everyone. It wasn't my intention." None of this was my intention. I didn't want to leave the warmest bed I'd ever known and face a soul-eating monster across a dark table.

Calista continued to shift her gaze back and forth in disbelief.

"Let's just drop it."

"Is this because of last night?" Her anger started to fade and was quickly replaced by hurt. "Every time we get closer, I feel you pull away. And it fucking hurts—"

"No, that's not why."

"Then...then explain to me why you just disappeared like that. Why would you scare both Khazmuda and me like that? Why you would hold up everyone for a whole day because you needed to be alone—"

"Calista." I couldn't tell her the truth. Couldn't tell Khazmuda the truth. It would kill them both. "Do you trust me?"

She hesitated when asked the question. "Talon, of course I do—"

"Then let this go."

Her eyes continued to flick back and forth in unease, like that wasn't enough for her. But she didn't say another word.

I pulled her into me and locked my arms around her, my chin dipped to rest on the top of her head, my arms like solid bars of a cage. I squeezed her against the plates of my armor because I didn't want to let go. I wanted to feel her little body against me and close my eyes, get the horrible vision out of my head, to treasure the peace and joy in my life before it was savagely ripped from my grasp.

We boarded the galleon and set sail at dawn. The waves were calm at this hour, the sun barely crested above the horizon over the edge of the world. The winds were in our favor and filled our sails in the direction we wanted to head, and the large ship glided through the water with ease.

I stood at the bow of the ship and looked at the open sea beyond, still shaken by the image burned in my head. Movement in the air caught my eye, and I spotted Khazmuda soar through the skies, his black body distinct against the backdrop of blue and pink with fluffy white clouds.

I want answers, Talon. He turned his head to tilt his gaze to me down below.

Calista accepted my silence, but Khazmuda wasn't so understanding. *I'll give them to you when the time is right.*

What secrets do you keep from me?

Everyone has secrets, Khazmuda.

Not I. I keep nothing from you, Talon Rothschild.

I looked out at the ocean again, feeling the pain of guilt.

I feel the weight you carry. Let me carry it with you.

I ignored his words even though it pained me to do so. *Queen Eldinar said it may be a week of sailing. Will you make it that far?*

Don't question my strength.

It's not a matter of strength but endurance—and you weigh a great deal. You said yourself that you'd gotten fat. I hoped the tease would lift his mood, lure him away from the subject I wanted to avoid.

If I need to rest, I can float.

You don't know what lurks under the surface.

I'm an enormous dragon. I'll take my chances.

"You're a sailor."

I pulled my eyes away from Khazmuda when I recognized the queen's voice. I turned around to face her directly.

"My men told me you gave a hand on our departure."

"It's a beautiful ship. A type of craftmanship I've never seen." The ships I'd sailed had been well made and withstood the storms, but the attention to detail didn't compare to the one built by the elves. "It makes the water feel still."

"The ocean has a spirit just like all the flowers in our forest. And she shared her secrets with us."

I'd touched the spirit of the ocean myself and felt her salty tears heal my wounds. I didn't expect to share that belief with someone like Queen Eldinar.

She stared at the side of my face. "Do you enjoy being back at sea?"

"I do." The smell of the salt. The spray of the ocean. The way the light danced off the surface in the distance. It was a moment of respite I desperately needed.

She looked ahead once more, no longer in her armor but in a white gown with long sleeves. She appreciated the sunrise in silence, standing a foot away from me as the breeze blew her hair over one shoulder past her face. "Calista is in your chambers?"

"Yes. She needed sleep." Because she'd been awake for an entire day, worried for my well-being. Once we'd set sail, she'd climbed into bed and immediately knocked out.

Queen Eldinar pivoted her body to face me. "Then perhaps it's a good time for us to speak."

I didn't face her right away, knowing exactly what she wished to discuss. "I'd like to watch the sunrise first, if that's alright, Your Majesty." I knew my sunrises and sunsets were limited. This might be one of the final few I'd ever see ...if not the last.

She pivoted her body back to the ocean and watched the sun reflect off the surface of the water. "Of course. Let's watch it together."

She had the biggest accommodations on the ship, a full dining table where she could confer with her general and her soldiers. She sat at the head of the table with a glass of wine before her, surrounded by the glow of the candlelight.

I'd already had a glass of wine in the silence, and I helped myself to another. General Ezra was absent, and I was grateful for it.

With her hands together on the table, she stared at me, her eyes as blue as Bahamut's.

It made me grateful Calista had eyes green like emeralds...that I could stare at endlessly.

"You know what answers I seek, Death King."

I held her gaze, my fingers resting around the stem of my glass.

"I would rather you share this story with me as a friend. I respect you too much to interrogate you."

I'd hated this woman when I met her, felt rage any time I looked at her. But now, I felt affection for her. I'd saved her life for Calista, but at this point, I would save her life because I wanted to.

"Not a single one of my men saw you leave or come back. And these aren't ordinary men. These are soldiers and warriors who survived the great battle, the best, those who are entrusted with my protection. I've lived over a thousand years and have seen magic and found many secrets in this world, but I've never watched someone disappear into thin air."

I wouldn't be able to deflect her with a poor lie. Wouldn't be able to ask her to pardon her curiosity. "I will speak to you as a friend. But will you guard my secret as a friend?"

Her intelligent eyes absorbed my words without reaction.

"Will you take this secret to your grave, Queen Eldinar?"

She continued to sit in silence as she considered the question.

"Even your husband cannot know." He was the worst person to know.

"I never make a promise I can't keep, but I've never made a promise to withhold knowledge without understanding the significance of that knowledge or its repercussions." She stared at her hands for a long moment as she seriously considered the situation before her, comprehending the gravity. The silence lasted minutes, not seconds, her intellect at work. Then she lifted her gaze and met my stare. "It's unwise to make this promise, but I will make it, nonetheless. I suspect you carry this burden alone, and if I don't carry it with you, no one will."

Her words elicited emotion from me that I didn't expect, and my eyes immediately flicked away to recover from the unexpected blow. Her prejudice against me had made me question her faculties, but now there was no doubt she was one of the most intelligent people I'd ever met. "Thank you."

"I'm ready to listen, Death King."

I didn't know where to start. Didn't want to admit the decision I'd made had been reckless and foolhardy. "You know my father was the King of the Southern Isles. That he was usurped by my uncle. Not really my uncle...

because the blood has been diluted over the generations. He used the dark elves who reside in that land to control the dragons we'd lived with peacefully for generations... and took everything from me." My eyes dropped to the table as I spoke. "He burned each member of my family alive."

I didn't know her reaction because my eyes were down, but I suspected her expression hadn't changed at all. Not because she was heartless, but because she was a monarch who had to face cruelty with a hard face.

"I loved every member of my family. My father. My mother. My sister. My brother..." All of their deaths still hurt me. "But what hurt most of all..." I'd had decades to accept the loss, but no amount of time would make this one better. The guilt wouldn't allow me to let it go. "They burned my wife...and she was pregnant with my daughter." I kept my eyes on the table and focused on the texture of the wood to stave off the tears. "I tried to send her away on a ship...but he knew."

"I'm sorry, Death King."

"Call me Talon."

There was a long pause. "Then call me Eldi."

I lifted my head to look at her.

"It's what my parents used to call me. How my husband and other close friends address me in private."

"I—I feel honored." More honored than I'd ever been.

"Continue your tale, Talon."

I held her gaze for a moment before I looked down at the table again. "Khazmuda saved me, and over those decades, I spent my time trying to forget what happened. I tried to take my life, but Khazmuda fused with me to spare me. I sailed the seas in the hope everything would just go away, but it never did. No matter how fast I sailed our galleon, I couldn't outrun my misery."

She listened with patience and didn't try to rush me.

"When you're a pirate, you meet a lot of people in a lot of places. My captain told me a tale of Bahamut, God of the Underworld. He told me where to find him, so I sailed there."

The tension rose like a fire that was growing in intensity. She said nothing, but the air around her had changed.

I lifted my chin to look at her once more. "I asked him to make me powerful enough to defeat my enemies, to avenge my wife and child...and the rest of my kin. He gave me the ability to command the dead, told me free dragons still existed in the world, and gave me the tools I needed to reach this moment. But it came at a heavy price."

"Talon..." Her hard confidence disappeared as the sadness flooded her eyes. Disappointment was in her voice, the kind that was heavier than a rain cloud in a storm. "When is this debt owed?"

"Once the battle is finished—whether I win or lose."

She brought her hands underneath her chin and dipped her head slightly, her mind lost in thought.

"When I disappeared, it was because Bahamut took me. He's angry that I defended the Great Tree and the God of Caelum when my purpose is to serve him. I made no apologies because I feel no remorse. The dark elves were foul creatures, and they deserved death."

"They would have been good allies for your war."

I gave a slight shake of my head. "I'd rather win it the hard way than the easy way."

"What else did he say to you?"

"I tried to end the agreement and spare my soul, but he won't let me go." An invisible power had bound me to him. I couldn't undo what had been done. And no living creature could undo it. As mighty as Khazmuda was, even he was powerless against a god. "I said I would forfeit the powers he gave me, but he said it was too late."

"The God of Caelum has shared little of him, but she's mentioned his unspeakable cruelty."

A cruelty I would endure for eternity.

"I wish you hadn't made that deal, Talon."

"I was in a different place when I made it." Too depressed to care about anything other than Uncle Barron's death. I wanted him to burn in Khazmuda's flames and scream just the way my family had screamed in agony. "But if I hadn't made it, it wouldn't have led me here." It wouldn't have led me to Calista on that starry night in the middle of the desert.

"You're in a much different place now because you love again."

I stared at the table.

"She doesn't know..."

I shook my head.

"And Khazmuda?"

"No."

A sorrow as heavy as mine filled her eyes. "Will you tell them?"

"I—I can't." I couldn't tell Calista what was to come. It would destroy her joy and her smile. It would ruin what we had. It would ruin the first happiness I'd felt in a very long time. "I can't see the look on her face. And Khazmuda...that would kill me." I wasn't sure who would be more devastated. "To tell them it's coming will poison every day we have left together. It'll be all they think about."

She gave a slight nod in agreement. "You're right."

"I'll just drop dead, and they'll never know."

She lowered her gaze to the table.

"I think it's best if they never know." It would be hard enough to lose me, but to know I would spend eternity in an insufferable existence when they couldn't stop it was far worse. They couldn't know.

Her eyes remained down.

"I—I loved my wife so much."

She lifted her chin to look at me.

"I'll always love her. So, I didn't expect to ever feel this way for someone." I didn't expect to meet a woman who I would care so deeply for. Someone who would heal my wounds and make my heart beat again. Someone I would die for. Just when I touched the sun, just when I felt

spring bloom in my heart, it was already dark and winter.
"She needs me...and I'm about to abandon her."

Chapter 10

Calista

I had to accept the fact that I would never know where Talon had gone.

He'd just vanished. I was jerked awake by his abrupt departure, my head dropping onto the pillow because his chest was suddenly gone. I jolted upright and looked into the dark bedroom, the flames barely alive, but only saw shadows.

Our journey on the galleon had been smooth for days, but it turned rocky when he sailed into storm clouds. The rain pelted the deck, and the ship swayed back and forth, making glasses and candles on tables knock to the floor. I'd never been on a ship, and I quickly learned that I was susceptible to seasickness.

I remained below deck in our chambers alone while Talon helped the elves navigate the ship through the storm. I wanted to help, but since I had no experience on the sea, there wasn't much I could do except stay out of the way.

I sat against the headboard and felt my body rock back and forth, doing my best to stay calm and not let the sickness spread to the rest of my body. The storm lasted from day to night. At some point, it stopped because I'd fallen asleep and woke up to a still boat and a quiet day.

Talon wasn't beside me, and I hoped he was okay.

I dressed and climbed to the deck, feeling the sunshine on my face when I emerged at the top. The sea air blew through my hair and removed any remaining tendrils of nausea that resided deep in my stomach.

I spotted Talon at the bow of the ship in plain trousers and a long-sleeved shirt, like he preferred to sail as a man rather than a king. Beside him was Queen Eldinar, in her usual gown and elegance. They were both facing the ocean ahead, but they appeared to be engaged in conversation.

I ascended the steps then approached them from behind, seeing the landmass in the distance between them. I stilled when I realized that was our destination, an island far off into the sea with nothing else around for leagues. It was still small at the moment, too small for details or dragons in the sky. "Looks like we're almost there."

Talon turned around to look at me, his eyes kind but mostly exhausted. "Yes."

Queen Eldinar turned to regard me. "Before you stands Thalian, guarded by our soldiers who pledge their lives to the defense of the last free dragons."

I stepped between them and looked across the calm ocean to the island that was still too far away to make out. My hand shaded my eyes from the light so I could see better, but even then, the details of the land were unknown. "I can't wait to see Inferno again. I've missed him."

"Judging by the wind speed, we'll be there tomorrow morning," Talon said. "Would have been there much sooner if that storm hadn't assaulted us." He looked at me. "I hope you didn't get sick. Sailing isn't for everyone."

"I felt a little unwell, but it passed." I looked up to Khazmuda in the sky, who continued to glide above our boat. I can't even imagine what you're feeling right now.

I feel it in my heart—and I still can't describe it.

You don't have to wait for us, Khazmuda.

Talon and I have worked toward this for a long time. I want to share this with him.

"Khazmuda wants to wait for us."

"I know," Talon said. "He has more patience than I thought." He looked up at his dragon overhead, a slight smile on his lips.

Queen Eldinar regarded Talon with a look of affection, a look she continued to give him after he'd saved her people and their forest. "It's not patience that steadies his wings—but loyalty."

His eyes remained on Khazmuda, and then, slowly, the smile started to fade and he addressed the queen. "How will we proceed, Your Majesty?"

"Khazmuda is welcome to visit with his kin. And I'm sure Inferno will be pleased by your arrival, Calista. Macabre is the leader of their society. A mighty dragon with intelligence as fierce as his talons. He is ferocious but, after earning his trust, very kind. He's the one you'll need to convince."

"Can't I speak to each dragon individually?" Talon asked.

"You can pursue this endeavor however you wish," Queen Eldinar said. "But Macabre is a proud dragon, and if you pursue this without his support, you'll be climbing an endless hill."

"He sounds like a dictator," Talon said coldly.

"He's very protective of his kin," Queen Eldinar said. "He considers the well-being of each dragon his personal responsibility. Despite everything we did to protect their kind, it took a long time for him to trust us. He was suspicious of us for years, waiting for us to show our true colors hidden by our false kindness. Try to remember that his distrust is valid, because many of their kind were killed in the Great War long ago. Neither of you lived at the time and neither did your recent ancestors, but Macabre and I remember it well. It's men he trusts the least."

Talon released a heavy sigh. "It sounds like protecting Riviana Star and sailing to Thalian was the easy part."

"Do you think we'll succeed?" I asked Queen Eldinar.

"A difficult question to answer," she said. "If you'd asked me this same question a few weeks ago, I would have told you we wouldn't stand where we stand now. I would have told you that the Death King would never be my ally. I would have told you this moment never would have come to pass. But we are in sight of the secret lands where the dragons reside. I don't think it's likely you'll convince Macabre to leave the safety of this place and fight for you, but I don't think it's impossible."

I looked at Talon.

With eyes full of defeat, he looked at me.

"Perhaps Inferno will be of help. He's been there a while."

"Perhaps," he said solemnly.

"And we know Macabre will like Khazmuda."

"I'm not sure what he'll think," Talon said. "Might regard Khazmuda as an outsider."

Queen Eldinar looked at the horizon once more before she silently excused herself and left the bow of the ship.

Talon ran his fingers through his hair as his squinted eyes looked at the blue horizon.

"You must be tired."

"It was a long night."

"I missed you." With every passing day, I grew more attached, and I didn't try to fight it. I let my heart beat on my sleeve. Let my eyes say the words that my mouth was too afraid to speak. I didn't just look at him, but stared deeply into his soul.

He slowly turned back to me, his eyes suddenly sad. "I missed you too."

When we woke up the next morning, the island was close.

Lush and green with a tall mountain in the center, it looked like a beautiful paradise. The shores were white, the air was warm, and the trees were different than they were on the mainland.

I didn't wear my armor and sword because I didn't want to provoke the dragons. It wasn't like I had any chance against them in a battle anyway. I wore one of my dresses with my sandals, the air too hot and moist for anything else.

Talon wore his uniform and armor anyway, his cape billowing behind him as he stood on the bow, looking like a king about to conquer another land in his name. But his sword had been left behind in our quarters below.

We sailed closer to the port, the wooden dock extending far into the cove of clear blue water. Structures were visible along the shore near the water, other galleons with cannons waited along the sides. It was a battle station, but I suspected no one had ever sailed to Thalian. For a thousand years, the island had probably remained untouched.

As we approached the dock, guards appeared to take the ropes thrown overboard to secure the ship. Their armor was different from the elves, a brilliant teal that had a shine like the sun. It was a perfect mixture of the trees and the water, a color that camouflaged them into the scenery of the island.

The three galleons were secured to the dock, and then Queen Eldinar disembarked first, followed by Uncle Ezra. Everyone else followed suit while the Thalian guards secured the ships and unloaded the supplies packed inside.

Talon took his place by Queen Eldinar, and they walked together like they were equals. I trailed behind with my uncle, seeing the two monarchs leading the way, looking like king and queen of a joint territory. They were both beautiful people, so it would be easy to assume they were husband and wife as well. I'd never been the jealous type, but seeing just how breathtaking Queen Eldinar always was, day and night, made me feel a little self-conscious. Even on my best day, I never glowed the way she did.

We crossed to shore then entered the grouping of buildings erected along the coast, each one of them with a view of the water and the gentle waves that rolled to shore.

More guards were ready to receive the queen, and when the first one stepped forward, I assumed he was the one in charge. "Queen Eldinar." He bowed deeply, and so did the others who stood behind him. When their heads were dipped, they stayed that way for a long pause, like an exaggerated form of respect.

Queen Eldinar didn't smile, but there was a kindness in her eyes when she regarded her people. "Guards of Thalian, thank you for protecting this special place and guarding our scaled friends. We think of your sacrifice every day."

"Thank you, Queen Eldinar." He gave another quick bow.

Queen Eldinar turned slightly to Talon beside her. "May I introduce the Death King, an ally to Riviana Star and dear friend of mine. Please provide him suitable accommodations. He has an omnivorous diet."

"I can exist without meat while I'm in your lands," Talon said quickly. "Don't make any special provisions for me."

Queen Eldinar stared at him for a moment before she turned back to the commander of the guard. "The Death King has come to make a plea to Macabre. Once that's finished, we'll return to our lands. The soldiers I've brought will take the new rotation so you can return home to your families."

The commander didn't glance at Talon and accepted her words without protest. "Thank you, Your Majesty."

One of the guards approached Talon and gave a slight bow. "I'll escort you to your accommodations, Death King. This way." He took the lead and guided us down a dirt path past the buildings until he reached a single home at the far end, a humble abode but a private one. The door was opened for us to reveal a one-bedroom cabin with a bed, a fireplace, a small living area, and a private bathroom. "I hope this is suitable, Your Majesty."

"It is," Talon said. "Thank you."

Two other guards walked inside and placed our belongings on the couch. They didn't question who I was.

"We'll bring water and your meals throughout the day." He gave another bow before he left with the guards who had helped him carry our belongings.

Now we were alone together in a cabin, the ocean visible in the window, the air far warmer here than it was back at home. I looked at the artwork on the wall, images of seashells and exotic birds. We'd finally arrived in the place we desired most, but the moment didn't feel real. It wouldn't feel real until I looked Inferno in the eye.

Then I heard his voice in my head. ***CALISTA, I FEEL YOUR MIND… BUT IT CAN'T BE YOU.***

I smiled. It is.

HOW CAN THIS BE?

It's a long story. A very long one...

I CAN'T WAIT TO HEAR IT. BUT FIRST, I WANT TO SEE YOU.

I want to see you too. "Inferno knows we're here."

A thud sounded outside.

I looked out the window and saw Khazmuda's dark scales against the white shore.

Talon headed toward the door. "There's our ride."

We left the house and walked across the white sand to where Khazmuda sat, his dark eyes like coal in the bright surroundings. He lowered his body so we could climb up his side into the saddle that had been secured before we left.

Talon helped me up first then climbed up and sat behind me. Like he did on the horse, he secured his arm across my waist to keep me in place before he grabbed on to one of the spikes that protruded from Khazmuda's spine. "Hold on."

I grabbed on to his arm then felt us launch high into the sky, my hair immediately whipping around and striking him in the face. The world grew small below as we rose up with the mountains. Khazmuda soared over the land in search of the mighty red scales.

I FEEL YOUR MIND GROW BIGGER.

"We're getting closer," I said. Where are you?

THE VALLEY AT THE NORTH PINNACLE. IT'S MY FAVORITE PLACE TO WATCH THE SUNSET.

"He said he's at the northern tip," I said.

Khazmuda spoke directly into my thoughts. ***I feel his mind.*** Khazmuda changed direction and soared over the land that seemed uninhabited.

"Baby, look down."

I looked down into the greenery below and saw brilliant scales in the grass. Several dragons lay there basking in the sun, each of them displaying different colored scales that reflected the light of the brilliant sun. "Wow, there're at least five of them."

Talon's arm tightened on my waist as I leaned to the side like I was a child about to fall off the couch. "Hard to believe, isn't it?"

Khazmuda dropped in altitude as he approached the valley Inferno described. Then I saw his brilliant red scales contrasted against the cool grass, large in size like Khazmuda, with his head held high in pride.

"I forgot how beautiful he is."

Khazmuda landed more gently than usual, probably because I was a rider instead of just Talon. He dropped his belly to the ground so it would be easy for me to climb down as well. Talon went down first, then helped me get my feet on the ground.

Once I felt the earth beneath me, I ran to the dragon with mighty red scales, the dragon I loved with the same intensity as Khazmuda. I felt a smile pull at my lips as I ran to him, feeling so free I could sprout wings and fly.

He dipped his snout to receive my hug, his eyes affectionate and warm. ***IT'S BEEN SO LONG SINCE I'VE SEEN YOUR FACE.***

I collided with his snout then grabbed on to hug him, to hug a dragon as best I could.

He dipped his head into me then released a low hum, a sigh of satisfaction.

"Your scales are even prettier than I remember."

I KNOW.

I chuckled before I pulled away to look at him. "We have a lot to catch up on."

WE DO. He raised his head and looked past me. The second he set his eyes on Talon, they narrowed in distinct disdain. ***THE FIRST THING YOU CAN DO IS***

EXPLAIN WHY YOU'VE BROUGHT HIM HERE.

Talon stepped forward but kept his distance, Khazmuda behind him. He looked upon Inferno with a hard gaze, like he expected to be unwelcome...or could read the rage in Inferno's eyes.

I turned back to Inferno. "Talon has proven himself to be a man of good, not evil."

Inferno shifted his gaze to me. ***THE LAST TIME YOU SAW HIM, YOU EXCHANGED BLOWS WITH YOUR SWORDS—***

"A lot has happened since. After you left, General Titan marched to Riviana Star to take me, and he would have succeeded and burned down the entire forest if Talon hadn't come to my rescue. He saved me and the forest. When the dark elves realized that the elves had a battle to the south, they decided to take the Realm of Caelum from within the forest. We were outnumbered because they struck an alliance with Behemoths and goblins. Without Talon, we all would be dead now." I lowered my voice to make sure Talon couldn't overhear me. "I've forgiven him for everything, and now he's the man in my heart."

Inferno had stared me down with annoyance the entire

time, but he must have seen the sincerity in my gaze because his hostility slowly waned.

"You can trust him."

Inferno stared at me for a moment longer before he released a loud sigh from his nostrils. ***HE MAY BE A KING, BUT YOU'RE THE QUEEN OF MY HEART. I THINK YOU DESERVE MORE.***

"Even if that were true, he's the only man I want."

Inferno continued to stare at me. ***YOUR AFFECTION FOR HIM IS PROFOUND.***

I blinked at the observation, feeling the sting of truth in my heart. "It is..."

The disappointment in his eyes was evident, but it slowly started to fade. ***THEN I WILL TRY TO LOVE HIM AS WELL.***

I felt the affection burn my eyes. Felt the rush of gratitude. "Thank you." I pressed my palm to the soft scales around his snout and rested my head against the side, so close to his razor-sharp teeth but completely unafraid.

When I turned back to Talon, he was where he'd been a moment before, still staring at us. "It's nice to see you again, Inferno."

I spoke aloud for Inferno. "You as well, Death King."

"Queen Eldinar granted us passage to these lands so we can make our plea," Talon said. "Have you had any success of your own?"

NO.

Talon's eyes tightened in disappointment.

BUT I HAVEN'T MADE A PLEA OF MY OWN. I'VE SPENT MY TIME TRYING TO BUILD A RELATIONSHIP WITH THE DRAGONS. THEY'VE WELCOMED ME TO THIS ISLAND, BUT THEY CONTINUE TO TREAT ME AS AN OUTSIDER. THEIR RELATIONSHIPS HAVE ENDURED FOR A THOUSAND YEARS, SO IT'S NOT EXACTLY EASY TO ENTICE THEM INTO FORMING NEW FRIENDSHIPS. I SPEND A LOT OF TIME ALONE, UNFORTUNATELY. BUT I'M STILL GRATEFUL BECAUSE AT LEAST I'M FREE.

Talon gave a slight nod. "I'm sorry to hear that."

THEY'LL OSTRACIZE ME EVEN MORE WHEN THEY REALIZE THE COMPANY I KEEP.

"What can you tell me about Macabre?"

HE HAS MANY MATES AND MANY HATCHLINGS.

"I thought dragons were monogamous?" Talon asked.

THEY ARE. BUT HE'S NOT.

"He sounds popular."

HE HAS VERY NICE SCALES.

"The more I hear about him, the less I like him."

HE WOULDN'T BE REVERED BY THE OTHER DRAGONS IF HE WERE UNKIND.

"Why would the female dragons be willing to share him with other mates?"

BECAUSE GROWING THEIR POPULATION IS OF THE UTMOST IMPORTANCE. A DRAGON IS PREGNANT FOR TWO YEARS BEFORE THEY LAY THEIR EGGS, AND ONLY ONE OR TWO OF THOSE EGGS WILL HATCH. THEY LOST SO MANY OF THEIR OWN IN THE GREAT WAR. MACABRE IS THE EQUIVALENT OF A KING, SO MANY FEMALES WANT TO HAVE HIS HATCHLINGS.

Talon crossed his arms over his chest as he considered what Inferno had shared with him. "I intended to speak with Macabre directly and ask for his aid to free the dragons in the Southern Isles. But now I fear he'll have no interest in speaking to me."

YOUR ASSUMPTION IS CORRECT. THEY HATE HUMANS. THEY WILL BE VERY DISPLEASED TO SEE YOU ON THIS ISLAND.

"Perhaps you and Khazmuda could convince him together."

WE CAN TRY. BUT I DON'T THINK THERE IS MUCH INCENTIVE FOR THEM TO LEAVE THIS PLACE AND RISK THEIR LIVES. EVEN THOUGH THE GREAT WAR WAS LONG AGO, THEY ARE STILL GRIEVING THAT LOSS. THEY'RE STILL HEALING. WE PROCESS TIME DIFFERENTLY FROM MORTALS. WHAT HAPPENED ONE HUNDRED YEARS AGO FEELS LIKE YESTERDAY. WHAT HAPPENED ONE THOUSAND YEARS AGO FEELS LIKE A YEAR. THEY'RE ONLY INTERESTED IN REBUILDING THEIR SOCIETY. AND SINCE THE SOUTHERN ISLES IS SO FAR AWAY, WITH A LANDMASS IN BETWEEN, THEY'LL NEVER BE AT RISK FROM YOUR UNCLE'S TYRANNY.

Talon turned quiet and looked toward the sea, standing tall as the breeze flapped his cape. His handsome face had hardened into consternation, the thoughts pounding behind his eyes and underneath his flesh. He spoke aloud, but he seemed to speak only to himself. "I didn't come this far for nothing..."

It hurt to see his disappointment and not be able to do anything about it. I couldn't rush off and confront Macabre myself. "The best thing we can do is to remind them how it *does* affect them. They may not know these dragons, but they're still dragons. And if the situations were reversed, they would hope their kin would come to their aid."

THE DRAGON POPULATION HAD DROPPED CONSIDERABLY SINCE THE AGE OF MAN. THERE ARE SO FEW LEFT. IT DOESN'T MAKE SENSE TO RISK WHAT LITTLE THEY HAVE FOR NO GUARANTEE.

"How many dragons live on this island?" Talon turned back to Inferno.

MAYBE SEVENTY ADULTS. THERE ARE FAR MORE HATCHLINGS.

Talon's eyes remained still, like he was thinking. "I hoped for more, but seventy is enough."

THAT'S ASSUMING EACH ONE OF THEM AGREES—WHICH WON'T HAPPEN.

"An attack of fifty dragons that no one sees coming is a

powerful attack," Talon said. "How long does it take hatchlings to grow?"

FOR THEM TO REACH FULL SIZE, AT LEAST A DECADE.

Talon shifted his gaze to the ground as he considered the situation, arms still across his chest.

I continued to rub Inferno's snout.

After several minutes of silence, Talon spoke. "The dragons are safe on this land, and they may remain safe for a long time. It's a beautiful place, but it's still an island, and at some point, they'll outgrow it. Their population can only increase so much. If they fight for us, not only will they be able to free their kin, but once King Barron is killed and that land is eradicated of evil, the dragons can claim it as their own. It's a beautiful place with more land than they could ever know what to do with."

WON'T YOU RULE THE SOUTHERN ISLES AS THE NEW KING?

His eyes dropped to the ground. "My only desire is to avenge my family. I've never cared about taking back the kingdom, just purging the asshole who sits upon the throne. The dragons can have it."

My heart raced in excitement. Would he give up his kingdom so he could live with me in mine? We could live together in Scorpion Valley or in Riviana Star. Or perhaps he would continue to rule Shadow Stone as the king while I was his queen.

THAT IS THE ONLY ANGLE WE HAVE, SO WE SHOULD USE IT. BUT PERHAPS YOU SHOULD GIVE MACABRE A CHANCE TO WARM UP TO YOU. HE'LL BE GREATLY DISPLEASED AT THE SIGHT OF YOU.

"That will be a waste of time," Talon said. "You're their kind and have been here for months, and they continue to ignore you. I came here for a purpose, and if I'm not transparent about that purpose, it'll only make him more suspicious. No, I will get to the point and get to it quickly. At least then he'll respect me."

I DON'T THINK HE'LL EVER RESPECT YOU, DEATH KING.

"Don't call me that," he said. "Talon is fine."

"What does Macabre look like?" I asked.

HE'S THE LARGEST DRAGON HERE, WITH SCALES THE COLOR OF SMOKE. ON A CLOUDY DAY, HE'S INVISIBLE IN THE SKIES. WHEN HE FLIES ACROSS THE

WATER, HE BLENDS INTO THE SURFACE. THE ONLY COLOR HE POSSESSES IS HIS EYES—WHICH ARE A STUNNING BLUE. HIS SCALES MAY BE DEVOID OF COLOR, BUT THEY REMAIN IRIDESCENT.

"Do you know where to find him?" Talon asked.

HE RESIDES IN ONE OF THE CAVES THAT HE SHARES WITH HIS FEMALE COMPANIONS.

"Then let's introduce ourselves." Talon turned back to Khazmuda so he could climb up his scales into the saddle.

"Now?" I asked incredulously.

Talon climbed onto Khazmuda's back and regarded me from his impressive height. It'd been a long time since I'd seen Talon atop his dragon, and I was reminded how regal he looked, his black armor matching the dark scales that protected Khazmuda's body. "He'll soon realize that humans are present on his island. Perhaps he should hear that news from us."

"I think we should ask Queen Eldinar for an introduction," I said. "That way, she can vouch for our character before we petition him for aid."

Talon considered my words. "She said she wouldn't help us convince him to fight for us, but you're right, that would be a better approach. We'll speak with Queen Eldinar and decide when to speak with Macabre."

Inferno dropped his snout to look at me. ***WOULD YOU LIKE A RIDE?***

I smiled. "It's been a long time."

CLIMB UP. I'D LIKE TO KNOW WHERE YOUR ACCOMMODATIONS ARE SO I CAN VISIT. He dipped his head farther so I could climb onto his snout before he lifted me to his back so I could grab on to one of his spikes.

Talon watched closely from where he sat upon Khazmuda, visibly worried about my riding a dragon alone without a saddle. "Inferno, go slow."

I KNOW HOW TO TAKE CARE OF MY QUEEN. He looked at me over his shoulder. ***HOLD ON, CALISTA.***

I grabbed on to one of the spikes.

Inferno jumped from the ground, but he took flight much easier than Khazmuda, gliding forward rather than launching into the sky. He gently rose in elevation then flew low over the ground, taking me back to the south, where our cabin was located. He soared over the water before he landed on the open beach, making as gentle of a landing as he could. He folded his wings then lay on his belly so I could slide down and land on the soft sand.

I hadn't felt earth this soft since the Arid Sands. A quick flashback came across my mind, remembering the sight of Khazmuda in the dark...and then the appearance of the Death King.

Khazmuda dropped down a moment later, and Talon hopped off his dragon and landed in the sand on steady feet. Despite the heavy armor he wore and the heat from the humidity, he seemed unaffected by the discomfort.

"We'll speak to Queen Eldinar," Talon said. "And let you know the plan." We left the sand and made our way to hard ground before we walked down the path between the buildings. The birds were loud in the canopies of trees, the world such a vibrant color it made me squint. It was different from Riviana Star, but just as beautiful.

It was easy to distinguish Queen Eldinar's royal chambers because they were the grandest and had the most guards. Four of them were posted outside the double doors and more along the surrounding deck, protecting her from no one on this secret island.

When we entered, Queen Eldinar had changed out of her white dress and now wore a green one with thin straps that exposed her shoulders, the hollow of her throat, and most of her chest. It was also a short dress rather than a long gown, and in her hair was a flower crown full of exotic flowers of pink and orange.

She could wear a sack covered in mud and still be the most beautiful woman in the room, but right now, she looked more god than mortal. She sat at a table with plates of fresh fruit that the guards had prepared for her.

Uncle Ezra sat with her, so transfixed by her appearance it took him a moment to acknowledge us. "Are your accommodations suitable?" He rose from the chair and addressed us with his hands behind his back.

"Yes," Talon answered. "Thank you."

"Take a seat," Queen Eldinar said. "We're all weary from our travels."

"You're right, so I'll be brief," Talon said. "I'd like you to introduce us to Macabre. I think meeting him in your presence will make him less guarded. Is that something you're willing to do?"

"Of course. I've already informed him of your presence, so you won't frighten the dragons with your unexpected appearance."

"You spoke to him?" Talon asked, slightly perplexed.

"You forget that I also have the gift." A slight smile moved into her lips. "Macabre felt my mind when we reached these shores. We treat each other as fellow monarchs, but throughout time, that relationship has deepened into a friendship."

"And his reaction to our arrival?" I asked.

She paused for a long time, sitting straight in the chair without back support, her blond hair perfectly placed around her shoulders like someone had arranged it. "He was displeased. His hatred for humans is something that will persist for as long as he lives. But I gave him my word that you're a friend to the elves as well as the dragons and you would never betray their location. I also informed him that you and Khazmuda are fused, and while he didn't approve of that relationship, it did convince him that you truly are an ally to his cause—because no dragon would fuse with a human unless he loved him."

Talon gave a nod in appreciation. "When can we approach him?"

"Tomorrow at sunset. It's best to give Macabre time to accept your presence on the island. We'll overwhelm him if we approach too quickly. I also need time to recover from the journey. I do far better on land than at sea."

I'd hardly seen her on the ship, but when I had, she'd looked as poised and refined as usual. If she had been fighting seasickness, she gave no signs. "You hide it well, Your Majesty."

"A monarch can never appear weak," she said. "That is my burden."

"Then we'll meet here tomorrow evening," Talon said. "I hope you feel better tomorrow."

She smiled slightly. "I'm sure I will, Death King. Enjoy your evening. The island is a beautiful place."

Talon must have grown tired of his heavy uniform and armor because he left it in the closet and wore only his trousers. After we had dinner, we sat together on the beach and looked out at the gentle water. The sunset was on the other side of the island, but we could still see the sky change to faint colors of pink and orange. We sat that way for a long time, enjoying the view in comfortable silence, the birds growing quiet as the sun disappeared.

The waves were so small the water seemed more like a lake than the ocean. "The waves are so gentle."

"It's because of the reef."

"The reef?"

He pointed out to sea. "It's hard to see now that most of the light is gone, but there's a coral reef that surrounds most of the island. The elves must have picked this location to build their dock because there's a break in the reef at the point. It catches most of the waves, so everything after that is gentle."

"Where did you learn that?"

"Home," he said. "We had reefs as well..."

I stared at the water, the light continuing to fade.

"This place reminds me of it in some ways. It was warm like this in the summer, just not as humid."

"I'm excited to see it."

"It won't be the same."

"But some things never change."

He left the sand, retrieved fallen branches and dried palm leaves, and put them in a pile before me. Then he grabbed a match from his pocket and lit it on fire. The flames burst high once they came alive but then quickly burned down to a calm level.

He returned to his spot beside me, leaving a foot between us.

I watched the fire burn as the ocean disappeared into the darkness. The air was considerably cooler now that the sun was gone, and the fire was welcome. I continued to look at the flames as I thought about the journey here, about the fact that I was in a place I hadn't known existed until I'd stepped onto that pier.

I turned to look at Talon beside me.

His elbows rested on his propped knees as he stared into the flames, his dark eyes seeming lost in them. Seconds passed, and he didn't blink. Didn't blink for an entire minute. He hadn't shaved during the journey, so the shadow at his jawline was the thickest it'd been since I'd known him. Normally, his jaw was well-kempt, but I liked this grizzled appearance too. It didn't matter what he did with his hair or what he wore. He was still the most handsome man I'd ever seen. My heart felt full for the first time in a long time...since before my mother died. "Talon."

His eyes remained on the flames a moment longer before he turned to look at me, his stare a mix of fatigue and sorrow. The cuts between the muscles of his arms had long shadows because of the brightness of the fire. His hardness was on display, the scars he'd collected through his journeys.

The feelings I harbored were packed into a tight ball inside my chest and locked away, but the bars of that cage were becoming weaker with time. Those feelings had been there before he'd come to Riviana Star, just ignored because I refused to acknowledge what burned in my heart. But now I had to acknowledge it...and wanted to embrace it. "I—"

"I don't know if we'll be able to convince Macabre, and if we can't, I'm not sure what we'll do. Even with the black diamonds, I don't know what we're up against."

I hesitated because he'd never interrupted me before, not unless we were in a heated argument. But he completely cut me off like he didn't hear what I said or didn't want to hear it. "Black diamonds...?" I'd spent a decade digging for them in the Arid Sands, but I had no idea what they were. "What are they for?"

"They're different from other substances because of their absorbency. Darker colors absorb more light and, as a result, give off more heat. They work the same way—but with energy."

I became so intrigued by this that his interruption seemed inconsequential. "Energy for what?"

His dark eyes continued to stare into mine. "When we fought each other outside that forest, you were fused to Inferno. You remember how different that felt?"

It was hard to believe we'd ever raised our swords to each other. It was hard to believe I'd ever tried to run from him, when now I wanted to be with him always. My life had always been about survival so I'd never thought about what my future would look like, but now I pictured a little boy with the same dark hair and eyes. I pictured a life with them that I'd never considered, even in my dreams. "Yes, I felt powerful."

"Because Inferno shared his abilities with you. You have the same blood, so he can transfer those powers to you. But that energy is finite. In a battle that can last hours or days or a week, you can drain that energy. And if you take too much, your dragon will die."

I pictured Inferno collapsed on the ground, men moving in to harvest his teeth and spikes for weapons. "Then I won't use his powers."

"You *need* to use his powers," he said. "We need everything if we're to win this war."

"So, the black diamonds supply additional energy?"

"Yes. It allows you to use his power and the energy from the diamonds. Once that's expired, it'll start to drain from the dragon. It's unfortunate that despite the unity of the fuse, the energy is only harvested in one direction. It feels selfish to use Khazmuda's energy in battle when he's also fighting himself. I wish I could use my own."

"I do too." To wield my sword with Inferno's energy felt selfish. "How did you learn this about the black diamonds?"

"I didn't learn it. It was shared with me."

"By who?"

He looked away. "Bahamut. He told me where to find them, and that was why I conquered your kingdoms."

He'd needed the men for his war, but this was the bigger reason. Flashbacks of that night came to me, seeing the mighty black dragon rip my castle apart. Feeling the burn of the sun on my back from digging in the sand all day. The memories hurt, but nothing could change the way I felt for Talon now. It was as permanent as a scar.

"I'm sorry."

"I've already forgiven you, Talon."

"I know you have," he said quietly. "But I'll be sorry for the rest of my life...and for all eternity."

I watched him watch the fire, the flames dancing in his empty eyes. "How do you use the diamonds?"

He was quiet for a long time, as if he didn't want to continue the conversation he'd introduced. "As long as you're in contact with the diamonds, you'll drain them. I intended to place them into my armor to distribute the weight. I'll do the same with you."

"You should have all the diamonds—"

"This battle is important to me, but your life is more important. I'm not sure if you'll even be included in the battle, to be honest."

"Why wouldn't I? You asked me to help you."

"And you have."

"You trained me with the sword. You told me I had the gift. You told me you needed me in battle."

"That was before..."

"Before what?"

He stared at the fire and let the silence simmer. His answer never came. "The black diamonds are rare. So rare that I've only found a few chunks and pieces. The piece that you and your friend discovered is the biggest one I've come across."

"If you don't want me in the battle, then it doesn't make sense for me to wear them."

"But you'll be close, and I want you to be unstoppable if you need to be."

"I'd rather fight for your family and the dragons who are imprisoned by those fiends—"

"You're more important than both of those things."

"I don't think so." I loved Khazmuda and Inferno with my whole heart. I knew if I met those other dragons who were imprisoned, I would love them too. "My life isn't more important than theirs."

"It is to me." He turned to look at me again, his eyes back to their signature intensity. "My family is dead, and getting yourself killed won't bring them back. I want the dragons to be free too, but not at the expense of the most important person in my life."

My heart tightened into a fist and squeezed so hard it hurt. I felt my soul slip away into his grasp. Felt my entire being fuse with his just the way I fused with Inferno. The connection was beyond words, beyond anything I'd experienced. My body moved before my mind realized it, and my fingers were deep in his hair with my aching mouth on his. I kissed him with a fire that burned hotter than the one he'd built in front of us.

He rolled me onto my back on the sand, snatching the reins out of my hand so he could take the lead. He held his body over mine as he caressed my mouth with his, giving my bottom lip a gentle bite before he turned his head and kissed me, before he pulled away and brushed my nose with his and went in for another white-hot kiss.

The sand was still warm from being exposed to the sun all day, and I sank into its softness as he held himself over me, kissing me as the flames heated his back, his hands tugging at my bottoms to get me free.

We were visible in the light of the flames to anyone who watched, but Talon dropped the front of his trousers and positioned himself between my open thighs, sliding into place like a key in a lock, and then he sank, his dick invading a land he had already claimed in his name. His hand was back in my hair, and he kissed me as he rocked into me, silencing our moans with the passion of our lips.

Chapter 11

Talon

When I woke up the next morning, Calista was still dead asleep. She didn't wake up when I left the bed, but she turned over and got wrapped in the sheets, hogging all the covers.

I dressed in the clothes I found in the dresser, a short-sleeved cotton shirt and trousers, and walked down the pier until I found a sloop I could handle on my own. Fishing gear was already inside it, and I set off over the clear water and made it past the break in the reef.

Khazmuda's powerful voice sounded in my mind. ***Good morning.***

Where did you sleep?

Inferno showed me his favorite beach. We slept there together.

Sounds nice.

What are you doing? I can feel your mind recede like you're moving at a distance.

I almost didn't say out of fear of his reaction. *Fishing.*

Why?

I miss it. And I didn't have much time left to enjoy the things I loved. *Used to spend the day out on the boat with my father and Silas when I was a boy. All I wanted to do was get out of the sun and go home...and now I would give anything to have another day like that.*

I see.

I lowered the sails when I found a quiet spot and dropped my line in the water along with the net, hoping I would catch something in the next hour. I wasn't sure if Calista would eat it because she seemed to have turned vegetarian after her stay with the elves, but that was okay.

Would you like company?

You'd scare everything away, Khazmuda.

That's right. Sometimes I forget how terrifying and ferocious I am.

I smirked. *No, you don't.*

You're right. I don't.

How are things with Inferno?

Despite the fact that he's been on an island with dragons, he's lonely. He's happy I'm here.

I'm glad you two are getting along.

His scales are magnificent.

I smiled again. *Not as magnificent as yours.*

There was a heavy pause. ***Thank you, Talon.***

I returned to the beach and cooked the fish over a fire. I didn't have a lot of spices on hand, so I made do with what I had. Fruit was easily accessible from the trees, so I included that in the dish, using the sweetness to complement the saltiness of the fish.

Calista came out moments later, wearing a dress with her eyes still waking up. She dropped to her knees on the sand beside me, her dress rising up to the tops of her thighs. "Is that fish?"

"I went past the reef in one of their sloops."

"You caught that?" she asked in slight surprise.

"I told you I used to be a sailor."

"Wasn't that a long time ago?"

"It's like gripping a sword. Once you learn, you never forget." I removed the pan from over the fire and placed it in the sand to cool. "I made enough for two, but don't feel pressured."

"I definitely want some. It smells great."

I divided the dish onto two plates, and we ate in front of the fire, the sun still low in the sky, so it was a cool morning. The waves were gentle, the fire was low, and we ate together like we'd done it together every morning for the last twenty years. The moments I cherished the most somehow also hurt the most.

"You're a master of the blood. The master of the sea. And now you're a master of cooking." She ate everything off her plate before she set it aside. "Did your father teach you how to cook?"

I made a slight scoff. "No. He wouldn't know the difference between salt and pepper."

She chuckled. "Then how did you learn?"

I finished my plate and set it aside. "I lived in a hut alone in a fishing village for a year. Picked up on things as I went along."

We sat together on the beach until the sun started to heat the land. Then we returned to our cabin on the sand, showered, got back into bed, and made the day pass within the blink of an eye. Before I knew it, it was nearly sunset.

A part of me wanted Macabre to say no so I could draw this out as long as possible and cheat Bahamut. But as a god, he seemed to see everything, seemed to know everything. Even though he was barred from Riviana Star, he knew exactly what had happened there.

The two of us walked to Queen Eldinar's royal chambers and waited outside until she was ready to join us.

"Do you know what you're going to say?" Calista wore the same olive-green dress she'd worn when we arrived here, the color making her green eyes stand out. The queen was always regal in her presentation, a woman whose beauty rivaled that of the natural world, but she didn't have the fire that burned within Calista. She didn't have her strength or grit. She didn't have her heart. Perhaps my vision was skewed by the beat of my heart, but Calista's beauty was so powerful, it was like staring straight into the sun.

Calista stared at me.

I stared back.

Her eyebrows rose.

My eyes narrowed in confusion.

"I asked if you know what you're going to say."

If I'd heard her, I must have forgotten, lost in the eyes that looked like emeralds. "Yes." I hadn't given it any thought, spending all my time with Calista by the sea. Choosing to cherish the present rather than worry about the future.

The double doors opened, and Queen Eldinar appeared with General Ezra at her side, the personal guard who never left her presence, who guided her as his monarch but also, selfishly, as his wife. "Follow me." She stepped off the deck that led to the front door and made her way to the dirt path between the trees, going in the opposite direction of our seaside cabin.

Calista and I followed her for ten minutes, walking along the shore as the sun disappeared over the horizon.

She stopped on a vacant beach, a circle of large bonfires lit to illuminate the area for the meeting. She walked onto the sand barefoot then stopped, her gown moving in the breeze that blew in from the ocean.

Khazmuda landed behind me after I told him where we were. Inferno landed beside him then stepped to Calista before he dipped his head to look down at her, like she was his hatchling.

She tilted her head back to look up, and the biggest smile entered her face. A smile so beautiful and genuine that I couldn't do anything but stare. Couldn't do anything but memorize it to savor it for the hard times ahead.

Inferno rubbed his snout against her cheek before he stepped back.

Calista looked ahead, and slowly, her smile disappeared, but a hint of it was still in her eyes.

I continued to stare.

She must have felt it because she turned to look at me.

Her green eyes reflected the fires, looking like brilliant emerald flames dancing to the beat of her heart.

Another moment I wanted to memorize.

"Macabre approaches." Queen Eldinar continued to stand several feet in front of us, prepared to greet the mighty dragon with scales of smoke.

I looked forward and waited, the blue sky deepening into shades of pink and purple. In the next twenty minutes, it would be dark, and the temperature would become cool and pleasant. I turned to the sky and saw him above, only noticeable because the sky had hardened in the sunset.

His scales truly were dark like smoke, but still iridescent like a pearl. With a wide wingspan that rivaled Khazmuda's, he was a large dragon that could terrorize an entire village on his own.

He dropped to the ground with an increasing speed like he didn't intend to slow down before he landed. He didn't widen his wings when he was close to the earth, choosing to land with enough force to send a tremor through the ground. Sand splashed around his talons like disturbed water.

In the light of the torches, he looked even more incredible, his scales shining from every angle. He had the same kind of elegance as Queen Eldinar, holding himself fully upright like an invisible crown sat upon his head.

He stared at Queen Eldinar for a short moment before he shifted his gaze to me. It instantly turned hostile, like I was as unwelcome in his lands as Queen Eldinar claimed. He didn't need to speak a word to tell me how deep his disdain burned, how much he wished he could kill me for threatening the only home he had left.

"Macabre." Queen Eldinar was a speck in comparison to his height. She was normally the biggest person in the room because of her power and beauty, but she was quickly dwarfed by this powerful dragon.

He resisted her voice for a moment before he switched his gaze back to hers.

"Thank you for coming," she said. "I understand how difficult this is for you."

He projected his voice outward and included me, probably because Queen Eldinar told him I had the gift for speaking with dragons. ***It is.*** His gaze shifted back to me. ***I like him even less than I thought I would. I can smell his arrogance the way I can smell a horse in a stable. Just because one dragon was naïve enough to fuse with him doesn't earn him any allegiance from us. I'm disappointed that you allowed him to come here.*** He had a tougher spine than most men I'd fought, speaking his mind right to my face without even giving me a chance to speak.

"I didn't like him either."

Macabre turned his stare back to her.

"My opinion of his character was the same—until he changed it. He didn't earn my respect because he desired it. It happened because of his altruistic dedication to others. It happened because I saw a hero instead of a villain. It happened because I saw the heart beneath the flesh. If you give him a chance, you might feel the same."

***I already gave men a chance—and look what happened*.**

I decided to jump into the conversation. "I'm not like the men who came before me. You're right to assume that humankind has dangerous intentions and can't be trusted. You're right to assume that they'll always be a threat to you. But I've never been like the rest of my race. I've had a stronger relationship with my dragon than I've had with most humans. I would lay down my life for him."

Macabre continued his ruthless stare.

"History will repeat itself. Men will always want power and immortality—and they'll come after you to get it. I'm not offended by your distaste for my kind because I hate them just the same." My own distant uncle slew my entire family for power. Destroyed an entire bloodline. Burned a pregnant woman alive. "I'm a friend to dragons, all dragons, and I respect and fear you."

You should fear me, human.

"My name is Talon."

Human*.** He looked at Queen Eldinar again. ***Why do you subject me to this introduction?

"Because he has something to tell you. Before you listen to him, I want you to understand what he's done for

Riviana Star. Humans from the south tried to take the forest, but Talon stopped them with his sword and his powers. When Riviana Star was threatened by dark elves and the Real of Caelum nearly compromised, Talon saved it. I was already on my knees from all the knives that pierced my armor, but I survived because Talon took the blades that were meant for me. If Riviana Star had fallen, you would be on your own, Macabre. Your only ally in the world would have perished."

Macabre shifted his gaze back to me. ***I'm sure this human had his reasons for helping you.***

"One reason," I said. "And that's the woman who stands beside me." I chose to be honest in the hope he would trust me. The more I tried to sell myself, the more suspicious he would become. "Her love for the forest made me love it too. And when the Realm of Caelum was at risk, I defended it with my blade and the powers bestowed upon me—because my family dwells on the other side. Because her family dwells on the other side. Because one day, she'll travel there too." I looked into his powerful eyes and saw someone similar to myself, someone who had lost their trust in everyone. "I had no affection for the elves before I saved Riviana Star, but now that affection runs as deep as the ocean. But from the moment I was born, I was taught to respect dragons. Taught that they were more than immortal beasts with the gift of projectile fire. That they were friends and allies. I should have died a long time ago, but Khazmuda saved me, not once, but twice. There's nothing more I can do to prove my love for your kind than everything I've already done."

This puzzle is missing a piece. It's clear you want something from me since you're so determined to earn my favor. Make your request so I can deny it.

Everything I'd said meant nothing to him. I might as well have just stood there in silence.

Queen Eldinar stepped aside, leaving it up to me to figure this out.

I stepped forward, away from Khazmuda and Calista. "My father was the King of the Southern Isles many years ago. For generations, we shared a border with King Constantine, King of Dragons."

Dragons didn't wear expressions the way people did. Their eyes didn't dilate and they didn't frown or smile, so it was hard to know if that information meant anything to him. He continued to stare without blinking.

"We coexisted in harmony. We never ventured into their lands, and they never fed on our livestock. We were always allies, but life had been peaceful for generations, so there was never a reason to combine our forces against an adversary. Well...that all changed one horrible day. A distant family relation staged a coup against my family, and he used the power of the dark elves to force Constantine and his kin into mental subjugation. He attacked the Southern Isles with the dragons as unwilling participants—and he burned each member of my family alive." No matter how many times I shared this story, it still fucking hurt. "The only reason I stand before you is because Khazmuda rescued me just before they burned me."

Macabre shifted his gaze to Khazmuda. ***Why were you able to resist the dark magic while the others could not?***

I don't know. But they almost succeeded. It felt like a blade that punctured my skull and slowly inched closer to my brain. I somehow forced it out and felt Talon's agony. I thought he was a dragon that needed help.

Why did you save him instead of your kin? Accusation was heavy in his tone.

Because they couldn't be saved. They were lost...

Macabre continued to stare him down. ***You fused with a human. The very race that enslaved your kind.***

They may be the same race, but they aren't the same people. One bad apple doesn't mean the whole tree is rotten. We've been fused for several decades, and our love, friendship, and connection has deepened through that time. I don't love him the way I would love a mate or a hatchling, but I love him just as deeply.

"Thank you, Khazmuda."

Macabre's eyes shifted back to me, still cloudy with suspicion.

"Khazmuda and I intend to free the dragons of the Southern Isles. But we can't do it alone. We can't do it with all the armies I've claimed. We need dragons to fight with us. Otherwise, we have no chance."

So you ask us to fight alongside you.

"Yes."

There is no chance of success, Talon. Even if I agreed to help you, we would be mentally enslaved by the dark elves the moment we reached the Southern Isles. We would be trapped in the same mental prison. This plan of yours is doomed. The idea of any dragon being forced to serve humankind is like a

mark against my scales, but I will not risk the last of our kind for them.

His plan is not doomed. It takes the focus of many elves and several minutes to enslave a dragon. They took Constantine first because they knew he would be the hardest. Chaos and horror ensued after that, and they tied us down and trapped us one by one, using our own kin to pin us against the ground. In the heat of battle, there simply won't be time for that kind of opportunity.

You're still asking me to kill other dragons, something I won't do. Their actions are not their own.

"I don't want to kill the dragons either. But if the dragons aren't distracted by their own opponents, they'll eviscerate us down below. I just need enough time to kill my uncle and slay the dark elves. Once the elves are gone, the dragons will be free."

Macabre stared at me for a long silence. ***Even if you presented an unshakable plan, my answer would not change. I feel for the dragons who were conquered by dark magic, but our survival is of the greatest importance. We are still recovering from the Great War the***

mortals have forgotten because they're all dead.

I'd expected this, but it was still disappointing. "Dragons don't die, Macabre. That means they're enslaved for eternity. A cruelty so unspeakable it hurts just to think about it." A cruelty I would have to endure myself. "If you choose to remain on this island—"

You can paint me as a coward all you like, but it won't change my answer. If this were reversed, I would not expect them to come for me. I would expect them to protect the last line of dragons.

"You would expect them to leave you, but you wouldn't want them to."

I've given my answer, Talon.

"This island won't hold you forever. It's not big enough for creatures your size. Your kin live forever, so if you continue to produce hatchlings, you'll consume all your natural resources and turn it into a wasteland. You will be forced to leave, and then where will you go?"

By then, we'll have a much bigger population and, therefore, will be a more formidable adversary. We'll take whatever lands we wish

and burn the humans the way they tried to burn us.

A jolt of rage hit me, but I couldn't act on it. "So, you only care about yourself."

He was still as he stared at me. ***Yes.***

"So, you conquer the humans, piss them off, and then one day, they rise up and conquer you. The cycle never ends. I have a better idea. Help us save the dragons of the Southern Isles. Claim the lands that were taken from Constantine. Live in peace by the sea, on more land than you could ever need, alongside your kin whom you saved from damnation." I was so fucking close but so damn far away. Macabre was the most stubborn dragon I'd ever met. "Please."

Don't pretend you care that deeply about the dragons. All you care about is your revenge and your crown—

"I will not take the crown. As I already told you, I'm not like other humans. I need to avenge my family, but I also need to see the dragons fly free again. My uncle's actions were not my own, but I feel responsible because I knew he had a ploy up his sleeve—and I didn't stop it." Everything that happened was my fault. I didn't just lose my family, but the dragons lost their entire civilization. All because I didn't have a damn spine. "The guilt has gnawed at me for decades. I will not find peace until I fix it—*all of it*. I realize it's a lot to ask, I do. But I need your help. Khazmuda and Inferno simply aren't enough to take on all their dragons. Neither is my power over the dead."

His eyes narrowed. ***You wield the power of a god.***

"Yes..."

The God of the Underworld does not share his gifts freely.

"Trust me, it wasn't free."

All he did was stare at me.

"Please..."

I warned you my answer wouldn't change—

"How can you go about your life after what I just told you? There are a hundred dragons who are *enslaved* by dark magic. They're treated like fucking horses. They endure an existence so horrific, they wish for death. And you're going sit here on your fucking island and watch the sunset? I spoke with King Constantine many times, and he was the bravest and fiercest dragon I ever knew. If he sat where you sit now, he would have agreed to the fight the second he knew others suffered. Because his scales are harder than yours will ever be."

Queen Eldinar spoke with a warning in her tone. "Talon."

Macabre stared at me with eyes of smoke.

"I meant what I said."

Constantine was a king. I am no king.

"You're right," I snapped. "You're a coward. You're a coward who likes to sit in his cave and eat and mate all day long. You don't care about the suffering of others when your life is too perfect—"

"*Talon.*" Queen Eldinar warned me again.

I ignored her. "But what if Queen Eldinar decided not to help you? What if she left you to your fate while she sat comfortably upon her throne and watched the sunlight flood through the trees? What if she abandoned you the way you're abandoning your own kind? You would be dead, Macabre. Your head would be mounted on the wall in a fucking museum. I didn't care for the elves before I met them, but they're the only race I've ever known to care for others as much as they care for themselves. That should inspire you to do the same. You're a disgrace to your kind—"

"That's enough." Queen Eldinar didn't raise her voice, but her displeasure was evident. "Talon, you've had your opportunity to make your plea to Macabre. It's time we go our separate ways."

"He says he's no king, so that means I have the right to ask each dragon individually," I said. "He does not have the power to decide for everyone."

They will not listen to you.

"I have a feeling they'll listen to me better than you have."

Queen Eldinar came to my side and addressed Macabre. "Thank you for agreeing to listen—"

Macabre pushed against the sand and took flight, moving a large amount of mass in very little time. He disappeared quickly, getting so high in the sky that the flames from the bonfires couldn't reflect off his scales. Then he was gone, and his absence was felt.

Queen Eldinar stared at the bonfires for a long time before she turned to look at me. Like a mother disappointed in her child, her blue eyes were heavy with quiet resentment. "That was not diplomatic."

"He's a coward."

"Macabre is a dear friend. Please don't insult his character in my presence."

"I stand by what I said."

Her disappointment continued. "I've given you your opportunity, Death King. Now it's time you search for another solution."

"Doesn't this bother you?" I asked.

All she did was stare.

"You've dedicated your lives to their protection, and when the time comes for them to fight for someone else, they do nothing."

"They've suffered a great deal, Death King—"

"So has everyone else in this world."

No matter how angry I became, she retained her calm. "We can continue this conversation tomorrow when you're yourself once more."

"I am myself, Your Majesty."

She stepped closer to me. "I know this is what your heart desires most. I understand the disappointment is simply too much to bear. But you've come so far in your journey —and I know this is not the end. You will find a way."

"I don't know—"

"*You will find a way.*"

Chapter 12

Calista

Talon was the angriest I'd ever seen him.

So angry, he was beyond words.

After we returned to our cabin, he sat outside on the sand in front of the fire he made and didn't say a word. Didn't acknowledge me beside him. Just stared into the fire with the eyes of a madman.

"Queen Eldinar is right," I said. "We'll figure it out—"

"Calista." He steadied his voice, trying to control the wrath that wanted to explode. "The last thing I want to do is attack the person I care for most, but this is a disappointment that has only grown and festered since it was implanted in my flesh. Please leave me be." He said all of that without taking his eyes off the fire.

I let the silence trickle by as I absorbed his words, knowing nothing I could say would counteract his anger. So, I left him there on the beach alone and went into the cabin we shared. When I got under the sheets, I just lay there, lost without him beside me. He'd become the person I shared my bed with, and without him there, I felt lost. It made it hard to sleep, and it was a long time before I drifted off.

When I woke up, the morning had already passed, and it was afternoon. I could tell by the light through the windows. And it seemed like Talon had never returned. I hadn't heard the front door open in the middle of the night.

I left the bed and looked out the window to where the dead bonfire sat in the sand. Talon wasn't there. I wondered if he'd gone fishing again. Or if he'd gone for a walk. Or if he was with Khazmuda. The island was small enough that I could communicate with both Khazmuda and Inferno, each of their minds different and distinct from each other. I pushed my mind to Khazmuda. Is Talon with you? I haven't seen him since last night...

Yes.

Glad he's okay.

We had breakfast, and then he fell asleep. He was up all night.

Doesn't surprise me.

His anger burns like lava.

Yeah...

I'm disappointed as well. Dragons are known for their bravery and ferocity. Macabre showed none of those traits. He despises Talon for being human, but he seems more human than dragon to me.

Maybe we could talk to him again.

That'll be a waste of time.

Maybe you could talk to him. Dragon-to-dragon.

He has a poor opinion of me since I'm fused with Talon.

Well, I have a poor opinion of him for being so judgmental.

As do I. I've lost my kin just as he has. My pain isn't deeper than his, and his pain isn't deeper than mine. But I've managed to see the good in people. Not all humans are like Talon's uncle. A lot of them are good, like the two of you. I've seen it with my eyes, felt it with my heart.

Whether we convince Macabre or not, I know we'll find a way.

Perhaps.

You don't think so?

I think the only foe that can challenge a dragon is a dragon.

I built a new bonfire on the sand and lit it with the matches Talon had in his pack. I ate dinner alone and watched the sun disappear over the horizon. When it grew dark, it was just me and the flames, and I pulled the blanket I'd brought from the cabin closer around my body to fight off the cold.

I watched the fire crackle and pop as it smoldered in the heat. Listened to the wildlife on the island, the crickets and the frogs chirping and croaking into the night. It'd only been a day of separation from Talon, but it was long enough to make me ache. To make me miss him more than I ever had. To make me feel as if I'd lost a piece of myself.

The sound of shifting sand caught my attention, and then he was visible in the flames, in just his trousers, like he'd gone to the cabin first to shower and change his clothing. He'd shaved too because his jawline was smooth.

He took the seat beside me, his arms moving to his knees, his eyes on the fire.

I didn't say anything right away, just treasuring our reunion. The disappointing events from the night before left a lingering sadness, but I still felt joy at his presence. There was no misery strong enough to overcome the happiness I felt at the sight of him. I wanted to kiss him but knew that affection wouldn't be reciprocated when his mood was still so foul, so I leaned in and pressed a kiss to his arm, to one of the big muscles that bulged under his skin. He was warm to the touch, and I hoped I would feel more of that heat when we went to bed that night.

He turned to look at me, eyes still angry but not as potent as they were yesterday.

"How are you?" I asked quietly.

"The same." He looked at the fire again.

"Queen Eldinar is right. We'll figure it out another way."

He released a sarcastic scoff. "Unless there are other dragons out there who aren't cowards, then I don't think so."

"We have the armies of the kingdoms and your command of the dead."

"That won't be enough."

"We'll need to figure out a way to make it enough. Perhaps we could infiltrate the castle and assassinate your uncle—"

"I don't want to assassinate him. I want him to watch his world fall apart before I burn him alive. Before I make him watch his sons burn alive."

An unease prickled my skin. "You—you wouldn't do that, would you?"

"They were responsible for everything, just as much as he was," he said. "And even if they weren't, I would still do it. He burned my mother and my sister and..." He clenched his jaw and stared at the fire. "I feel no empathy for him or his kin."

I watched the side of his face and let the conversation die. "Should we make another attempt to convince him?"

"I burned that bridge."

"Then maybe I could try."

"He won't listen to you either. He knows you're my woman."

I would never grow tired of hearing that. I'd been the possession of a man once before, and it was the most horrible experience of my life. But being Talon's possession made me feel safe, cherished, and protected. "I like being your woman."

His eyes remained on the fire.

"I love it, actually."

He continued to stare like he didn't hear me.

Maybe now wasn't the best time for a confession. We'd come so far, and now we were lost at sea. Talon had never looked so defeated. But light shone the brightness in the dark, and I wanted to be that light. Pressure had built up inside my chest like water in a geyser, desperate to shoot into the sky and release. So much emotion with so little room to store it. "And I—"

"There's something I need to tell you."

I flinched at the coldness in his words. Felt winded like I'd been knocked off my feet. The unbridled confidence I'd felt just a moment ago had been destroyed by the tone of his voice. Fear came next, the anxiety and the uncertainty. "I'm listening."

He took his eyes off the fire, not to look at me, but to look up at the stars in the sky. He stared at them for a long moment before he dropped his chin once again. When it seemed like he would speak, another wave of silence passed, this stretch longer than any other one we'd had.

It made me feel worse. I believed Talon would never hurt me, but the seed of doubt dropped into the earth...and it started to grow. "Talon, you're scaring me—"

"I was married." Both of his hands tightened into fists as if he squeezed invisible swords.

I was winded again, in absolute confusion because it was the last thing I expected him to say. He'd had another life before our paths crossed in the Arid Sands, but he'd never hinted of a past love. When I'd asked him if he'd ever loved someone, he never answered.

"My father didn't want me to marry her because she wasn't of noble birth, but I loved her, so I married her anyway. We were married for a couple of months before we started our own family. She was six months pregnant when my uncle came for the throne..."

I knew the end of the story the second it began. I braced for it like I was riding a horse over a cliff.

His hands tightened even further. "I tried to save her. I sent her on a ship out to sea. But after my uncle had killed every one of my family members except for me, he dragged her out. Tied her to the stake and..." He started to breathe hard, his fists so tight his knuckles turned white. He didn't speak again, and I was spared the horrific details.

I expected to feel jealous that he'd been married, that he loved someone so dearly, that his love still endured because he couldn't finish telling the story. But I didn't. All I felt was pain...horrible, throbbing pain. "Talon..." My hand grabbed on to his arm, and I felt tears burn in my eyes.

He held his breath to stop his tears and locked his gaze on the fire as if that would make him forget. "She screamed my name until the very end...and I couldn't save her. I failed both of them."

My hand remained on his arm to comfort him, but nothing could soothe such a loss.

"I'm sorry I kept it from you."

"Don't apologize," I whispered. "You weren't ready."

He closed his eyes for a moment, allowing himself to breathe again like an invisible weight had been lifted off his shoulders. "I have to finish this."

"I know."

"I have to butcher him and burn him."

"We will."

"I have to rip him apart until there's nothing left." Tears escaped the corners of his eyes and streaked down his cheeks. "I will burn his sons. I will burn his wife. I will burn every fucking person he's ever loved. They will all turn to ash and fill my chamber pot."

I let him seethe. Let him burn.

The tears continued their slow progress down his cheeks. "I lied to you. Riviana did speak to me. To reward me for protecting the Realm of Caelum...she told me I had a daughter."

More tears flowed from my eyes. I tasted the salt.

"Her name is Lena."

My hand remained on his arm, crying with him, crying for the little girl he'd lost.

"I wanted to be king. I wanted to rule the Southern Isles. But what I wanted more than anything...was to be a father."

My tears deepened into sobs. I should comfort him instead of giving in to my own heartbreak, but it was too much for me to contain. "I'm so sorry..."

He closed his eyes again, new tears trailing down his face.

"I'm sorry," I repeated. "I'm so sorry."

He remained that way, still as a statue, doing his best to compose himself, as if emotion was a sign of weakness. He eventually recovered and opened his eyes, which were wet and red, but calm. "I'm not leaving this island unless Macabre and the others leave with me."

Talon wasn't himself the rest of the night. He barely said two words to me and remained distant. When we went to sleep that night, he stayed on his side of the bed and didn't come anywhere near me. He even rolled onto his side and turned his back to me.

I knew it wasn't personal, but it still felt personal.

When I woke up the next morning, he was still asleep in the same position as when I'd closed my eyes. He was never awake after me, so I knew he was tired...or depressed. I got dressed and left the cabin, the air cool in the morning, giving a slight chill. I crossed the beach and then pushed out my mind to Khazmuda's. Are you awake?

Yes.

Can I speak to you?

Always.

I stood there alone for a few minutes before Khazmuda's black scales appeared in the morning light. A direct contrast to the beautiful world of blue water and white sand, he looked like he didn't belong in this serene place.

He made a gentle landing and folded his wings. ***I'm assuming you wish to speak of Talon since he's still asleep.***

"Yes."

His rage has been constant. I can feel it even when he's asleep.

Last night felt like a hazy dream, but it all came back to me vividly. "He told me about his wife..."

Khazmuda paused as he stared at me, his dark eyes absorbing my stare. ***He told you about Vivian.***

"Yes." The memory broke my heart all over again. No one deserved to die that way. To be burned alive while life glowed inside you.

It's a horrible story, but I'm glad he shared it with you.

"A part of me wishes he hadn't told me," I said. "It makes me sick."

Now you truly understand him. Why he needed to conquer your kingdom for your

army. Why he forced prisoners to dig in the Arid Sands. Why he seemed empty of heart and soul when you met. After she died, I told him we needed to plan our revenge, but all he wanted to do was sit on a rock all day. He eventually moved to a small village and became a fisherman…then a pirate. I was deeply frustrated by his indifference and searched for free dragons on my own. But in hindsight, I understand he was in shock. His heart and soul were destroyed by what he saw, and he simply couldn't process it. It's like a hatchling that tries to fly before he can walk.

"How long ago was this?"

Over twenty years now. But no passage of time will make either of us forget.

"Yeah."

He continued to regard me. ***How does this make you feel?***

"Heartbroken."

I know it must be hard to know he pledged himself to another.

The Talon who was happily married was a different man than the one I knew today. He would have been happy and open and vulnerable. If I'd met him in that time period, I probably wouldn't even recognize him. "In some ways, it hurts. It hurts to know that he loved someone else so deeply, that the love perseveres even decades later. But he was a different man than he is today. I've fallen for the broken version of him because I was just as broken on the night we met. Our connection is deep because of our struggles. It endures the greatest hardships because the foundation is thicker than bedrock. That was then...and this is now."

You're mature for someone so young.

"I always assumed he had a long list of lovers."

It's not the length of the list that matters, but the quality. Therefore, there are only two names on that list.

A small smile spread my lips. "Thanks, Khazmuda."

He dipped his snout down and gently rubbed the side of my head with his smooth scales. ***Of course, Pretty.*** He pulled away and looked at me once again.

"We need to convince Macabre to join us." It felt like an impossible task. After Talon had insulted his character, there was no going back. If Macabre didn't feel obligated to do the right thing, he would feel less obligated if he hated the person who asked for help.

I don't see how, Pretty.

"We have to. Now that I know what happened to Talon, I have to figure this out."

Dragons are the most stubborn creatures.

"But not more stubborn than me," I said. "Could you take me to him?"

Khazmuda turned his head and looked at the cabin. ***Without Talon?***

"I don't think Talon will be an asset at this point."

Khazmuda continued to consider it.

"It's not like I can make it worse."

Perhaps. He lowered himself to the sand, letting his belly hit the earth. ***Let's try.***

Khazmuda carried me up the mountain to the cave Macabre occupied. It was visible even from a distance, the blackness distinct in contrast to the beautiful colors of the tropical paradise.

We came in for a gentle landing on the grassy field that led to the edge of a cliff. There were no trees, so there was plenty of room for dragons to land or lounge. I climbed down his side then looked into the cave.

It was so dark, I couldn't see a thing. "Shall we go in?"

Even if they don't like you, they won't hurt you. Not when you're here as the queen's guest.

"I wasn't worried about that, not when I'm with you."

He dropped his snout and rubbed it against my shoulder. ***Thank you, Pretty.***

We slowly entered the cave, the light disappearing as we became engulfed in shadow. It seemed to go on forever until we spotted the light in the distance, the light of a low-burning fire. We continued, the details of the cave coming into view once we drew closer to the light.

Then I noticed the reflection of light on many sets of scales. Five dragons were spread throughout the large cave, all sleeping near the walls. I spotted Macabre toward the back of the cave, snuggled close to two dragons I assumed had mated with him last night.

Unbridled annoyance burned inside me because Talon's accusations had been correct. Macabre preferred to enjoy this easy life than to think about others less fortunate. He'd rather sit on his scales all day than help those in need.

Macabre seemed to realize we were there because his eyes suddenly popped open. He stared right at me, his eyes the same color as the smoke that rose from the fire that was about to go out. He slowly rose to his feet, his lovers sliding past his scales, and made several steps forward to approach us.

But he stopped by the fire, his hostility evident.

But my hostility was evident as well.

Do you have a death wish? The powerful voice came into my mind.

Khazmuda issued a low growl.

"Do you?" I countered.

Macabre looked at Khazmuda for several hard seconds before he returned his attention to me. ***You come to my home without an invitation. You would be a fool to expect a warm reception.***

"And you would be a fool to assume our previous discussion was over."

It is over.

"It's not over until you agree to help us."

He tilted his head slightly, his eyes wide and focused. ***My decision will not change.***

"Why?"

I already told you I wouldn't risk the rest of my kin—

"But Talon is right. You are at risk. Maybe not today, and maybe not in a hundred years. But one day, you will be. You can be proactive about it now and save the rest of your kind in the process."

He stared for several seconds. ***No.***

This was infuriating. So infuriating I wanted to scream. "How can this not bother you?"

I never said it didn't bother me.

"But you continue your life of leisure." I looked around at the female dragons who lounged in his cave, seeing him as the most desirable mate among the dragons, the alpha.

I don't appreciate your judgment.

"And I don't appreciate your indifference."

You would do well to remember that you're a stranger. A human who has come to my island without my consent. I will not share my deepest thoughts with someone I don't know. What's more, I don't like your male companion—and I barely tolerate you.

"Queen Eldinar speaks highly of him."

For reasons I still don't understand.

"Because he saved their entire race and, by extension, your race—and the afterlife."

Even if they perished, our island would have remained a secret. And dragons have no afterlife.

"Wow, you really are selfish. All you think about is yourself..."

I was just explaining—

"You don't even care about the elves. The very people who saved you. I've only met two dragons, and they are both brave and selfless and kind. I guess it was stupid of me to assume all dragons are that way. Because they clearly aren't."

He didn't even try to refute my claims. ***Please leave my cave now.***

"I'll petition each dragon individually. Some of them must care."

You can try. But I've informed them of the disrespect your companion showed me, so they've all closed their minds to you—as well as to Khazmuda and Inferno.

I'd assumed only a human could be a dictator, but it looked like any race was capable of corruption. "Inferno was one of the free dragons who remained in this world and came to this island for a new start, but you shunned him as an outsider instead of opening your lands and your hearts. After the compassion Queen Eldinar showed you, I don't understand why you're incapable of showing it to others."

All he did was stare.

Khazmuda spoke to me privately. ***This is hopeless, Pretty.***

Leave my home and never return—and leave my island.

When Khazmuda returned me to the beach, Talon sat on the sand in front of the dead fire. He was in the shade of a palm tree as he looked out at the water, in just his trousers, like he'd come out there as soon as he woke up.

Khazmuda dropped me off then opened his massive wings and departed to the skies.

I joined Talon by the cold campfire. "Good morning."

His arms rested on his knees, his hair matted from the way he slept on the pillow. He stared at the fire like it still burned. "Khazmuda told me about your conversation with Macabre."

I'd assumed I couldn't make it worse, but I somehow had. "I didn't think it was possible to dislike a dragon."

"Just like Khazmuda said, one bad apple doesn't mean the tree is rotten."

"I know, but he's blatantly selfish," I said. "When I reminded him what you've done for the elves, he said their island would have persevered even if the elves had been killed. Didn't care whatsoever about Queen Eldinar. He made no effort to make Inferno accepted here. Honestly, he's a fucking asshole."

A painful smirk moved over his lips. "I caught on to that."

"I don't know what to do." It really did feel hopeless. It was impossible to convince someone who didn't have an ounce of empathy. Who only cared for himself. "You can tell he doesn't care about the other dragons at all. That he hasn't lost a moment of sleep over it. That he's too busy fucking all the females who live in his cave."

He massaged his knuckles on his knees, like he felt old pains return to the joints. He had been livid and fiery last night, but today, he seemed subdued and hopeless. There had always been a fight inside his bones, but that fight seemed to have died.

"I don't know what to do."

He remained silent, eyes still on his hands.

"We'll figure out a way." It sounded like a lie, but I wanted to believe it. Needed to believe it. I wanted to avenge Vivian and Lena as much as he did now. Wanted to save the dragons Talon spoke so highly of. When he didn't say anything, I looked at the side of his face.

He continued to stare at his hands.

"Do you think we can do this without the dragons?" I asked, hoping he had an answer to this dilemma.

He remained quiet for a long time, like he had no intention of speaking. "I haven't received word about the Southern Isles since I left long ago. I have no idea how it's changed, how many dragons live, even if my uncle is still king. But when I left, there were a hundred dragons in the skies raining down fire and burning us all. Even with my armies and the dead, I can't fight enemies in the air. Khazmuda and Inferno will either be slaughtered or imprisoned."

"If we kill the dark elves, it'll free the dragons."

"But I know nothing about the elves. I don't know their numbers or their organization. I assume my uncle offered them something in return for their participation, but I'm not sure what that would be."

"Then we can travel to the Southern Isles and investigate. Figure out the structure and make a plan."

"They'll spot our dragons leagues away."

"Then we can fly somewhere nearby and sail."

"It's been a long time, but they could recognize me."

"But they won't recognize me."

He finally turned to look at me.

"I could become a maid in the castle. Learn whatever I can and report back."

"That's risky."

"Every part of this journey has been risky, Talon."

He looked at the cold fire again.

"I think that's our best option."

"Maybe," he said quietly.

The Talon I knew was authoritative and decisive, finding a path even if it was riddled with obstacles. But now, he was overcome with defeat, a depression that seeped so far in his flesh it hit the bone.

I wanted to make it go away. "What was she like?"

He stilled at the question before he stitched his fingers together. "I told you about her because I thought you should know. Thought it would help you understand why I have to do this and there is no other option but success."

"It did help me understand."

He continued as if I hadn't spoken. "I never want to speak of it again."

My eyes dropped at his words.

"So much time has passed that it's hard for me to picture her face. If I saw her again, I would recognize her, but my mind is unable to recall her appearance on memory alone. I loved her deeply, and I will always love her, but the passage of time has decayed my heart and my mind, and I'm not the same person I was when I loved her. I've learned to let her go. She died because I failed her as a future king, a husband, and a father. I don't deserve to speak of her. I didn't deserve her when I had her. I will strike down the man who took away her life in her honor, but it still won't exonerate me."

"I think you're being unfairly harsh—"

"I didn't ask for your opinion, Calista."

I stilled again as if he'd struck me.

"This is the last time I'll speak of it."

I spoke with the guards at the double doors, and once they gained permission from Queen Eldinar, they allowed me entry into her royal chambers.

I entered the wooden cabin with the husk roof, seeing vases of flowers everywhere, the grand dining table outside on the patio that faced the mountain. Queen Eldinar was seated there, flower stems on the table in front of her while her hands worked with a pile of twigs.

My uncle sat in a nearby chair, watching her work like he was content just to be with her.

I approached the table and waited for her to acknowledge me.

My uncle shifted his gaze to me but said nothing, wearing a casual shirt instead of his armor and sword.

Queen Eldinar secured the twigs with a tiny piece of string before she looked at me. "Take a seat, Calista."

I pulled out the chair and sat down beside her.

She returned to her work with the flowers.

"What are you doing?" I looked at the tropical flowers on the table, an array of bright colors like pink, orange, and purple.

"Making flower crowns for the hatchlings," she said with a smile. "After they saw mine, they wanted some for themselves. They'll look so beautiful against their glorious scales." She tied another section of branches together, completing half of the circle. She finally gave me her full attention, her hands together on the table. "Will the Death King be joining us?"

"I came alone."

She gave a slight nod. "We'll depart tomorrow morning. As much as I love it here, I can't leave my kingdom for long."

"I understand."

"What do you seek?"

I could tell Talon was in a dark place, just as he had been when he'd become a fisherman and a pirate. In a state of shock, he needed a moment just to exist as he recovered from the painful disappointment. So, I decided to take matters into my own hands. "I spoke with Macabre again. I know Talon said some impolite things to him, but now that I've spoken to him privately, I'm in agreement.

He's one of the most selfish beings I've ever encountered."

Queen Eldinar took in that comment in silence, retaining her composure and her reaction.

"When I reminded him of what Talon had done for the elves, he said it wouldn't have mattered if your race had perished because the island would have remained a secret. My father gave his life to keep this island a secret, and Macabre doesn't give a damn about that either. When I asked to proposition the other dragons, he ordered them to block me from their minds. He may be a dragon, but underneath those scales is a monster."

Her composure remained perfectly in place as she regarded me with those piercing blue eyes. "I like to bestow my wisdom upon the young. It gives them invaluable perspective. So allow me to share some with you. In life, we do good things and expect nothing in return. We helped Macabre and his kin because we wanted to. We offered them protection and salvation in exchange for nothing."

"Not even love and loyalty?" I asked incredulously. "Because he clearly feels neither for you. You're his servants. Just as all the females in his cave are servants—"

"Macabre's personal life is none of my business, just as my marriage to a human is none of his," she said calmly.

"If you came here to poison my mind with insults to Macabre's character, I would rather spend that time completing my flower crowns for the hatchlings. Are we finished?" Her tone sharpened.

I didn't want to take this conversation in this direction, but I had to. "We can both agree that your race, your forest, and the afterlife would be gone if Talon hadn't saved it. And I know we can agree that your hatred toward him has blossomed into affection and friendship."

"What's your point, Calista?"

"He came to your aid—and now it's time you come to his."

A cloud suddenly passed over the sky and blocked the sun. A shadow came across the land and the mountain. It matched the change in atmosphere, the way everyone at the table was provoked by what I just said.

Her expression slowly hardened, her eyes turning sharp like the blades she wielded in battle.

I held my stance.

"I gave Talon the dragons, as we agreed."

"In exchange for killing the dark elves, a feat at which you hoped he would fail. But he's done much more. He saved everyone—including you. Like it or not, Your

Majesty, you're indebted to him for a lot more than an introduction to a stubborn dragon."

Her eyes flicked back and forth between mine, her hostility slowly rising. "This conversation should happen between monarchs—"

"He's too broken to speak. Macabre's refusal has cut him down at the knees. He's devastated because he's bound by his honor to do this and succeed. So I will do it for him. You will command Macabre and his kin to fight with us."

"I can't command him to do such a thing—"

"Then you will pledge your army to us and ask him to support you—"

"Don't you dare interrupt my queen." Uncle Ezra wore no armor, but he looked as formidable as he appeared on a battlefield. "You forget that you speak to Riviana Star's longest reigning monarch, a queen who is more deadly and more beautiful than the sun. Interrupt her or disrespect her again, and I will personally escort you out of these chambers. I don't give a damn if you're my niece."

I looked at my uncle and saw the ire in his eyes.

"It's alright, Ezra." Queen Eldinar spoke quietly. "She can speak to me that way in private—because I'm her aunt."

A rush of warmth moved through me, bringing a rouge to my cheeks that had nothing to do with the heat and humidity. The last woman to show me love was my mother, and I hadn't known it since she died. I stared at the queen for several seconds, touched by her gesture of maternal affection. It made me falter before I continued. "You will pledge your army to fight with us. You will tell Macabre you've done so and ask him to join you. You said you've built a deep friendship with him. If that's true, I can't imagine he would deny your request."

She stared at me for a long time, her eyes as clear as the sky. "I don't appreciate being coerced like this."

"I would never coerce you. It's a request that you can deny."

"Then I deny it," she said quickly. "I will not pledge the elven army to fight for a cause that doesn't concern us or involve the very beings I've given my life and service to protect."

And just like that, my plan went out the window. The disappointment hurt more than the first time because I didn't have a backup plan. That meant we would have to sail to the Southern Isles and find another way.

I sat back in my chair and looked at the flowers upon the table, the ones she would attach to the flower crowns she would gift to the little dragons she clearly cared for.

There was nothing left for me to do but leave, but I didn't want to return to Talon without something to lift his spirits.

"Calista."

My eyes found hers again, waiting for another rejection.

"I will pledge the elven army to your cause, not because you asked, but because it is my wish. Because I've come to care deeply for the man who's claimed your heart. I don't agree out of obligation, but desire. Desire for Talon, the Death King, the rightful King of the Southern Isles, to avenge his family and his people—and find peace."

All I could do was blink, shocked by what she'd said.

"I will ask Macabre to fight with us. But I can't promise he'll agree."

When I returned to the cabin, Talon was on the beach, dragging branches and debris into a pile at the center so he could light the bonfire like he did every night. Khazmuda lay on the sand with his head on his claws, his eyes following Talon as he walked around. Once Talon was finished preparing the bonfire, he stepped back and let Khazmuda light it.

A blaze erupted high into the sky then slowly burned down to a reasonable height.

Talon took a seat in the sand, his mood still hopeless and lifeless.

I arrived at the campsite and saw Khazmuda shift his eyes to look at me.

Talon barely acknowledged my presence.

I dropped down to my knees and looked at the side of his face.

He continued to stare at the fire and ignore me.

I waited for him to turn to me.

It took minutes, but it finally happened. His eyes were hostile and guarded, like the last thing he wanted to do was talk.

I didn't bother with context or an explanation, just blurted it out. "Queen Eldinar has pledged her army to fight with us. And she's going to ask Macabre to join her."

He blinked several times as he processed that.

Khazmuda lifted his chin from his talons and straightened.

Talon's eyes shifted back and forth between mine. "How...? What did you do?"

"I spoke to her but can't take the credit," I said honestly. "Because she said she cares for you...and wants to help you find peace."

Talon remained in silent shock, his dark eyes piercing mine with the sharpness of daggers. The haze of melancholy slowly burned in the heat of the sun, and the determination and ambition were awoken anew. He left the sand and lifted himself to one knee, his hands cradling my cheeks as he regarded me with new eyes. "You are the reason I've made it this far. And you're the reason I'll make it to the end."

Chapter 13

Talon

It was evening when I approached the royal chambers. Calista and I had had dinner by the fire on the beach, spending most of our time outside because it was too beautiful to stay indoors. The cabin was only used for sleeping and lovemaking.

The guards let me through, and General Ezra greeted me. He didn't wear his armor or weapons, dressed casually like he and the queen would retire for bed soon. He regarded me with his eyes that reminded me of Calista.

"I wish to speak to Queen Eldinar, if she'll have me."

His stare was hostile. "And I know what you wish to speak of." He moved away and walked toward the dining table, which was empty with the exception of a few flowers. He nodded to a chair then moved into the other room.

I sat there alone for minutes, candlelight illuminating the corners of the room. A large window showed the deck outside, the mountain that looked like a dark mass. I waited for her, dressed in my uniform and armor as a sign of respect, despite the heat.

She emerged a moment later, barefoot and in a green dress, her blond hair in perfect ringlets down her shoulders. When she came to the head of the table, General Ezra pulled out the chair for her, not as her general, but as her husband.

He looked at me again, his stare angry, and then silently excused himself.

When he was gone, Queen Eldinar addressed me. "Forgive him. He's upset by my decision."

"I don't blame him. You've just fought two battles."

"Peace is merely a pause between conflicts."

"There's been a lot of conflict for you—all caused by me and Calista."

Her hands came together on the table. "The dark elves were always our woodland adversary. They marched on our border so quickly that it's clear they'd organized that strategy long ago. The battle against General Titan simply rushed it."

"General Titan wouldn't have been there—"

"You're determined to carry all the blame, aren't you?" A slight smile moved on to her face.

"I just understand General Ezra's perspective. While I appreciate your offer more than you'll ever know, it feels selfish to accept it." A different version of me would have accepted the aid without further thought, only concerned with my triumph. But I'd come to care for the people I'd once hated. "If you were to withdraw your decision, I would completely understand."

She stared at me with those sharp eyes. "The only thing that will make Macabre feel obligated to fight is if I fight as well. You and Calista have both shared your poor opinion of his character, but he's more than he seems."

I had yet to see it.

"There is no other way."

"Even with an ironclad plan, many of you will die." I didn't want to misguide her expectations. "You know the dark elves are cunning. Even with my command of the dead, we almost lost the battle of the Great Tree. I don't know what to expect across the sea, but I suspect it will be deadly. Your population has already been decimated..."

"It has."

"Not to mention, Bahamut will collect payment immediately." My eyes shifted away at the realization. I'd never wanted something to pass and not pass simultaneously. I'd never felt both relief and disappointment at once. When Macabre denied my request, a weight was lifted off my shoulders but then twenty knives pierced my ribs. "My peace will be very short-lived."

Pity entered her gaze. "You said there are a hundred dragons enslaved in the Southern Isles."

"Yes."

"That's too many. Creatures so beautiful and intelligent should not be treated as such. I risked my life to save Macabre and the others. I consider it one of my greatest accomplishments as Queen of Riviana Star. I would like to save more—if I can."

I gave a slight nod. "But you face more than men. You face dark elves and dragons."

"I know what I face," she said calmly. "You can waste this beautiful night trying to dismiss my help, or you can accept it."

I bowed my head and gave a sigh.

"This is exactly what you wanted, Death King. I expected to feel your gratitude, not your disappointment."

"I'm not ungrateful," I said quickly. "I just care for you."

Her eyes softened as a gentle smile moved over her lips. "You continue to surprise me, Talon. You possess more love and compassion than any human I've ever met—except my husband."

"I wish there were another way."

"But there is none."

"Could the others fight while you remain in Riviana Star?"

Her smile changed into a sad one. "I'm not the kind of monarch that sends her army to do her bidding. I'll fight alongside my army. I'll die alongside my army. Just like you. I know I have more to lose since I have a nearly immortal life-span, but if my life is claimed in the battle, I know the God of Caelum will accept me with open arms of love—because you saved it." She stared at me for a while. "And I know Macabre will look after me like a hatchling. He'll look after my husband as well since he knows our love is true."

It was hard to accept her words when I felt so much guilt. When I'd first met Queen Eldinar, her company had felt like the tips of a thousand knives against my skin. Now I saw someone I would take a blade for.

"I will speak to Macabre in the morning. After he accepts, we'll make the return journey and finalize our plans. You'll need to prepare your army to set sail. I'll prepare mine for the same."

Now that this felt real, my heart started to race. My future was set in stone, an eternity as a pawn to the God of the Underworld. But the other details remained unclear. If I lost the battle and forfeited the lives of other free dragons, lost other people I cared about, it would all be for nothing. I wouldn't get revenge for Vivian and Lena—and I would have to suffer for eternity anyway.

"You're afraid."

My eyes found hers again. She could read my expression as well as Khazmuda could feel my emotions. "Yes. Decades have been spent preparing for this moment, and now that it's here...I feel unprepared."

She stared at me for a while, her eyes possessing depths so vast, the light didn't reach the bottom. "You command the kingdom of men to the north, command the dead, have allies in both elves and dragons. You're as prepared as you can be, Talon Rothschild, King of the Southern Isles."

"I will never be King of the Southern Isles..."

"You will, for a moment, and you will savor that moment with everyone you cherish most."

When I returned to the cabin, Calista wore one of my shirts with nothing underneath, sitting on the couch in front of the fire she'd built without my help. She looked at me when I walked inside, green flames in her eyes.

The guilt felt heavier every time I looked at her.

Her eyes showed her curiosity, but she didn't question me about the conversation I'd had with Queen Eldinar.

I removed my armor and uniform and stripped down to my boxers. The window was open, so the sound of the ocean was audible over the crackling flames. I grabbed the bottle of scotch I'd taken from their stores and sat on the couch beside her.

She was beautiful without even trying, her bare feet resting against the edge of the table, her elbow propped on the back of the couch as her hand supported the back of her head, her dark hair a lovely curtain.

I took a drink as I looked at her, stunned that someone could be so gorgeous without even trying. After I put the canteen on the table, I leaned back and continued to look at her, unable to deny the connection that had grown stronger over the last few days. I'd thought I would push her away when I told her about Vivian, but she showed no sign of hurt or resentment. Seemed to care for me more and not less. My plan had backfired, and not only did I bring us closer together, but I deepened the feelings I tried so desperately to fight.

Calista stared at me in the light of the fire, her thoughts unknown behind that calm face.

"She'll speak with Macabre in the morning."

"I think he'll say yes."

"I do too."

"I'm sad to leave this island, but it's time to go."

I was sad to leave it too. It was easy to picture a life here, Khazmuda taking us for a short vacation from our duties, watching the sunset, and making love in front of the bonfire on the soft sand. But then I pushed it away, because there would be nothing after the battle. Once it began, it would be the last thing I ever did.

"Talon."

My eyes shifted to hers again.

"Where did you go?"

Just like the queen, Calista could read me. Read me like an open fucking book. "Your uncle disagrees with her decision."

Her eyes filled with sadness. "He cares for her more than himself."

"I know he does." He wore his heart on his sleeve, just the way I had when I was married. I never played games. Always remained faithful even when I didn't have to be. Made my wife feel secure by making her feel cherished every day.

"She's so beautiful, she doesn't seem real."

I watched her speak, watched the light hit the angles of her face perfectly.

"She's like living magic, and my uncle is deep under her spell. I don't agree with all the parameters of their relationship, but I can't blame my uncle for his obsession because she really is the most beautiful woman I've ever seen." Her eyes shifted away as if she had pictured Queen Eldinar that very moment.

A sarcastic smirk moved on to my lips as I stared at her, seeing a woman who was so beautiful, a single look had changed my life forever. "I still remember the night we met with vivid clarity."

She turned to look at me.

"The glow of your skin in the torches. The fight in your green eyes. The way you walked right up to the mightiest dragon in the land without hesitation. All it took was a single look and a brief interaction, and I was hooked on your line for the rest of my life." I hadn't been with another woman since I'd seen her, even when we were leagues apart and she wanted nothing to do with me. "I tried so hard to resist, not to care for you, but I was cast under your spell, and I've been imprisoned by it ever since. Your uncle may think she's the most beautiful woman in the world, but I disagree." I'd tried to pull away from this woman, to put a barrier between us to make this all easier for her in the end, but then moments like this happened...and I couldn't fight it. "You are."

She stared at me for several hard seconds, her eyes emotional but encased in disbelief. She continued to look without needing to blink, staring at me where I sat on the opposite end of the couch. Then she moved for me, showing more confidence than she ever had, and cupped my face as she brought our mouths together, kissing me with a passion that made her tremble.

My hand slid into the fall of her hair, and I fisted it as I felt the rush of emotion and desire, an adrenaline burst only she could give me. Rendezvous with my concubines had been just a means to an end, a display of power, but with Calista, it was deep and full of ache, a connection so raw it hurt.

She straddled my hips and cupped my face with both hands as she kissed me, sitting right on top of my hard dick through my boxers. She breathed into my mouth before she turned her head and kissed me another way, taking what she wanted without an ounce of hesitation.

I still remembered our first time together, how much patience and encouragement it had taken for her to let me in, for her to embrace our physical intimacy as something beautiful rather than violent. Now she took me like that had never happened.

It turned me the fuck on.

I lifted my hips slightly to pull down my boxers and get my dick free.

She lifted her shirt over her head to show her tits.

I tugged her underwear to the side because I was too anxious to wait for her to get them off. I wanted to be surrounded by her slick tightness because I was a man with a beautiful woman on my lap. But I also wanted to be inside her because it was medicine in my veins. It healed my broken heart. It brought peace to my chaos. It slowed down time, made me forget the future and the past. It made me live in the moment…and cherish every second.

Chapter 14

Calista

When Talon and I arrived at the royal chambers, Queen Eldinar still hadn't returned from her conversation with Macabre. My uncle sat at the dining table with a cup of coffee in front of him, wearing his regular clothes because he seemed to have dropped his guard while on the island.

He was quiet and uninterested in our company. Didn't offer us anything and hardly looked at either of us. It seemed like we weren't there at all.

It made me feel guilty.

Before I could address the tension in the room, Talon spoke. "I tried to talk her out of it."

My uncle slowly turned his head to look at Talon. The stare said everything his lips didn't.

"Multiple times."

Uncle Ezra looked away, and the conversation seemed over before it started.

"He's not mad at you," I said. "He's mad at me." He wouldn't hesitate to snap at Talon if he were angry, especially when Queen Eldinar was absent. So his anger must be directed at me instead.

When my uncle didn't speak, I knew it was true.

"I'm sorry—"

"You're sorry?" He turned to me, eyebrows raised. "My wife has done enough for the dragons. She's done enough for Riviana Star. She's the one who stood in front of the Great Tree before the Death King joined the battle. And now you want her to travel across the world to raise her sword once again? How dare you ask this of her."

My eyes dropped in guilt.

"I can't protect her from this. I would beg her to stay behind, but I know she won't."

Talon intervened. "With all due respect—"

"This conversation does not include you." He said it without taking his eyes off me. "This is my wife. I'm supposed to die in the next few decades, but she's supposed to live on for a very, very long time. I will never forgive you if she perishes—"

"General." Talon not only raised his voice but added his ire. "That was uncalled-for, and you know it."

I couldn't lift my gaze. I felt like shit. I wanted to help Talon, but I'd betrayed the only family I had left.

My uncle didn't apologize. "I pity those dragons. Of course I do. But I care about my wife a lot more than anyone else on this earth, and now she's involved in another war that doesn't include us—"

"*Protego Nia.*"

We all stilled when we heard her voice behind us.

My uncle turned to regard her, and the sight of her instantly loosened his tight expression.

She approached the table, her white gown trailing behind her. "General, you're excused."

He remained in his chair, looking up at his wife as if he didn't know how to obey an order he'd never received before. His anger slowly softened into unspoken remorse. "Your Majesty—"

"I said, you're excused."

He stilled in the chair, emotion entering his face.

She waited for him to leave.

I felt responsible for all this turmoil.

After a heavy moment, my uncle rose from the table and walked out of the building.

Queen Eldinar lowered herself into the chair he'd just occupied and moved his cup of coffee aside. She sat straight, her hands coming together on the table like the exchange had never happened. "I apologize for my general's behavior. When we agreed to our nuptials, I made it very clear that our personal relationship couldn't affect our professional one. He seems to have forgotten that."

"He just loves you," I whispered. "So much..."

"Even so," she said gently. "As Queen of Riviana Star, I've chosen this path for my people, and as General of Riviana Star, he's to support that decision. His job is to prepare the armies for victory, no matter how unlikely that victory seems. He failed me."

"His job is also to protect you," Talon said. "As both a general and a husband. That's all he's trying to do, Your Majesty."

She stared down at her clasped hands. "Enough of my woes. After a long conversation with Macabre, he has agreed to join us in battle. He will not command the dragons to serve but will ask them to join. Some must remain behind to care for the hatchlings and ensure there are enough to continue their survival. He suspects forty will join him."

After the fruitless conversations with Macabre, I was shocked that he'd agreed so quickly when Queen Eldinar asked. "I can't believe he changed his mind so easily. When I spoke to him, he made it clear he wouldn't budge under any circumstances."

"Our love has lasted a century. It's deeper than the bedrock below the soil. It's deeper than the center of the ocean. The version of him you met is very different from the version I know. I knew he would deny your request no matter how you presented your plight, and I knew he would never let me fight for the remaining free dragons without his hard scales for protection."

I still couldn't believe this had happened.

Talon seemed in shock too because he didn't speak.

"We will begin our journey home tomorrow. Macabre will meet us there once he's determined how many dragons will accompany him. By galleon, it takes us a week to reach our destination, but if he flies at normal speed, he can reach land within a day. Khazmuda and Inferno can remain behind and join him if they wish."

"I think that will be best," Talon said. "It's harder for Khazmuda to glide at our slower speed rather than to fly normally."

"Then we're in agreement," she said. "We'll leave first thing tomorrow."

I didn't care for the journey here, being stuck on that ship with limited places to go, but having Talon below deck with me made it bearable. "Please don't be angry with my uncle. I promise you he means well."

"Trust me, I know he does," she said gently. "But the behavior is inexcusable nonetheless."

"You—you will forgive him, right?" Did I just ruin a marriage? And not just any marriage, but my uncle's? "When I spoke to you, I didn't mean for any of this to happen. I didn't mean to cause strife between the two of you—"

"Child." She gently placed her hand on mine. "Yes, you instigated this decision. But the situation had weighed heavily on my mind this last week. If Macabre had never agreed and you failed in your attempt and those dragons remained enslaved, it would have troubled me the rest of my days. The elves wouldn't be enough to defeat King Barron later on, so there is only one chance of success. It is now. I want to free the dragons. I want to help Talon. I want to rid this world of oppressive regimes because that is not the way of life."

The next morning, we packed up our belongings and boarded the galleon. Supplies were loaded under the deck for the return journey. Fresh fruit had been harvested from the island that would prevent the onslaught of scurvy, something Talon had suffered from more than once during his time as a pirate.

Once everyone was aboard the ship, we were untied from the dock, and the sails were dropped to catch the wind. The direction of the breeze was in our favor, and we sailed away from the tropical paradise quicker than I wished.

I watched it disappear with a twinge of pain in my heart.

Talon continued to help the other elves get the ship out to sea, someone who was younger than the others but had a lifetime more of experience. He turned into the captain of the ship, and none of the elves objected.

I continued to watch the island disappear, growing small in the distance.

Queen Eldinar appeared beside me, dressed in one of her gowns, a flower crown upon her head. "I'm sure you'll see it again someday."

"I hope so." I would love to stay there with Talon, living in solitude and away from the chaos of the world. Our time would be measured in sunsets and meals. We would never wear shoes because our feet would always be in the sand. Life would be simple and slow.

When I looked at her, I saw my uncle lingering behind her, in his full armor, with his heavy blade across his back. His eyes were on the island in the distance. It was hard to know where their relationship stood when they were in the presence of others.

I switched my gaze back to her. "I hope you two worked it out." It'd been heavy on my mind, the thought always there when I wasn't occupied by something else.

She turned her head to look at me, her hair blowing elegantly in the breeze. "There's nothing to work out, child. The elves have a different approach to confrontation than humans because of our longevity. There are very few actions that can't be forgiven. Your uncle's display of love is not one of them. But nonetheless, he needed to be reminded of our obligations to our roles in this society."

"I'm glad you aren't mad at him."

"Never."

When I felt the relief in my body, the smile followed.

"The times ahead will be challenging. There's a chance one of us may die, perhaps both of us. No one is meant to live forever, but we're all meant to die with purpose. This is a purpose worth dying for."

I'd never known anyone so pragmatically brave. Humans were only concerned with themselves, but the elves were willing to make sacrifices for others. I knew Talon would be the same way once he reclaimed his throne.

She turned to watch the island slowly disappear, growing farther and farther away.

Side by side, we watched it fade in the distance, becoming a smaller speck on the horizon, the breeze flapping our hair around, until the speck was no more...and it was gone.

Talon and I sat together at the small table in our cabin below deck, the lamp in the center of the table burning low through the frosted glass. So far, it'd been a smooth ride with minimal rocking, so I hadn't suffered from seasickness.

He was just in his trousers, his hard chest bare in the light of the lamp, not the least bit cold even though it was chilly on the open sea. He seemed particularly interested in a crack in the table because he stared at it for a long time.

"You said you don't want to be King of the Southern Isles."

His eyes flicked up to mine.

"Why?"

He stared back, the gold flecks visible in his eyes in the light of the lamp.

"I know you want to avenge your family, but why not sit on the throne that's in your blood?"

He continued his hard stare.

I waited for an answer, waited for the answer I wanted to hear—that he intended to live with me.

He finally looked away. "I just don't."

A twinge of disappointment burned. "Then what will you do?"

His eyes stayed down.

"Will—will you live with me?" I didn't know why I asked for reassurance when he made his feelings for me clear. He made them clear when he stared at me. When he kissed me. When he said beautiful things.

His eyes shifted back to the crack in the table he'd been staring at earlier. "If I were to survive...yes."

Warmth should have filled me in that moment, excitement for the future, but the way he said it gave me pause. Made me read between the lines when I should have only seen his words on the page. "You think you won't survive?"

He gave a slight shake of his head.

"Why?"

He didn't lift his head to look at me. "I just don't."

"You're the most powerful man I've ever heard of, Talon. You claimed my lands with a simple sweep of your hand. You defeated the dark elves entirely on your own."

He lifted his chin to look at me, his eyes hard with aggression that came out of nowhere. "There are beings far more powerful than me, Calista. There are forces and powers that I can't control. Tomorrow isn't guaranteed, and I choose to live one day at a time. So, let's not speak of the future. Let's just appreciate what we have right now, in this cabin, on this boat, in the middle of the sea."

We docked at the secret port hidden within the cliff face. Even when my legs were on solid ground, I felt the world rock as if I were still on the open sea. The ship was large and luxurious, but I still felt cramped in the cabin below deck, trying to stay out of the way of the elves who navigated the ship.

I missed the island more than ever.

Now, we would make the long journey back to the forest, riding for three days and sleeping on the hard ground for three nights. And once we reached the forest, I knew there would be no time for rest, just preparations for war.

We rowed back to the beach where the elves had made camp in our absence. Commander Luxe had made a station there and had taken care of the horses until we returned. They had spent that entire time sleeping on the hard ground, waiting for the galleon to appear on the sea, and that made me feel guilty for complaining—even if I never voiced those complaints out loud.

Instead of mounting our horses and riding back to the forest, Queen Eldinar instructed us to make camp to wait for the dragons. Khazmuda had informed Talon that they'd left just hours ago, so they would arrive by morning.

Talon constructed the tent we would share, along with our own bonfire, putting it at a distance from everyone else. He was back in his armor with his heavy sword across his back, the metal cool and cruel to the touch.

He lit the fire with his matches and brought heat to the campsite. The rest of the elves made camp, putting Queen Eldinar in the center with my uncle, in the safest position she could be in with her men around her.

I spotted Commander Luxe as he passed through the campsite, but he was careful not to look in my direction to avoid Talon's ire.

Talon had hunted before sunset, so he prepared the meal over the fire then divided it onto two plates.

"No thank you." I didn't want to be rude, but my diet had changed during my stay with the elves. I saw food differently, saw the consequences of an omnivorous diet. Fish felt different for some reason, far more removed.

Talon didn't show a hint of irritation before he tilted the plate and let my food join his pile, as if he'd expected me to say that but wanted to offer anyway. He sat in silence on the log, looking into the fire as his mind drifted to other matters.

We were close enough to the ocean that I could smell the salt in the air, but it wasn't the same as it'd been on the island. The humidity was like a gentle blanket of warmth on a cool night. The waves didn't crash against the shore in the same way. The ground was hard as stone, and there was no sand to slide between my toes.

Talon finished eating then cleaned his plate before he stowed it into his pack again. "I won't tell you what to eat or how to live your life, but we'll be on the move soon, and you won't have the opportunity to be particular. Your survival is more important than your morals. You need to eat well to stay alive."

My eyes shifted to his. "It feels different now."

"You can continue that lifestyle when this is over. Next time I cook something, you're going to eat it." Like we were back in time, he'd become the authoritarian I'd first met, locked up in a castle made of stone. But I dismissed his bossiness because I knew his intentions were good.

"Okay."

He stared at me for another moment, like he expected a fight rather than acceptance. When it didn't come, he looked at the fire again. "The dragons will join us in the morning. We should get some sleep."

"Does it feel weird being apart from Khazmuda?"

"I know it's temporary."

"But you've been side by side for so long."

"Not entirely," he said. "We were separated while I was in Riviana Star. And my time as a fisherman and a pirate was spent in separation. Our minds were always connected, but years would pass in which I didn't see his scales."

"It seems like your relationship has changed since then."

"It has," he admitted. "But like I said, it's temporary. If I couldn't speak to him whenever I wished, I would feel much differently. But no amount of distance can ever break the bond we share."

A smile melted onto my face. "That's so special." I'd had it for a short while with Inferno, but our relationship would never compare to the one Talon shared with Khazmuda. We'd fused for a time because it was necessary, but to fuse permanently was unnecessary. "Because you're fused with Khazmuda, you'll live forever?"

His eyes had shifted to the fire, but they came back to me. "Theoretically."

"So, what would happen if you unfused with him this moment?"

He stared at me for a while as he considered the question. "Time would catch up with me. I would age decades."

"And that means your uncle would look exactly the same."

"Yes."

Which meant if I didn't fuse with a dragon, I would age... and then die. While Talon remained frozen in time with centuries ahead of him. His attraction to me would die, and he would replace me with someone more youthful. It was a problem I didn't know how to address.

He seemed to pick up on my change of mood because he said, "What is it, baby?"

My eyes remained on the fire. "Nothing."

"I guess I know you well," he said. "Because I know that's a lie."

I tried to focus on the fire. "I just had the realization that you'll be young and handsome forever...and I'll get old." I would get old and useless. Once he'd squeezed every drop of youth from my body, he would replace me with someone else...and I would be alone.

He stared at the side of my face for a long time.

I should focus on the task immediately before us, but it was easier to get through it when I had something to look forward to. Like a quiet and full life with Talon. With children of our own. With peace and happiness that neither of us had gotten to enjoy.

"Baby."

I didn't want to look at him. "I already know what you're going to say."

"What am I going to say?"

"That we can think about this after we survive the battle."

He was quiet for a long time. "I don't think you understand what we're up against. Because if you did, you would be afraid. You wouldn't be thinking about what comes after because there's a good chance there will be nothing that comes after."

"I have dreams, Talon. And there's nothing wrong with that."

He looked at the fire again and turned quiet, his mood subtly hostile.

"I lost my parents young, and I've been on my own ever since. And then you came into my life. And even though the world is still chaotic and things are so uncertain, you're the one thing that is certain." I looked at the side of his face. "I want the dragons to be free. I want you to have your revenge. But I also want a life with you, and I'm not ashamed to say that. Whatever that life looks like, whether we're in Shadow Stone or Riviana Star or Thalian or the Southern Isles...I want it to be you for the rest of my life."

His eyes moved down to his hands as his arms rested on his knees, his fingers stitched together. The cords in his forearms and knuckles were visible because his hands were clenched tightly.

"I love you—"

"Calista." He released a sigh through his clenched teeth, the frustration popping like the sparks in the fire. His joined hands moved to his mouth, like he silenced himself too late. He sounded like a parent who'd lost their patience and scolded their child unnecessarily. He sounded like my words were a burden too heavy for him to carry.

I felt an invisible arrow pierce the center of my heart. My body had been alive seconds ago, but now it felt like it was on death's doorstep. My optimism had sunk to the bottom of the ocean like a galleon that had been struck by a cannon.

"This is as far as I go." He lowered his hands again and turned to face me, his dark eyes wide with ferocity. "This is it. Not another step."

Pain was more than an acquaintance. It was my closest friend, always there for every season of life, standing beside me in the shadows, watching my tears spill down my face. But this pain...felt like a stranger. It was somehow worse than every other pain I'd ever known —combined.

He clenched his eyes shut then turned back to the fire.

"Is it because of her?"

"I said I didn't want to talk about her ever again—"

"Well, I just told you I loved you, and you ripped me apart."

He bowed his head and released another sigh.

"I'm sorry that my feelings are such a burden for you."

"That's not it, Calista—"

"Then what is it?" Flashbacks struck me in that moment, remembering our conversation on the beach on the island, the way he interrupted me not once, but twice—because he knew it was coming. It wasn't an accident. It wasn't a coincidence. "Because I assumed you felt the same way. Would have put my life on it."

He continued to stare at the fire.

"You've told me how much I mean to you. Told me to never leave you. Say I'm the most beautiful woman. But I'm just another woman to pass the time? Because I'm not your wife, and I'll never be—"

He tried to bridle his anger, but his voice still seethed. "She has nothing to do with this, so don't mention her again."

"So, it's just me?" I snapped. "You want me for a night but not all your nights?"

"I didn't say that—"

"Then say what you feel, Talon. Because I'm tired of guessing."

He dragged his hands down his face like he found himself in a situation he didn't want to be in.

Ever since he'd come to Riviana Star, I'd felt like the most important person in his life. I felt loved and protected. I felt a kinship with him that I'd never felt with anyone else. Even though we lived in hard times, it felt easy with him. But apparently, I'd misinterpreted all of that. "You know what? Forget it." I went into the tent, not to go to sleep, but to grab my pack and leave the campsite. I came out of the flap and threw the bag over my shoulder.

"Calista."

I started to walk off.

"Calista." He came after me and grabbed me by the arm.

I twisted out of his grasp and shoved him in the chest.

He barely moved back. He didn't reach for me again, but his eyes looked desperate to touch me. "Please just listen to me." The irritation was out of his voice, and now there was a quiet plea.

I stared, still so angry I could breathe fire like a dragon.

He paused for a long time, like he was trying to find the right words.

I continued to wait. "Is it really that hard to talk to me?"

"Calista." He raised his voice slightly to silence me. "Listen to me."

"I am listening, Talon. I've *been* listening. But you continue to say nothing."

His eyes looked so heavy as he stared, like he carried an invisible weight that only he could see. "The last thing I want to do is hurt you. Your life has already been so fucking hard, and I don't want to make it harder."

"How would you make it harder?"

He breathed harshly for several seconds. "By dying."

"You don't know what's going to happen—"

"Calista, the battle will claim my life—"

"You don't know that." And I didn't want to think about it. Not for a second.

"This was never supposed to happen."

"What?" I asked.

"This." He gestured between us. "This was not supposed to happen. We were supposed to fuck and then move on. I should have had a fucking spine and ended it before it got this far, but I was weak, so fucking weak." He continued to breathe, his nostrils flaring. "I let my guard down because I assumed I was incapable of an ounce of feeling...and then you set my world on fire and made me burn."

"So, you wish this never happened?"

"No." He bowed his head and sighed. "I think *you're* going to wish this never happened."

I continued to stare, doing my best to keep my eyes dry.

"I'm sorry that I let it get this far." His eyes shone with sincerity even though the campfire was behind him. "I meant what I said before. This is as far as I go. This is as much as I can give you." He stood there in his trousers and nothing else, his chest rising and falling with the strenuous breaths he took. Longing was in his eyes, but it was guarded. "Let's forget this conversation...and finish this together."

I remained rooted to the spot as I soaked in those painful words. I'd given myself to him completely when he appeared outside Riviana Star, and my love continued to grow with every passing day. Now, I stood there with a broken heart, a woman deliriously in love with a man who refused to feel the same way. "If you couldn't love me because you still hold a vigil for Vivian in your heart, I would understand that. But refusing to give me all of you because you assume you're going to die...is just an excuse."

He inhaled a slow breath. "It's not an excuse."

"If you really think it's all going to end soon, then you should say how you feel while you still have the chance. You should cherish this time together because it's all we have left. Because I'm already in love with you, Talon. The damage is done. I'm already stuck. You're right. If this is how you felt from the beginning, then you should have kept your distance—but you didn't. Now, here we are." I raised my arms in defeat and dropped them again.

"I'm not going to spend the time I have left pretending I'm not madly in love with you. I'm not going to hide my feelings like I'm ashamed of them. So, you can go back to your tent and lie and pretend all you want—but I won't be joining you."

He shifted his gaze away in disappointment.

"I want to love you every moment that I still have you, and if you aren't willing to give me the same in return... then I don't want you at all."

"Calista—"

"I gave all of myself to you. Do you know how hard that was? After everything I've been through, all the pain you directly caused, and I still gave myself to you. And then you reject my love?"

"I didn't reject your love—"

"Then tell me you love me."

His gaze hardened at the request, his breaths no longer labored.

I didn't expect him to say it back, and I was still disappointed. I already felt worthless, and I didn't want to look weaker. Already put my heart on the line and watched it get trampled under his boots. Didn't want him to take anything else. "Goodnight, Talon..." I turned my back on him and headed to the center of the campfire.

I waited for him to stop me.

Waited for him to grab me by the arm.

Call my name.

But he didn't.

He let me go.

Chapter 15

Talon

I'd already had breakfast before everyone else was awake.

Because I'd never gone to bed.

I sat at the campfire alone and continued to feed the fire throughout the night, staring into the flames as the self-loathing and rage boiled in my blood. When the sun crested the horizon, the sky started to lighten. I looked around the camp and saw I was the only one awake, with the exception of a few guards on duty.

I wasn't sure where Calista had gone, but I suspected she went to her uncle's tent.

The light continued to rise, the white clouds becoming visible, rabbits and squirrels appearing in the distance as they started their day. My back was aching from sitting on that log all night, but I knew chasing sleep would have been a wasted endeavor.

In the distance, I saw Queen Eldinar in her white armor, no longer in the gowns she'd worn while out to sea and on the island. It was clear she was headed straight toward me, her crystal-blue eyes like beacons of fire.

I rose to my feet before she reached me and gave her a slight bow in respect. The only monarchs I'd ever respected were Constantine and my father. But she'd been added to the list as well.

"Your eyes are weary."

My heart was weary too. "Didn't sleep much."

"I assumed so." She stepped past me, away from camp. "Walk with me, Death King." She didn't wait for me, leaving the area where her people were gathered in anticipation of the dragons' arrival.

I came to her side and followed her gait. "You shouldn't wander off too far, Your Majesty."

"I don't fear for my safety," she said. "And I certainly don't fear for it when I'm in your company." She gave me a slight smile, the kind that barely grazed her lips but bloomed in her eyes.

I didn't know how to accept such a compliment, so I said nothing at all.

Her smile started to fade. "Calista joined our tent last night. Neither Ezra nor I questioned her."

"I'm sorry if she intruded."

"She is always welcome in our presence. Therefore, she can never be an intrusion. But I assume trouble has befallen you both."

My eyes flicked away. "I fucked up."

"How so?"

I gave a heavy sigh, but the weight of the situation continued to suffocate me. "I saw it coming a mile away, like a hurricane on the horizon, dark clouds swirling." When it reached me, I knew it would destroy my ship and everything below deck. "I dodged it as long as I could, but Calista's persistence didn't wane. She told me the one thing that I didn't want to hear, that she loves me."

She studied me for a while, absorbing my words with a pause. "You already knew the contents of her heart long before she said it. You can see love well before you hear it."

I continued to stare at the camp, wondering if General Ezra watched us or if he spoke with Calista inside the tent.

"What did you tell her?"

"That I didn't want more than what we have."

A sad smile crossed her lips. "Love is possessive. It wants all of you—not just a piece."

Calista had cornered me, and I had nowhere to run. I had to face the damage I'd caused. "What have I done..." I looked at the open valley and felt my mind burn in regret. "It'll kill her." I didn't know how it would happen. If she would be in my arms when Bahamut appeared with an evil smile and yanked me away.

Eldinar's eyes softened in pity.

"I knew this from the beginning, and I still did it." I knew my life wasn't my own, and neither was my soul. But I still grabbed on to Calista and didn't let go. I said things I should have kept to myself. I slept beside her when I should have been alone. Every time I told myself to walk away, I just walked into her arms instead.

"You can control your mind. You can control your body. But you can never control your heart. It beats for whomever it chooses. Don't punish yourself for what you can't control, Talon."

I looked at her again, the self-loathing crippling.

"What you feared most has already come to pass. There's no going back now."

"I almost told her." I wanted her to understand. Needed her to understand that I didn't push her away because I wanted to. Because I didn't want to hurt the person I cared for most. "But I couldn't do it. I couldn't give her that burden to carry. I'd rather her think less of me."

"Your time left together is limited. If you can't change what's to come, then you should enjoy what you have while there's still time to enjoy it. Whether you reciprocate her feelings or not, she'll still be devastated when you pass. There's nothing you can do, Talon."

I bowed my head in misery. "I also worry for myself."

"Meaning?"

Her presence would haunt me for all eternity. Her features would fade from my memory, and I would change beyond recognition. I would watch a monster eat my soul. But I would always remember how happy I was with her. "It'll just make it that much harder to die."

I spotted them over the ocean before Khazmuda announced their arrival. It was a sight to behold, dozens of powerful dragons soaring through the blue sky, their figures clear on a beautiful day. It was a sight I'd dreamed of so many times I assumed it would never come true.

We've arrived.

I'll never forget this moment. I wanted to freeze it in my mind to keep forever. We'd searched for these dragons for decades, scoured the countryside in search of the allies we needed to win an impossible war. And finally, it had happened.

How do our scales look in the sunlight?

Their bellies were cast in shadow so their scales were impossible to see, but I would never tell him such a thing. *Breathtaking.*

The dragons approached and landed past the campsite in the open field. It was hard to count them all, but I suspected there were at least forty, including Khazmuda and Inferno. Khazmuda was the most distinct of them all because he was the only one who was completely black, dark like midnight.

I approached him, feeling a lightness in my heart at our reunion. *How was the journey?*

Much easier than the first one. Where's Calista? He looked around near his claws, like he'd somehow missed her.

My heart gave a twinge of pain. *I'm sure she'll come by soon.*

Khazmuda continued to glance around like she was hidden in plain sight before he turned back to me. ***How did so much change in the blink of an eye? I can feel the pain in your chest. It's like a bloody wound that won't heal.***

It was a moment of triumph, all these dragons gathered together to usurp my uncle from the throne, but it felt empty.

Why won't you answer me, Talon?

Because I don't want to talk about it.

What did you do?

Why do you assume I did anything?

Because if she was the one to blame, you would be angry. But you aren't angry. You're depressed.

Being bonded with someone like Khazmuda felt like a gift most days. But sometimes, like today, it felt like a curse. *I said I don't want to talk about it.*

Then I'll speak to Calista—

"Just leave it alone," I snapped. "I'll tell you when I'm ready to tell you."

Khazmuda dipped his head farther to regard me. ***I'm here for you, Talon Rothschild. Always.***

The words burned like scotch on a cut. They hurt because I needed him, and it hurt to know I wouldn't always have him. We would be savagely yanked apart. I would reach out to my mind to him, and he wouldn't be there. "Thank you, Khazmuda."

He dipped his head and touched his snout to my shoulder.

A painful smile moved into my lips, and I rubbed his soft surface with my palm, appreciating the tiny specks of shine in his black scales, the shine that was only visible on a bright day like this.

I continued to rub his scales, comforted by his presence. No one else in the world could cure my blues the way he could. It was a connection that had built over decades. A connection that was as pure as the ocean and the sky.

"Death King."

Khazmuda pulled away.

I turned to face General Ezra.

Judging by the look on his face, this would not be a pleasant conversation.

"What can I do for you, General?" I assumed he'd come to yell at me for hurting his niece. If only he knew the full story. At least I knew Queen Eldinar kept my secret, even from her own husband.

He stepped forward. "I'm tired of these clandestine meetings you have with my wife."

That was not what I expected him to say.

"Speaking to her in secret. These private conversations in her cabin, on the deck, in her chambers, at the edge of the campsite—I'm tired of it. Just because you're a king who commands the dead doesn't make you worthy of her love. Continue to pursue her, and your army of the dead won't be enough to stop my blade from piercing your heart."

I blinked at least three times in complete shock. "General, I do not desire Queen Eldinar—"

"I've grown suspicious of your conversations but told myself I was just a jealous husband. But now that you and Calista have separated, I'm more convinced of your ambitions to pursue my wife."

It was so ridiculous I could barely find the words to respond. I'd been broken since Calista had left my side, thinking about the one person I wanted most but couldn't have. "Calista and I aren't separated. We're just...having an issue." I assumed she hadn't shared the details of our conversation with her uncle. They weren't close enough for that kind of heart-to-heart. I'd shared it with Queen Eldinar because she was the only person besides Bahamut who knew what would happen to me when this was done. "And whether we're together or not, all I desire from Queen Eldinar is her friendship."

General Ezra's anger was still rampant, his eyes shifting back and forth between mine. "I'm no idiot. My wife is the most beautiful woman in the world, and you're a very pretty man. Youth frozen in time with magic and powers that can't be rivaled...a man my wife calls a hero. Once you defeat the Southern Isles and claim my wife as your own, you will literally rule the world."

His assumptions couldn't be further from the truth. It almost made me laugh. "If I were to survive this war, there's only one woman I would marry. And it's not your wife. I won't deny that Queen Eldinar has the beauty of a flower frozen in bloom, but my heart belongs to someone else."

He continued to look angry, like he wouldn't believe me, regardless of what I said.

"I understand your insecurity. Your life will feel long and full, but to Queen Eldinar, it'll feel like a mere moment. She will remarry and have children with someone of her own race. Everyone seems like a threat to you because you feel like a pawn until she finds her king. But for what it's worth, I do believe that her love for you is true. I believe she'll be devastated for a long time once you're gone."

His anger gradually started to fade, his breaths coming out slower as he processed my words.

"I speak to Queen Eldinar in private because there are things I can tell her and no one else. I have very few friends. In fact, I have one, and that's Khazmuda. Queen Eldinar is the only monarch I've met besides Constantine whom I actually respect. I didn't expect to form a friendship, but that friendship has become a lifeline to me."

His eyes dropped like the anger had passed and he felt foolish.

"Don't worry, this can stay between us."

He lifted his gaze and looked at me again. "Calista didn't share your troubles, but I know sorrow is heavy in her heart."

As it was in mine.

"The way I feel about my wife is the way Calista feels about you," he said. "I can see it every time she looks at you."

I'd seen the same look...a long time ago.

"Please don't hurt her."

"Trust me, whatever she feels, I feel it tenfold." And I would have to carry that alone because she would never know the truth. "My youth is preserved because of my connection to Khazmuda, a gift I never asked for. The only reason Macabre agreed to this battle is because of his love for your queen. I'm sure if she asked him to fuse with you so she can be with her love always, he would agree."

His eyes flicked away for a while before he looked at me again. "That's not the way of the elves. We protect the dragons, not use them."

"You wouldn't be using him if he wanted to grant you this gift—and I suspect he would. I have no love for Macabre, but I have a deep love for his race. They're mighty creatures with killer instincts, but their hearts love infinitely."

"His hatred for humans is also infinite."

"I still believe an exception would be made to grant Queen Eldinar happiness. To have the love of her life until her time comes and you both go together. If he'll risk his life to protect her, he'll do this."

He continued to stare at me like he'd never been angry at me in the first place.

"Something to think about."

Chapter 16

Calista

The sight of all the dragons gathered together was so powerful I forgot my misery...just for a moment. With different colored scales and in a variety of sizes, they were a spectacle. Marvelous and beautiful, wonderful to behold.

Queen Eldinar walked beside me as we approached Macabre, the dragon that was bigger than most of the others, his scales dark like smoke from a forest fire. Upon her approach, he lowered his belly to the earth so he could dip his head and regard her face-to-face.

Macabre didn't wear the vicious stare he had when he looked at me. His expressions weren't as discernible as they were on humans, but the love was still visible in his gaze.

It was the first time I saw the good side to Macabre, witnessed all the things Queen Eldinar had said.

She stepped forward and raised her palm to feel his snout, to glide her hand across the soft scales. His teeth were bared and visible, but she stayed below his lip, his warm breaths making her hair fly every time he exhaled.

I assumed they were speaking with their minds.

But I felt like I knew the details just watching them interact. It reminded me of the way I embraced Inferno, the way my heart burned when I looked upon Khazmuda.

A shadow approached, a black contrast against the blue sky, and I turned to see Khazmuda walk over with Talon at his side—and my uncle.

My eyes went to Talon against their will.

His eyes were already on mine.

I held his stare for a moment, feeling the pain and disappointment all over again. Then I flicked my gaze away and ignored him, pretended I hadn't noticed him in the first place. I was still angry about our conversation, but I was even more pissed that he'd let me walk away. That he'd let me slip out of his fingers after everything he'd done to earn me.

Inferno approached from the left, his scales hot as fire.

I forced a smile when I looked at him, but I didn't feel it deep inside.

Queen Eldinar stepped back from Macabre. "This is a historic moment for all our races. The union of dragons, elves, and humans. I've witnessed many things in my long life, but I did not expect this." She turned to regard Talon as he stood beside Khazmuda. "I think the first thing we need to do is bury the animosity that lingers among us. We're allies now. We will fight for one another. We will die for one another." She continued to stare at Talon and silently encouraged him to speak.

I didn't want to look at him. Tried to resist the urge. But my eyes shifted to his on their own.

He still looked at me, like he didn't care about the queen or Macabre, only me. After a long stare, he shifted his gaze to Macabre. "It takes tremendous courage to do what is hard instead of what is easy. I meant those hurtful words when I said them, but they're moot now because you've proven just how mistaken I was. It means the world to have you here—and I hope you will forgive my harshness."

Macabre stared at him for a long time.

Queen Eldinar shifted her gaze from Talon to the gray dragon as the silence lingered.

I won't forgive you today or tomorrow. But one day, if we live long enough, I will.

That was exactly what I expected from him. "I'm sorry for the way I spoke to you as well."

Macabre shifted his gaze to me. ***You were passionate, but not disrespectful. There is nothing to forgive.***

Queen Eldinar addressed us again, turning her head back and forth between us because I stood so far away from the other three. "It's time we begin our preparations. Now that the Death King is our ally, we have nothing to fear from the kingdoms across the mountains. The dragons will be safe outside the forest for the time being." She looked at Talon. "Do you have a plan, Death King?"

Talon stood there in his armor and uniform, his cape flapping elegantly behind him in the wind, making him look like the king he was born to be. Handsome and tall, he looked like a living portrait that would line a hall of kings who came before him. "I need to prepare my army to sail across the sea. The journey will be long and arduous."

"And will they sail straight to the Southern Isles?" Queen Eldinar said.

"No," Talon said. "I have other allies in the south who will come to our aid. If we sail to their lands, they will grant us hospitality until we're prepared for battle."

"Who are these allies?" Queen Eldinar asked.

Talon hesitated for a moment, as if he didn't want to say. "Pirates."

My uncle turned to regard him in slight judgment.

Queen Eldinar said nothing.

Talon felt the unspoken pressure to speak. "The Southern Isles have a substantial fleet of ships. This battle will take place by land, sea, and sky. They're the best sailors I've encountered, have taught me everything I know, and we need someone with expertise to help so many ships arrive there safely and discreetly."

Queen Eldinar continued to stare at him. "It's difficult for me to accept an alliance with plunderers and thieves...but I trust your judgment, Death King."

"We have no other choice," he said. "We can't sail across the sea for weeks and go straight into battle. My soldiers need sustenance and rest. And we need time to study the terrain before we move in. We only have one chance of success. It must count."

"Then you plan to return to the Southern Isles yourself?" Queen Eldinar asked.

Talon was quiet for a long time, like the idea of returning home made him sick. "Yes. I need to know what to expect. I need to know the number of dark elves. The size of their army. If the dragons are still enslaved. It's been over twenty years since I've been in those lands, and it must have changed in that time."

"What if you're recognized?" the queen asked.

"Anyone who supported my family was killed long ago. The only people who would recognize me would be my uncle and his immediate family. All I have to do is stay away from them—and I intend to."

"And I can investigate in his stead as well," I said. "If he needs to avoid detection."

Talon turned to look at me.

I was careful to avoid his stare.

A heavy silence landed on us all.

Queen Eldinar spoke again. "Then we shall return to Riviana Star. The dragons will be safe outside the forest. Their only enemies are the Behemoths and monsters to the east, but they'll be no match for forty dragons."

No.

She continued. "The Death King will prepare his army to set sail, and we'll join his fleet. Khazmuda will guide the dragons to the hideout. Then Talon will investigate the Southern Isles, and we'll begin our assault. Any objections?"

It was quiet.

"Then we're in agreement," she said. "Let's ride."

It was a wearying couple of days. The return journey felt far longer without Talon by my side. We rode separate horses, and instead of sharing a tent with my uncle, I slept with Inferno, perfectly warm under his wing while I was tucked in my bedroll.

But I was sad. Lonely. Empty.

Talon didn't come for me, and other than the stares he gave me whenever we were in the same vicinity, it seemed like he had no interest in doing so. When he said he wouldn't give me more, he meant it.

That made me feel worse, because none of it seemed real anymore.

I collected a pile of rocks and gathered sticks from the countryside for a campfire, and Inferno lent his fire to light it. Then we sat across from each other in silence. Inferno had hunted when we'd made camp and eaten his catch whole.

I continued to eat the nuts and berries in my pack. It was enough for me, but probably because I didn't have an appetite. My misery was like a cloud that constantly rained on me. I didn't understand how a love could burn so hot and then turn to ash so quickly.

I FEEL YOUR SADNESS.

My eyes lifted from the campfire. "Sorry."

YOU'VE BEEN SAD SINCE I ARRIVED.

"I would turn it off if I could."

WHAT HAPPENED BETWEEN YOU AND TALON? YOU ASKED ME TO GIVE HIM A CHANCE, BUT NOW YOU DON'T EVEN SPEAK.

My eyes moved back to the fire. "It's complicated."

WE'RE AN INTELLIGENT RACE.

"I didn't mean you wouldn't understand. I just mean... I don't even know what happened. We were happy, and then I told him..." The humiliation always stopped me. When I told him how I felt, I'd expected him to say it back, and then we would make love in the tent...and everything would feel right. "I told him I loved him, and he didn't say it back."

Inferno said nothing.

"Said he didn't want to take it any further than where we are."

Inferno blinked, his eyes like orbs in the firelight. ***I'M NOT VERSED IN ROMANCE, SO I'M UNSURE WHAT TO SAY.***

"You don't need to say anything."

BUT IF YOU LOVE HIM, THEN WHY DOES HIM NOT LOVING YOU CHANGE ANYTHING? LOVE IS UNEQUIVOCAL TO DRAGONS. IT IS INFINITE AND UNCONDITIONAL.

"Nothing will change the way I feel for him. But it's hard to give yourself to someone completely while they only give a very small piece. And his reasoning...he says he doesn't want to go further because he'll probably die in the battle."

THEN IT SOUNDS LIKE HE'S TRYING TO PROTECT YOU.

"By breaking my heart and destroying the time we have left together?" I asked incredulously.

GOOD POINT. BUT IT SOUNDS LIKE YOU'RE THE ONE DESTROYING IT BY CHOOSING TO LEAVE.

I couldn't believe Inferno, of all beings, would take Talon's side. "The whole thing sounded like an excuse. He even admitted he never wanted our relationship to deepen the way it has. I think I was just someone he wanted to fuck, but it lasted longer than it should. And now I want a commitment when he doesn't. So, he's blaming it on the battle and other nonsense instead of just being straight with me. I left him because I've already given him too much, and I won't give anymore."

IN MY BRIEF INTERACTIONS WITH TALON, HE'S SEEMED LIKE A MAN WHO CUTS STRAIGHT TO THE CHASE AND DOESN'T PLAY GAMES. SO WHY WOULD HE MISLEAD YOU?

"Because I've been through a lot of shit, and he doesn't want to kill me." He couldn't bring himself to say that I meant nothing to him, that I was just a woman he wanted to screw in the meantime, but not for a lifetime. He couldn't dump me the way he did with other women because it was more complicated than that, so he played games instead.

DO YOU WANT ME TO EAT HIM?

"No."

BURN HIM?

"I appreciate the offer, but no."

I CAN TAKE JUST AN ARM OR A LEG.

I smiled because I realized he was trying to make me laugh. "No, Inferno. I don't think Khazmuda would like that."

I DON'T KNOW. KHAZMUDA HAS TOLD ME HOW IRRITATING HE CAN BE.

"It's okay, but thank you."

He continued to stare at me over the fire. ***I'M SORRY YOU'RE HURTING. IT MAKES ME HURT.***

"I'll be okay." I said it as sincerely as I could. But I felt the pain of the lie I told. It was hard to imagine ever feeling okay, not when the first time I had ever felt okay was when Talon came into my life. Now I had to go back to my old life...alone. "Eventually."

When we finally arrived at Riviana Star, my entire body was tired. Sore from riding the horse all day and stiff from sleeping on the hard ground. I'd felt this way when we'd boarded the galleon, but it was far more manageable with Talon. My hand rested on his heart when we slept at night. His muscular legs between my thighs when we made love. Inferno was a great companion, but he would never replace the love I'd lost.

We stopped outside the forest, and Queen Eldinar instructed some of her men to care for the dragons in the fields outside the line of trees.

Talon approached to address the queen, but his eyes were on me. "Prepare to depart Riviana Star and meet me in Shadow Stone when you're ready. My men will prepare the ships for our departure."

"We'll meet you there, Death King," she said. "It's been a very long time since I've been in the lands of humans. I'm not sure what they'll think of us."

"They'll welcome you because I command it," Talon answered. "The world will be a different place once this battle is won."

"I hope so," she said. "Travel well."

He gave her a nod and stepped away.

We'd been apart for days, but it would still be strange to watch him leave my side. We'd been inseparable for a long time now.

Instead of leaving our presence, he came closer to me.

Queen Eldinar dismissed herself and turned to the forest.

My heart immediately jumped out of my chest like it had wings. The terror and the excitement of his proximity drove me into an internal frenzy, but I managed to keep a straight face as I met his gaze.

His hard eyes stared into mine for a long time, for seconds that grew into a solid minute.

I still felt it. That desire that burned me to ash then consumed everything around me. That profound depth of emotion that made it hard to breathe. But there was also rage...so much of it.

"I need you to come with me."

Disappointment kicked me right in the stomach. Days had passed and he didn't chase me, so I'd come to accept he would never rectify this. But he somehow continued to disappoint me, destroy what little hope I had left. It took me several seconds to speak. "Why?"

"The black diamonds."

"That doesn't concern me."

"I need my blacksmith to fuse the diamonds into our armor."

"Then take my armor with you and bring it back when you're done—"

"Calista."

I turned silent at the sound of my name, hearing the power in his voice.

"I don't want us to be apart."

"Why?" I managed to keep my gaze on his even when I wanted to look away, to seem braver than I really was.

But his eye contact was more intense than mine. Far more potent and intrusive. "You know why."

"I don't know anything anymore."

His eyes gave a wince like I'd stabbed him.

"I've been miserable all by myself, and you seem perfectly fine."

"I haven't felt this shitty in a long time."

I felt myself step back, wanting to dismiss his ire as well as his emotion. My eyes shifted away because it was painful to look at him and know he was no longer mine. "I'm not coming with you."

"You *are* coming with me."

"Then you'll have to make me," I snapped. "Because I don't want to see or speak to you if I don't have to. And if you don't want to look like the biggest asshole in the world in front of Macabre and his kin, then you'll just go."

His eyes contained his rage, building up further because it had nowhere to go. "I never said I didn't want to be with you."

"I know what you said. I'm someone you fuck but not someone you marry—"

"That is not what I said." He raised his voice so loud that it drew attention from the nearby elves as they dismounted their horses and prepared to return to the forest. He looked so angry, he was on the verge of unleashing his army of the dead to rip me apart.

"But I know it's what you meant."

His eyes shifted back and forth between mine at lightning speed. "I will die in this battle—"

"If you really believed that, you would never let me go. You would hold on to me so tight, I wouldn't be able to breathe. Soon, you'll be King of the Southern Isles and the Northern Kingdoms, and I'm not good enough to be your wife—"

"I told you Vivian was of low stature, and I married her anyway."

"You loved her, and you don't love me," I said. "That's the difference."

His face turned beet red like he was so mad he might do something he would regret. The veins popped in his forehead like rivers on a map. The fire in his eyes burned so brightly, it produced heat. He trembled slightly, all of his rage packed inside his body and dying to burst out. "Maybe what we had wasn't real for you to think so little of me. For you to assume that I would treat you like some whore who got too attached. To ever think, for a fucking second, that I don't care about you."

I did my best to fight the tears that wanted to bleed from the wound in my chest.

He continued to tremble like he was about to strike me.

His words hurt me. They hurt me when they should provoke nothing.

He abruptly turned around and walked off. Moved through the sea of people to where Khazmuda waited in the field. His eyes were on Talon like he watched the entire thing, aware of Talon's pounding rage through their connection.

Talon climbed up Khazmuda's side quicker than I'd ever seen him, and then Khazmuda launched from the ground and into the sky at breakneck speed. Then they were gone…turning into a speck within seconds because Khazmuda flew like he feared for his life.

I stood there alone…and felt my soul crack in two.

Chapter 17

Talon

Despite the length of my absence, everything remained in order. Commander Navarrese had continued to run my affairs in my absence and give no indication that I'd left my throne. "Prepare the armies for departure. We set sail when the ships are ready." Once I'd become king, I'd ordered the manufacture of enough galleons to carry my entire army across the sea. When I'd made that demand, Commander Navarrese had looked slightly puzzled but obeyed the order. It took a long time to build that number of ships, and I was glad I hadn't dragged my feet on it. Otherwise, this battle would have been delayed even longer. "And I need to speak to the blacksmith."

"Right away, Your Majesty." He gave a slight bow then left the room.

I sat behind the desk and looked at all the matters that required my attention and realized none of it mattered. Not a single scroll. Not a single complaint from one of the stewards or the Scion Priest in his church to the west.

Nothing mattered—because I finally had what I'd wanted all these years.

Who would oversee all this nonsense when I was dead? I didn't know. Perhaps it would be Calista since she was the heir to Scorpion Valley and I had already slain all of King Theodore's kin. Or perhaps it would be Queen Eldinar, extending her borders to the south and ruling over the humans as well as the Southern Isles. Either one was a good choice.

Calista would marry and pass her bloodline through her children... And I couldn't finish the thought. Because Calista would only marry for love, and that would mean she loved someone other than me.

I thought I was too angry to care, but perhaps there wasn't enough anger to ever stop me from caring.

The blacksmith entered and disrupted my thoughts. "You called, Your Majesty?"

"I need armor." I came around the desk then pulled out the key from its hiding spot.

"Do you have an issue with the armor I already provided to you?"

"No." I unlocked the door to the cabinet built into the wall and pulled out the few black diamonds I'd managed to find. "You will flatten a third of these diamonds and secure them into my armor. Anywhere is fine." I started to remove the pieces of my outfit and laid them on the table.

"And the rest?"

"You'll make a new armor set with Calista's measurements. Include a third."

"And the remaining third?"

"Make another set similar to Calista's, but pretend she's four inches taller."

It was clear he wanted to ask questions, but he didn't want to ignite my anger. "It shall be done."

"I need it as soon as possible."

"Then I'll get to work on this now, Your Majesty." He gathered the pieces on the desk and departed my office.

I sat alone in my royal chambers, nursing a glass of scotch in front of the fire, blocking out Khazmuda because I didn't want to entertain his questions when I was pissed off and drunk.

"Your actions are admirable, Talon Rothschild."

My eyes remained on the fire even though I knew he was in the armchair beside me, where he usually appeared during these late-night conversations.

"It's a lot easier to lose someone if you hate them."

I didn't want to look at him. Couldn't get the last image of him out of my head, a monster eating a bowl of someone's soul. I had been young and foolish when I'd traveled to his lands and made that agreement. Too lost in my rage, I didn't care about forfeiting my life and soul... until I found a reason to live again.

"And she definitely hates you."

I'd hated her in that moment because of the way she'd spat all over me. The way she'd jumped to the most ridiculous conclusions instead of seeing the love I had for her written all over my face. All I had to do was tell her how I felt and correct her... But Bahamut was right. It would be easier for her in the end.

But it wouldn't be easier for me.

"You've found the dragons, as I knew you would. You've convinced the elves to come to your aid, something I hadn't foreseen. And now, with the armies you rule, you'll sail to the Southern Isles and finally get your wish. How does it feel?"

Empty.

"How does it feel to get everything you've ever wanted?"

It was what I'd wanted in the past, but now everything had changed. I loved a dragon the way I loved my brother. I'd fallen for a woman the way I'd fallen for Vivian. I'd finally come to know peace after searching for it on the seas for decades. Now, what I wanted more than anything was to go back in time and undo what couldn't be undone.

"I thought you would be more excited, Talon. As excited as I am."

I wanted him to leave but wouldn't ask him to go. He could take me to the underworld whenever he wished, give me another taste of what waited for me in a black-and-white world below. The last thing I wanted to do was provoke him to take me away from this world for days like he'd done before.

He hadn't shown me his true colors until the decision was made. Until there was no way to go backward, only forward. I'd have to face an eternity in his company, and I wasn't sure how I would do that when I couldn't even look at him now.

"You won't look at me."

"I'm afraid of what I'll see." Not the handsome man with the blue eyes and shiny armor. But the monster that was eight feet tall with sharp teeth that dripped with his drool. A being unlike any other I'd seen in the flesh.

"You should be afraid, Talon Rothschild."

Khazmuda pushed into my mind over and over, like a needle against the skin, applying enough pressure until the skin was punctured. Blood flowed as his voice sounded in my head. ***You've ignored me for two days. You will ignore me no longer.***

I was just as angry as the moment I left. I didn't desire company, not even Khazmuda's.

Talon.

The blacksmith is producing the armor. The ships and army are being prepared—

Those things don't concern me. You're what

concerns me. I watched your interaction with Calista but couldn't hear the words.

They weren't meant to be heard.

We're so close to battle, and you're spending that time attacking Calista—

Trust me, it's the other way around.

Talon. His frustration was audible in his tone. ***What happened?***

I knew I couldn't dodge Khazmuda. Not when we were connected like this. *I told her I didn't want anything more, and now she assumes I just wanted to fuck her and leave her.* After every conversation we'd had, every moment we'd shared, the fact that I'd told her about Vivian, how could she possibly believe any of that horseshit?

I think that's a fair assumption.

I felt my anger rise again. *How?*

If you don't want anything more than what you have, then that means it'll never be more than what it is. Which means you don't want her to be your mate and you don't want to have hatchlings with her. That means you think she's an unsuitable partner.

It means I think I'm going to die in the battle, and I would be a fucking asshole to let her believe we would be together forever when I knew full well we wouldn't. Maybe I look like an asshole, but I'm just trying to protect her.

You aren't going to die, Talon.

I closed my eyes because the pain was too much.

I will burn anyone who comes near you.

I didn't speak. Couldn't do it.

When Khazmuda spoke again, he was gentler. ***Whether you live or die, all you have is this moment. And you're wasting it. Of all people, I thought you would realize that better than anyone.***

If I'd known my last night with Vivian would be the last time we were together, I would have done things differently. We hadn't fought, but we hadn't made love. Her pregnancy had made her insecure about her body, and no matter how much I'd shown my desire, she'd dismissed my advances. Now, I wished I'd done something more to make her feel attractive. I wished I'd made more of an effort to spend time with my mother and sheathed my favoritism for my father. Even if everything was going to end the same, I had a few things I would have done differently.

After Calista left with Inferno, you sat exactly where you sit now, simmering in your anger and wasting time until you finally did something about it. When General Titan marched on the forest, you dug your boots into the earth like a stubborn mule until the very last possible second. Now, here we are again, sitting here and wasting time. Why don't you learn, Talon?

Shame flooded me.

You can't change what's to come. But you can change every moment that comes before it. I could die. Calista could die. All three of us could perish. And I think it would be a lot easier to die knowing everyone I love knows how much I love them. I know your heart, Talon. I know it feels the same way.

Chapter 18

Calista

Riviana Star didn't feel the same as it had when I left.

Talon had been with me, and we'd made a life together in each other's arms. Our nights were filled with passion, and our days were filled with adventure. When I stepped into my tree house, I could feel his presence everywhere, as if he were right next to me, as if he would project his mind and appear in the armchair or at the head of the dining table.

Our last conversation continued to play in my mind and made me feel guilty, as if I were the one at fault. I'd ripped him apart in retaliation for ripping me apart. My pain had nowhere to go but out, so I unleashed my destruction on the person who'd hurt me most. Since we were close to battle and all our lives could be forfeit, I should have held him close rather than pushing him away.

But I'd accepted less than what I deserved my whole life, and I wasn't going to do it anymore. It didn't matter how much I loved him—I wouldn't settle for a man who found me disposable. I'd told him I loved him I don't know how many times, and each time, he winced like he didn't want to hear it.

It made me angry all over again.

Queen Eldinar informed her people that they would fight to save the dragons across the sea, and once her announcement was made, all other projects were halted to prepare for battle. New armor and weapons were produced, and with the exception of a few elves who would remain behind, everyone packed their belongings for the long trip.

Talon had taught me the blade several times, but I still lacked the skills that Queen Eldinar and my uncle possessed. I could hold my own for a time, but not forever, not when I wasn't fused with a dragon. That extra strength, that aided focus, made me comparable to the other great warriors.

It took several days to prepare for departure, and on the last night, I stayed in my tree house alone, wondering if I would ever see this place again. If I chose to stay behind, no one would stop me, but I felt like my purpose was in that battle, whether I lived or died.

No matter how angry I was with Talon, I wouldn't abandon him.

I sat at the dining table with a cup of tea, looking at the fireflies floating outside the window and bringing a glow to the canopy and the forest. The music from the Great Tree was quieter than usual, somber because of the mass exodus that was about to happen.

I should go to sleep, but I hadn't slept well in several nights. Tonight would be no different. I would lie there and reach for someone who was gone. I would think of someone who didn't think of me with the same desire.

The front door opened.

It was late, and I expected no visitors, especially the kind that just let themselves into my personal space without invitation. There was no danger in the forest, but I got to my feet and rounded the corner in preparation to grab my sword.

But I stilled when I saw him.

Talon.

I sucked in a deep breath that almost sounded like a gasp. I hadn't been sure when we would see each other again, but I hadn't expected it to happen in Riviana Star, in my tree house, at this hour.

His armor was different now, with pieces of the Black Diamonds fused into different parts, the shine distinct against the matte appearance of his chest plate and vambraces. His cape was still at his back, and the hilt of his sword was visible past his head. He stared at me from where he stood in front of the door, his eyes dark like the underworld.

I was still frozen in place, still in disbelief at his appearance, even though an entire minute had passed.

Then he walked up to me, his boots loud against the wooden floor, taking his time as he crossed the room and came up to me.

He could kiss me or strike me. I wasn't sure which would happen.

He stared at me harder than he had before, his eyes shifting slightly between mine, a mixture of anger and desperation.

My heart raced so quickly I could feel my pulse in my neck. I felt like I was in free fall and glued in place at the same time. Even after all the harsh words that were said, I couldn't deny that my heart beat for him as much as it always had, since the night he'd told me what had happened to his family and we'd made love in the tent, since he'd swooped down from the sky and killed General Titan with a dagger to the mouth, since he'd slept with me through the night and dropped his guard.

"I thought keeping my distance would make this easier for both of us, but it hasn't. It's only made it worse, and now I hate myself for the time I wasted. For the nights you could have been in my bed. For the moments we could have shared. For the love we could have had. I'm sorry that I chose wrong."

I continued to breathe hard, surprised by all that.

"I'm sorry."

I looked into his eyes and saw the gold flecks in his gaze, the sincerity that shone through.

"I meant what I said before. That I believe this battle will claim my life. That these final days will be our last. I know it'll kill you—and that kills me. After everything you've endured and lost, you have to endure this too."

"You aren't going to die—"

"But our hearts were already sewn together. I finally gave my heart to you when I slept beside you, but you had earned it long ago, so long ago I can't recall the moment it happened. But that was the moment I couldn't fight it anymore. I thought I would love one woman all my life... but now I love another."

I could feel the tears burning behind my eyes, feel them try to break down the dam that kept them from the surface.

"I love you with all my heart, Calista."

I inhaled a deep breath as the fire in my eyes started to burn hotter.

"I've loved you a long time—and I will love you always."

This was what I'd wanted when I told him I loved him, to hear him say it back...and *feel* him say it back. All the anger and resentment I felt disappeared when his words hit me with a sincerity so potent it burned. "I love you too" The tears broke free and released from the corners of my eyes.

His hand cupped my face, and his thumbs swiped each tear away before he brought his forehead to mine and stared down at my lips. We stayed that way for a long moment, savoring the connection between our hearts and our souls.

I felt all my pains ease and my scars heal. Felt my heart calm from a raging river to a steady stream. The peace his love granted me was more profound than the serenity I found in this very forest.

He pulled away and tilted my head back to look at my lips, to rest his thumb in the corner as he continued to regard me with soft eyes. "If I were to live..." His eyes stayed on my mouth. "I would marry you...and have children with you, and we would live among dragons and elves and humans—all as equals."

I hadn't slept well in days and neither had he, but that didn't stop us from spending our night together locked in the throes of passion. We'd made love before, but it was different this time. Slower. Deeper. Our eyes connected at a depth we'd never experienced before.

He was always on top of me, exerting his muscles like they never fatigued, bending me in ways he liked so we could be as close together as possible. He rocked into me with his thick arms locked behind my knees, giving me the length I could handle, his head dipped to brush his nose against mine and kiss me.

My hands planted on his chest, and I felt his heart beat steadily under the skin, felt the vibration like a drum, the source of his love. It was the first time every single barrier between us had been removed, when it was the two of us and nothing else, our hearts pure and visible on our sleeves.

It was hard to believe I'd ever hated him. That I'd wished him a violent death. Not when he'd become the love of my life, my future husband, the man who would father my children. My hand cupped his face, and I brought his mouth to mine for a kiss, our lips like clouds that came together to form a single entity. I breathed into him as I felt my chest tighten, because if he was killed in battle, I really would be ruined.

He kissed me back without breaking his pace, filling me with his size and claiming me as his, marking his territory in a deeper way than he had before.

I spoke against his mouth. "I love you." I'd already said it to him several times before, but I wanted to say it again, to celebrate my commitment to him and hear him say it back. My fingers dug into his hair as I watched the same love burn in his eyes like a glorious sunset.

"Baby, I love you."

It carried on until sunrise, and by then, we were spent and exhausted and fell asleep. Our rest was short-lived because we were both roused by the heat of the sun as it entered the open window.

I awoke in his arms, his head on my pillow, his eyes tired from the long night we'd had.

I kissed the corner of his mouth.

He turned into me and kissed my hairline.

"I don't want to leave."

Sadness crept into his gaze, a slow infection that quickly turned rampant. "Nor do I."

"I wish we could stay like this forever."

He held my gaze without blinking, a hint of alarm moving into his face. It disappeared quickly like it never happened, and he rolled onto his back to stretch. Then he left the bed and stood up, his back to me, his tight ass like a rock. "If only..."

When we approached the royal palace, Queen Eldinar already stood outside with my uncle, giving orders to Commander Luxe as they prepared to depart the forest... possibly forever. "Fifty of our strongest must remain behind to protect Riviana Star from outside invasion. Now that the dark elves have been defeated, I suspect the forest is safe, but we must safeguard the Great Tree."

Commander Luxe nodded. "It saddens me that I won't join you in battle, Your Majesty."

She stepped forward and gave him a slight smile. "I've given you this task because I entrust it to no one else. You don't need to raise your sword with me in battle to serve me—because you're serving me in a much deeper way."

He stared at her for seconds before he gave a slight bow. "Please return, Queen Eldinar. I speak for everyone when I say you're the greatest ruler Riviana Star has ever known. Without you to guide us, we would be lost."

"I appreciate your kind words. Every monarch in our history has served our people well, and I'm certain my successor, if I perish, will do the same."

He gave her a final nod. "Fight well, Your Majesty."

"You as well."

He walked away and left the clearing.

Queen Eldinar turned to regard us, her eyes on Talon. "My scouts informed me of your presence in our lands. I didn't expect to hear from you so soon."

Talon stepped forward then set his pack on the ground. "I've come to bestow a gift upon you, Your Majesty. I hope you'll accept it." He kneeled down, opened the pack, and revealed an armor set that was stunning in black, reflective in the sunshine. Chunks of black were along the sides of the torso, black diamonds he'd harvested from the Arid Sands. He rose to his feet and presented the chest piece. "I had my blacksmith prepare this in our forge. The dragon scales are impenetrable."

She stared at it for a long time before she looked at him again. "This is a kingly gift. But I can't accept it, Death King. I will not protect my body with a dragon's sacrifice."

"It was not a sacrifice," he said. "Khazmuda offered."

"Even so—"

"It's a gift, Your Majesty. Khazmuda wanted to honor the sacrifices you've made for all dragons, including in the upcoming battle. With all due respect, your armor broke into pieces, and you nearly lost your life." He held it up slightly higher. "Dragon scales do not break."

She stared at it again, her eyes heavy with the weight of the gift.

"*Fleur Nia.*"

She hesitated before she looked at her husband.

"Please take it." The plea in his eyes came from the deepest part of his soul. His fear was on display, terrified of losing the woman he loved most. Emotion burned in his gaze as he silently begged her to put aside her beliefs to ensure her safety.

"Khazmuda's scales will regrow before the battle," Talon said. "You have not compromised him in any way. I would never allow him to be compromised." He continued to hold up the armor. "I know black isn't your color, but I think anyone who gazes upon Queen Eldinar of Riviana Star in midnight-black dragon scales will fear for their lives at the sight of you."

She stared at the chest plate a moment longer before she looked at him again. "I am honored to accept your gift, Death King."

My uncle stepped forward and gathered the pieces that Talon offered, holding it all in his big arms. "Thank you for protecting my wife." He looked at Talon as he said it, sincerity in his hard gaze.

Talon held the look before he gave a nod.

My uncle carried it into the royal palace, where Queen Eldinar would change.

She remained where she stood and looked at Talon.

"There's something else you need to know about the armor."

She didn't pursue the topic with questions. She let him answer her freely.

"Black diamonds are secured in some of the pieces. They're rare gems that can only be found buried in the sand in the desert to the west."

Her eyes shifted to me before she looked at him again. "Calista mentioned her time as a slave to your general. She spent ten years digging for those diamonds, and that makes it even harder to accept your gift."

"It's okay," I said. "Knowing that you're the recipient makes it worthwhile."

She stared at me for a long time and then looked at Talon again. "What is their purpose?"

"Energy," he said. "Even the smallest sliver houses a powerhouse of energy."

"I don't need it," she said. "My endurance is much stronger than any human."

"That's not what it's for," he said. "It's for your dragon."

She became confused, her head tilting slightly like she'd misheard him. "State your meaning, Talon."

He hesitated, like this conversation would be unwelcome. "Macabre only agreed to this because of his love for you. He would rather protect you in battle than let you fight without his scales, fire, and claws. And if he's willing to do that…I suspect he's willing to fuse with you."

Her eyes slowly narrowed in provocation. "The very reason we march to battle is because the dark elves forced the dragons into a fuse and control their minds—"

"Yes, *forced*," he said. "I have not forced Khazmuda into a fuse. He does it willingly, and that's why we have such a profound relationship. He's free to leave whenever he chooses. Calista was fused with Inferno for a short while, and then they unfused and went their separate ways. Just because dark elves decided to abuse their power doesn't mean it's wrong to fuse with a dragon—not if the dragon wants it."

Her eyes were still hard in anger, clearly offended by this conversation.

"Ask Macabre to fuse—and he will."

"I do not wish to fuse with him."

"But I promise you, he'll want to fuse with you," he said. "Because you'll have his strength and his focus, and you'll be an unstoppable force in battle. He's joining this battle to protect you—and this is the best way to accomplish that."

Fire continued to dance behind her eyes. "We don't use dragons—"

"With all due respect, Your Majesty. You're putting your life and the lives of your people on the line for the dragons. It's only smart to use their powers to increase our chances of victory. I understand you have an oath—but now is the time to put that aside. It's for the good of all of us."

She turned quiet.

"While you use their strength, you drain their energy. Because of their size, they have infinitely more energy than we do, but it's not unlimited. You'll drain the storage in the diamonds first before you tap into Macabre. Depending on the length of the battle, you may not even need the diamonds, but if this battle lasts days, then you might. You said you didn't want to use Macabre, and I'm giving you that ability. You can benefit from his powers without siphoning off his energy."

Her anger started to dim, but her discomfort was still obvious. She looked at her husband, who had returned to stand beside her.

He held her stare, standing perfectly straight with his thick arms by his sides, looking at her like he awaited a command.

"What are your thoughts, General?"

He inhaled a slow breath as he looked at her, staring at her as a husband, not a general of her army. "I agree with the Death King. We're the only race that's selflessly cared for them. The least they can do is share their gift with us—just during the battle. Knowing you'll be protected by their scales and have the power of a dragon in your veins brings me comfort."

"It's not about me, General. It's about—"

"It is about you, *Fleur Nia*. My obligation is to our army and our people, but I'm not ashamed to admit that I put you first always. I need you to live. I need you to return to this forest and rule for centuries. This is a temporary arrangement. The dragons know that we would never maintain the fuse against their will. They can trust us without doubt."

She stared at him for a while before she turned back to Talon. "I still don't like this. But I want to free those dragons bound by evil magic. I want Macabre and the others to return home and live the rest of their days in peace. I want my people to be victorious. I want you to succeed, Talon."

I knew Talon wouldn't have convinced her of this plan if it weren't for my uncle. He'd abandoned his role as general of Riviana Star and turned into a concerned husband who wanted his wife to live...even if he died.

"Then speak to Macabre," Talon said. "I'm sure he will agree, and once he does, ask him if the others will as well. Pair the dragons with your best fighters. I suspect my uncle's army will be no hardship for you, but we've learned from experience that the dark elves are a serious adversary."

We stepped out of the forest and entered the plains, the dragons sleeping in the sunshine or soaring in the skies, hunting for game.

No matter how many times I saw it, I would always enjoy it.

Queen Eldinar took the lead, protected in her black armor made of Khazmuda's scales, looking much different than she did in her all-white armor. An image of the Great Tree had been carved into her back, surrounded by a crest of flowers. Her long hair flowed in the breeze as she moved, her blades sitting in the scabbards at her hips.

Khazmuda landed before us, aware of Talon's presence as he drew closer. His eyes were on the queen, and he lowered his head to get a better look at her appearance. ***You're a fearsome queen, Your Majesty. All your enemies will tremble before your power and might.***

"Thank you, Khazmuda," she said with a slight smile. "And thank you for such a generous gift."

You're welcome, Your Majesty. My duty is to protect Talon in the battle, but I hope my scales will serve you in my absence.

"I'm sure they will," she said. "May I ask you something?"

Anything, Your Majesty.

"You don't have to address me as such. I'm queen to the elves, but to the dragons, I'm only a friend."

You'll always be Queen Eldinar to me.

She smiled. "You're sweet."

Ask your question.

"When you and Talon fused, who suggested it?"

Neither of us.

I could hear Khazmuda's words in my mind as they spoke. I knew Talon could as well, but my uncle was unaware of the dragon's side of the conversation.

"Then why did you fuse?" she asked.

Talon gave an unexpected sigh.

My eyes darted to him, seeing a hint of discomfort.

Khazmuda didn't speak. His eyes flicked to Talon.

"It's okay," Talon said. "You can tell her."

Queen Eldinar turned to look at Talon before she faced Khazmuda again.

Talon suffered a fatal wound...and only a fuse would spare him certain death. The same wound on my body would be inconsequential, so I absorbed that damage so he would live.

"What kind of wound was this?"

A dagger to the heart.

I looked beside me again to Talon.

He stared straight ahead, determined not to look at anyone.

Queen Eldinar stared at him for a while. "This wound was self-inflicted..." She read between the lines, interpreted the change in the energy that surrounded us.

I looked at the side of Talon's face.

Yes.

My heart squeezed so tight it almost burst.

"Is there a chance he did this in the hope you would fuse?"

No. He tilted his head slightly, as if put off by that question. ***Talon Rothschild tried to end his life because he had nothing to live for. He wanted me to let him go, but I saved him for my own selfish reasons.***

Queen Eldinar gave a slight nod in understanding. "What were those reasons?"

I didn't want to be alone…and I loved him.

"It sounds like this was during a time when you didn't know each other well."

We were forever bound by the events of that horrible night. It's hard not to love someone you pity so deeply. Talon didn't show his best characteristics during that time, but I knew they resided deep below the surface.

"And you've remained fused ever since?"

Yes.

"Why?"

Because I never want to be apart from him as long as I live. No distance can sever our minds. Even if we settle down with our mates and have our own hatchlings, our minds will always be connected. That relationship will never change.

"So you can honestly say that this is something you want?"

Wholeheartedly.

"And if you asked him to unfuse, do you think he would?"

Yes. Why do you ask these questions?

She was quiet for a long time. "Because I'm about to ask your kin to fuse with us, and I want to understand exactly what I'm asking before I ask it."

As long as it's a question and not a demand, you have nothing to fear, Your Majesty. I'm sure some will agree, while others will not. As long as their wishes are respected, there is no offense.

"This is my final question. Do you think I *should* ask?"

Khazmuda stared at her in silence, deep in contemplation. ***I don't understand your question.***

"Do you think it would be beneficial to all if I were to ask?"

Talon can surround himself with a shield of the dead to fight for him. That makes him a formidable opponent because he's untouchable. But without it, he's no different from General Titan or Commander Luxe. He's skilled with the blade, but so are his opponents. But with the strength I lend him, he's one of the greatest swordsmen who walks this earth. It's the reason he was able to defend your tree for as long as he did before you allowed him to call upon the dead. Having others with that power, even though they still won't match Talon, will undeniably affect the outcome of the battle. In that regard, yes, I think you should ask.

"Then I will speak to Macabre—in private. I'll respect whatever he decides."

He has the same love for you that I have for Talon. I know what his answer will be.

The elven army began its progression out of the forest to reach the open fields with the mountains in the distance.

They had been instructed to bring only what they could carry. The horses were left behind, and they traveled on foot so their mounts wouldn't be abandoned once they arrived at the harbor.

Queen Eldinar had been with Macabre for hours, alone in their spot on the field, her sitting on the ground as Macabre lay on the grass and faced her. From a distance, it seemed like their conversation went fine, but she wouldn't have been there for hours if there weren't conflict.

Talon and I sat together with Khazmuda in front of a campfire, the sun almost set over the mountains.

He sat with his arms resting on his knees, looking over the campfire to the field beyond, littered with dragons.

"They've been talking for a long time."

Talon gave no reaction. "He'll say yes."

"I thought so too, but now I'm worried."

"They're probably discussing other matters. Or he was appalled by the armor."

"I hope not...since it was freely given."

Khazmuda closed his eyes as he grew tired, like a dog on the rug in front of the fire.

"That was nice of you to give that to her," I said quietly. "You've grown so fond of each other." I was slightly jealous, but I never allowed it to consume me. Queen Eldinar was loyal to my uncle, and now that Talon had confessed his feelings, I knew his heart belonged to me. Whatever they shared was platonic.

"It's hard to earn my respect, but she did it without trying," he said. "I don't have any friends besides Khazmuda, so it's nice to have someone."

I felt a twinge of pain at his statement. "Are we not friends?"

A smile moved over his lips. "We are definitely *not* friends." He turned to look at me, that handsome grin lighting up his face. "And I would never want to be your friend. If I had to settle for that, I would lose my fucking mind."

He dissipated my insecurity and even made me smile.

He watched me, his smile slowly fading as he got lost in my eyes, staring at me like we were alone in the world with no one else around. Then his eyes turned sad, as they often did whenever he looked at me.

"Why do your eyes do that?"

"What?"

"Look so sad."

His eyes flicked away, and he looked at the horizon once more, the sky already almost dark because the sun seemed to sink into the mountains as if into quicksand. "When you have something you love, you have more to lose. Plunging that dagger into my heart was easy because I had no reason to stay alive. Death was preferable to my misery. But now...my life has meaning again."

"I think that's a good thing, Talon."

He didn't say anything for a long time. "Perhaps. Just wish it'd happened sooner."

"It happened when it was supposed to happen. You needed time to grieve. If we'd met too soon, it wouldn't have worked."

"I think I would have fallen in love with you at any time, under any circumstances."

This was a side to Talon he rarely showed. He was completely open and transparent, speaking his mind rather than masking his thoughts.

"When I met Vivian..." He hesitated before he continued, because anytime he spoke of her, it was like a knife was held to his throat. "I was smitten at the sight of her. I chased her and she ran, and I liked it because no one had ever denied my pursuit. There was an attraction there and I knew she liked me, but she still did whatever she could to avoid me. I cornered her and threatened to never let her go until she told me why. I just needed a reason." He stared at the fire as he swallowed. "That was when she told me she'd been raped..."

My heart broke for a woman I never knew. Didn't even know what she looked like.

"It had happened recently. By her own uncle..." His mood started to darken because it still bothered him after all these years. "She was still shaken up about it and not interested in me because she knew all I wanted to do was fuck around then move on to the next girl—which was a fair assumption. And if she hadn't been raped, she probably would have been fine with that, but she was a different person as a result."

"What happened?"

"She assumed that would scare me off and I would leave her alone," he said. "She thought wrong."

Now it all made sense, the way Talon was so patient with me, the way he saw past the violence and still saw me underneath. The way he was invested in my recovery, the way he wanted to heal me.

"It was a slow beginning, but from the moment I set eyes on her, there was nobody else. I took it at her pace, showed her there was no rush to do something she didn't want to do, and over time, she started to trust me. I fell in love with her long before I had her, so I didn't mind the wait. I never told her because I didn't want her to think it was some line to get her into bed. I waited until she said it first."

It was a little painful to listen to the tale of him falling in love with someone else, but I knew it was his story, his foundation, and it would always be a part of him and, therefore, a part of us. "What happened to him?"

"The uncle?" he asked. "I killed him."

Exactly as I expected. "Is that why...you were interested in me?"

"I think it was a part of it, yes," he said. "I knew what Vivian had suffered, and I didn't want you to suffer. She told me I put her back together, and I guess I wanted to do the same for you."

"Thank you for telling me that."

He stared at the fire. "I was a different man the night we met. I'm sure you realize that. And I hope you realize how much I've changed...because of you." He turned his head to look at me, his eyes soft once more. "I sailed the seas for decades looking for a solution to my problem, when all I needed to do was find you."

My eyes got lost in his gaze, seeing the gold flecks visible in the light of the campfire. I'd met him on a dark night in the middle of the desert, and while he was as handsome then as he was now, he did look different.

He leaned in and slid his hand into my hair, grabbing it at the back as he kissed me, giving me a slow and purposeful kiss by the firelight. His fingers fisted my hair, and he made love to my mouth with his. Ashes sparked into the night, and Khazmuda slept on, unaware of the way our hearts tangled in a knot so tight it would never come free.

I woke up at dawn.

I'd slept hard and deep throughout the night, recovering from the loss of sleep during my separation from Talon. Even though I was about to raise my sword in battle when I'd barely been in a fight, I felt no unease about it. Maybe it was because I believed Talon and Khazmuda would protect me. Or maybe it was because I was so deliriously in love I couldn't think straight.

Maybe it was both.

I silently dressed myself and let Talon sleep alone naked in the bedroll. I stepped outside to see the sky still slightly dark from the lingering night. The sun was approaching over the horizon, the mountains a dark silhouette from the approaching sun.

Khazmuda was still at the campsite where I'd last seen him, his chin resting on his sharp talons. He opened his eyes when he heard me.

I smiled and rubbed his snout. *Good morning.*

Morning. He released a quiet hum like he enjoyed my touch.

I looked around the campsite, seeing the elves still asleep in their tents, waiting for their queen to tell them to march. Dragons were in the field, most of them huddled together in a pile to keep warm throughout the night.

In the far distance, I saw Queen Eldinar approaching camp with Macabre beside her, her black armor brilliant even in the dull sunrise.

I wonder what Macabre decided.

He's agreed to the fuse.

How do you know? I turned back to look at him.

I can feel it.

Talon exited the tent a second later, fully dressed like he'd woken up shortly after I left, even though I'd moved as silently as possible. His sword was even hooked across his back, and with the sleepy look in his eyes, he was even sexier than usual. He'd entered that tent as my lover but emerged as a king, his armor unbreakable with its dragon scales. His eyes immediately went to me with a hint of affection in the look, like I was his sunrise. He came forward and, without saying a word, gave me a kiss on the mouth.

My eyes closed as I kissed him back, swept away in the simple embrace that long-term lovers exchanged. It was a greeting, not an act of lust, domestic affection my parents exchanged whenever they entered the same room together.

I thought I would never have something like that.

He turned to Khazmuda next and rested his palm against his snout for a moment, their eyes locked, an exchange of love there, a man with his dragon. Then he turned back to me. "Queen Eldinar has fused with Macàbre."

"Looks like you were right."

"A dragon loves more deeply than other creatures," he said. "It's their one weakness."

"Weakness?" I asked. "I think it's a strength. Because if Khazmuda hadn't saved you, you wouldn't be here now, about to save his race."

He gave me that signature hard stare, the kind that looked into my face endlessly.

Queen Eldinar approached our campsite, her eyes on Talon. "After much deliberation, Macabre has agreed to fuse with me. He's spoken to the other dragons, and over half of them have offered to do the same."

I couldn't believe it. "I'm so happy to hear that."

Her eyes remained on Talon. "They will only fuse with elves, not humans. So, if you have someone in your army who wishes to fuse with a dragon, that will not happen."

"I accept his terms," Talon said. "And that wasn't my intention anyway. The elves are the ones who have risked their lives to help their race. You're the only ones who've earned that right."

She gave a slight nod in appreciation. "Then I will pair my best fighters with the dragons who have agreed to fuse."

"With the exception of Inferno," Talon said. "He'll fuse with Calista."

The queen studied him with her intelligent gaze as she considered the request. "If he agrees."

"He will," Talon insisted.

"Then we shall begin the process," Queen Eldinar said. "And we'll meet you at the port of Shadow Stone."

"You can fly with us, Your Majesty," Talon said.

"Thank you for the offer, but I stay with my people —always."

I walked up to Inferno in the field. He was the last one to wake, like he'd been up later than the others or he was simply more tired than usual.

He opened his eyes first before he raised his head slightly. ***WHAT NEWS DO YOU BRING?***

"Macabre has agreed to fuse with Queen Eldinar. Some of the dragons have also agreed."

THAT DOESN'T SURPRISE ME.

"I was wondering...if you'd like to fuse again." We had been fused before because it was essential to our circumstances. We weren't bonded the way Talon and Khazmuda were, who wanted to spend their eternal lives in each other's company. "Talon prefers it because I'll be safer—"

NO EXPLANATION IS NEEDED, CALISTA. I AGREE TO THE FUSE BECAUSE I DESIRE IT. YOU'VE UNFUSED WITH ME BEFORE, AND I DON'T SEE WHY YOU WOULDN'T DO IT AGAIN.

"Of course."

AND I WANT MY STRENGTH TO KEEP YOU ALIVE. YOU DESERVE TO LIVE A LONG AND HAPPY LIFE, CALISTA.

My eyes softened. "Thank you." I wanted to live forever with Talon, but I would never ask Inferno or another dragon for such a gift. Now I understood why Talon's uncle had enslaved their kind to the south, just for the immortality. And I understood why they'd enslaved the dragons with dark magic, because they never would have agreed to give such a gift.

ARE YOU READY?

"Yes."

Inferno reached his snout toward me, pressing it against my palm. He closed his eyes.

I closed mine and felt the connection between us, an energy I couldn't describe. It was a moment of peace before the world tumbled and I felt my feet leave the earth even when I hadn't moved. My stomach churned before everything went still, and I opened my eyes to see that nothing had changed.

Inferno's wild eyes stared into mine.

Everything looked the same, but I felt different. I'd forgotten this feeling, the burn in my blood and the power in my veins. While I remained who I was, I felt a burst of energy that hadn't been there before, a strength in my muscles that defied their size.

YOU'RE FIGHTING FOR MY KIN. SHARING MY STRENGTH IS THE LEAST I CAN DO.

"I would still do it, even if you didn't want to share."

I KNOW. THAT'S WHAT MAKES YOU SPECIAL, CALISTA.

"I'll never be as special as you," I said. "Talon and I are leaving for Shadow Stone so he can prepare his army for departure. Would you like to join us or remain with the dragons and elves?"

I'LL COME WITH YOU. FROM THIS POINT ONWARD, WE SHOULD STAY TOGETHER.

"Okay. Maybe Talon can help me build a saddle. It's kinda hard to ride you without anything to grab on to."

I DON'T CARE TO BE SADDLED LIKE A HORSE, BUT I CAN'T REFUTE YOUR POINT. IT'S DANGEROUS FOR YOU TO RIDE ME, ESPECIALLY IN THE HEAT OF BATTLE.

"Then it's okay if I ride on Khazmuda on the way?"

IT'S PROBABLY FOR THE BEST.

"Alright. Then let's prepare to leave."

Chapter 19

Talon

With Calista in front of me on Khazmuda's saddle, we left Riviana Star and soared over the mountains, Inferno's red scales following behind us like a blazing ball of fire. On foot through the trails and mountains, the journey would take a week. But on the back of a dragon, it took merely a day.

The castle was visible even at a distance, the ocean stretching out behind it, the spires reaching high into the sky from atop the towers. It was made of dark stone, the same color as a headstone, so it never looked nor felt like home. Our keep was made of limestone, so it had a hint of brown, a far warmer color from a climate that could be humid in the summertime and absorb less heat. But it was still a beautiful castle, nonetheless.

We landed on the ramparts and dismounted Khazmuda, the weather a bit cooler than it'd been near the lush forest.

I will take Inferno to hunt. We're both hungry.

Return when you're finished. My blacksmith needs his measurements to construct his saddle.

Khazmuda flew off and joined Inferno, both of their scales beautiful in the setting sun.

Calista watched them go with a hint of a smile on her face. "Beautiful, aren't they?"

I'd seen Khazmuda fly through the air countless times, so my eyes stayed on her face, far more intrigued by her high cheekbones, full lips with the curve of a bow, and eyes that sparkled like a set of jewels. I knew I could look at her forever, would give my soul to have this moment for eternity. "Yeah."

When they were far in the distance, she looked at me again.

I wasn't sure why I did it, but my eyes flicked away like I hadn't been staring. My chest caved in, and my pain was squeezed from my heart like water from a wet towel. With every passing day, I ventured closer to the last place I wanted to be...and I couldn't stop it.

She scanned my bedchambers as she walked inside, studying the armchairs in front of the fireplace, desk in the corner, and the four-poster bed through the open doorway. She stopped and looked at it, probably remembering the night I'd fucked her then sat in the armchair while she slept.

She looked at the bed then the armchair. "Haven't been here in a long time."

"Neither have I." My bed had been full of whores and one-night stands these last decades. Now, it belonged to a single woman. The sheets smelled like her, and I didn't want her to leave. Walking into this bedroom felt like a step into the past, a time when I was a different man... and she was a different woman.

I removed my sword from my back and leaned it against the wall before I started the fire in the hearth. It wasn't winter anymore, but it was still too cold for Calista, judging by the bumps I noticed on her arms.

"Now what?" she asked.

"I'll prepare my men to set sail in the morning. It'll take a few days for my blacksmith to make Inferno's saddle. Then we'll be off, sailing to the south where the hideout is located."

"You're certain we'll be welcome among the pirates?"

I had no doubt. "Yes."

"You have a lot of faith in men who steal for a living."

Captain Blackstorm had become more than a superior, a friend instead. He might be disgruntled by the sheer volume of people I brought to his shores, but he would accept them and offer his hospitality. "I have a lot of faith in the men I knew."

She stared at the fire for a while before she looked at me again. "I have a question..."

"Ask."

"Why does Queen Eldinar have the gift?" Green flames danced in her eyes.

"I don't know."

"You said that some have the blood of dragons in their veins, that it's rare. How can an elf possess it?"

I shook my head. "My answer remains the same—I don't know. Queen Eldinar has opened her lands to us as well as her heart, but I don't think she shares all of her secrets —as she shouldn't. I suspect the relationship she has with Macabre has yielded her such benefits."

"You're saying Macabre granted her the gift?"

"Possibly."

"How would he do that?"

"I don't know," I said. "Anyone can fuse with a dragon if that's what the dragon wishes. But not everyone can communicate with a dragon as their equal. I suspect that the gift is transferred once a fuse has taken place, that even when you break apart, a piece of the dragon remains with you always."

"But if Queen Eldinar has the gift, that means she would have already fused with Macabre."

"Possibly."

"But he seems so against the practice."

"It would have been impossible for them to communicate otherwise," I said. "Perhaps it was only for a moment so they would be able to speak, and then they separated. Or perhaps they've been fused this entire time but pretending otherwise. She says she has the gift, but perhaps she was just fused."

"But why would she lie to us?"

I smirked. "Because otherwise, she would be a hypocrite. Her own people would overthrow her if they knew she'd broken their law and fused with a dragon. I doubt she even told her husband."

Her eyes shifted back and forth as she looked at me.

"I won't out her," I said. "She clearly has no mal intent toward the dragons, and that's all that matters."

She turned back to the fire, lost in thought. "That would mean Macabre lied as well."

"But he would do anything for her, so I'm not surprised." I stepped away and opened my closet to find the armor I'd had made before I left. I'd told my blacksmith to hang it up in the closet when it was finished. I carried it back to Calista and presented it to her, the same armor set I'd gifted Queen Eldinar.

Her eyes immediately scanned over it, taking in all the features, including the shine of the Black Diamonds that were secured to the surface the way a blade was attached to a hilt. Her stare lingered for a long time before she looked at me again. "You made me one as well."

"Because my woman deserves the same as any king or queen."

Her eyes slowly softened as they looked into mine. "You could have kept those diamonds for yourself."

"I would rather share them with the people I care for." I placed the armor on the table so she could admire it in the firelight. Dragon scales were hard as stone, and their external smoothness made them the perfect surface to deflect a blade and push off arrows. They were impenetrable to everything, including fire. Not once had this armor failed me. "Besides, you were the one who found some of these. They should belong to you." Knowing that I was the reason she'd lost ten years of her life had kept me up at night, but now I felt even worse about it. All that time she'd lost, all the torture she'd received, because my depression had turned me into a fucking lunatic.

She had the grace to pity me, her eyes soft with kindness. "I'm ready to go to bed."

"You don't want dinner?"

Her eyes flicked back and forth between mine before she moved into me, rising on her tiptoes as her palm cupped the back of my neck. Her soft lips kissed mine with the enthusiasm of a desperate woman. But she wasn't desperate for payment or pleasure.

She was only desperate for me.

I would never see the Realm of Caelum with my own eyes. I would only know it from tales that probably weren't based in truth. But when I was between Calista's legs, I felt like I was there. In a land filled with light, with pleasure that always throbbed at the fingertips, with a peace that only those who'd passed on could understand.

Wedged between her soft thighs with her nails digging deep into my ass cheek, I rocked into her, giving her only the amount that made her moan in pleasure and not wince in pain. Locked together in the throes of a passion that burned hotter than the flames in the fireplace, our souls grazed each other. I loved Vivian and would have spent my life with her without a single seed of doubt, but my bond with Calista was vastly different. The foundation was strong like a mountain range, formed through earthquakes and floods, withstanding time and all the forces of nature. Our love started as hate, but it still blossomed into a beautiful garden without an ounce of water, as if it was destined to be.

If only I'd found her sooner...

She squeezed my hips with her thighs and dragged her nails down my back. "Talon..."

I could feel her hit the precipice of pleasure then simmer there, slowly building until her desire had nowhere else to go. With watery eyes and nails sharp enough to draw blood, she came around me, her little pussy clenching me with an iron fist.

A wave of heat swept over me and made my spine melt to liquid. The pleasure we experienced together was different from my previous conquests. It was just so damn good, feeding the body as well as the soul. These were the moments that brought me the most joy...and the most pain.

What would she do when I was gone?

Would she be broken the way I was? Searching the world for answers she would never find?

I'd been on the verge of release, but when my mind drifted away, so did my body.

But with white knuckles, she pulled me back. "Come inside me."

And just like that, I was back as if I'd never left. My forehead rested against hers as I continued to thrust through her slickness. "Here it comes, baby."

I started the fire in the sitting room and sat in front of it, sipping my scotch in silent misery. This was how I'd spent my nights before Calista and even during the beginning of our relationship, and I fell right back into my old habits.

As a miserable drunk.

The more I let Calista in, the worse I felt. The highs were higher than the sky, and the lows were lower than the dirt that buried the dead. It was an act of torture, to feel so much joy when she looked at me with those green eyes and then to feel so much despair, knowing she wouldn't be able to look at me for much longer.

"I hope this is all worth it, Talon Rothschild."

My eyes shifted to the chair beside me.

Bahamut sat there in his midnight-blue armor, with blond hair, looking like a respectable king rather than a monster who devoured souls for sustenance.

"But even if it's not, it matters not. At least to me." A slight smirk moved over his lips.

I was more drunk off my misery than the scotch and spoke freely. "What is it about me that fascinates you?" He came to me often, sometimes to discuss matters of import, but most of the time, it was just to taunt me.

"You're a king."

"Because you made me one."

"You're the heir to the Southern Isles. Your predecessors all contain your blood as well as your honor and integrity. Most of the souls who come to me are those who are forgotten or abandoned. And when a soul is miserable and tainted, it doesn't taste the same."

I felt a rush of disgust when I pictured that bowl with my soul within it, ready for the taking.

"My power is fueled by the souls I consume. And the soul of a king...will give me power unlike any other."

"What do you need power for?"

He stared at me, a slight smirk on his lips.

I knew I would never get an answer.

"You'll see—once you join me."

I felt sick again, a taste in my mouth that the scotch couldn't mask. "There must be something I can do to make you reconsider."

His smirk remained in place. "The more you try to slip, the harder I grip."

"My uncle also has the blood of kings."

"Several times removed. Not interested."

"He took the kingdom from my family and enslaved the dragons."

"His allies did that. He himself is not that interesting."

I wasn't sure how much longer I could carry this weight. How much longer I could sleep beside Calista and hide the truth. Would it be better to tell her what would come, or would it destroy the happiness she could have enjoyed a little longer?

"There is one person I would accept as a substitute."

I stared into his cerulean-blue eyes, seeing the ocean that hugged the cliffs in my homeland. Bahamut could be beautiful like a flower one moment and then despicable the next. My heart raced a little quicker at the prospect of leaving this arrangement, of having Calista for the rest of my life. "Give me a name, and I'll make it happen." I didn't care how innocent the person was. I would do anything to be free, to spare my soul from the feast.

His smile widened. "You really despise me, Talon."

"I just want my soul back." I wanted to live with Calista and Khazmuda, to start a new life since my old one had been taken from me. I didn't realize how much I wanted to live until I had something to live for.

"Bring them to my borders—and we have a deal."

So I'd have to sail them across the sea to the little island that wasn't found on any map. "Fine. It shall be done after the battle."

He continued to wear that obnoxious smile.

"Give me a name." Khazmuda would help me hunt them down. I would tie them up and hand them over against their will. I didn't care how much they screamed and pleaded. I'd sail away from that island and never look back.

He stared at me for a long time, his smile slowly fading, his eyes hardening. "Queen Eldinar."

Keep reading for the conclusion we're afraid to get to. What will happen to Calista when Talon is gone? Or is there a way for him to escape his fate?

Made in the USA
Las Vegas, NV
06 January 2025